Love in Row 27

What happens when Cupid plays co-pilot?
Still reeling from a break-up, Cora Hendricks has given up on ever finding love. For herself, that is. To pass the time while working the Aer Lingus check-in desk at Heathrow, Cora begins to play cupid with high-flying singles.

Using only her intuition, the Internet, and glamorous flight-attendant accomplice Nancy, Row 27 becomes Cora's laboratory of love. Instead of being seated randomly, two unwitting passengers on each flight find themselves next to the person of their dreams – or not.

Cora swears Row 27 is just a bit of fun, but while she's busy making sparks fly at cruising altitude, the love she'd given up on for herself just might have landed right in front of her. . .

WITHDRAWN

Eithne Shortall studied journalism at Dublin City University and has lived in London, France, and America. Now based in Dublin, she is an arts journalist for *The Sunday Times* newspaper. She has been a committed matchmaker from an early age and, when not concerning herself with other people's love lives, enjoys sea swimming, cycling, and eating scones.

Published in paperback and e-book in Great Britain in 2017 by Corvus, an imprint of Atlantic Books Ltd.

10 9 8 7 6 5 4 3 2 1

A CIP catalogue record for this book is available from the British Library.

Paperback ISBN: 978 1 78649 203 6
E-book ISBN: 978 1 78649 204 3

Printed and bound by CPI Group (UK) Ltd, Croydon, CR0 4YY

Corvus
An imprint of Atlantic Books Ltd
Ormond House
26–27 Boswell Street
London
WC1N 3JZ

www.corvus-books.co.uk

Love in Row 27

Eithne Shortall

CORVUS

For my granny, whom I love.

Marsha Clarkson, Chief Executive
<m.clarkson@heathrow.co.uk>

Jul 23 at 11:11 p.m.

To: All Staff

Thank you all for attending this afternoon's briefing. The key points are clarified below:

While our recent security scare was a false alarm, it did highlight certain weakness in our operations. In consultation with the Home Office, we have agreed to cease self-check-in until our security system can be safeguarded.

All check-ins across all airlines will now be done manually by staff. Passengers will have to present, in person, at their check-in desk with reference number and identification in hand. Extra staff have been added across the board – so there is no need for concern about personal workloads. The airport authority is helping with costs in this regard.

The self-check-in kiosks have now been removed and placed in storage. Internet check-in will be disabled. We have been advised the restrictions could remain in place for up to one year. Staff will be updated as and when information is available.

As of tomorrow, we return to the old days of air travel, and we're going to do so with a smile. This is an opportunity to put customer service back at the centre of what we do. I encourage you all to go above and beyond for our passengers.

Marsha Clarkson

Chief Executive, Heathrow Airport Authority

<<DO NOT RESPOND TO THIS EMAIL>>

ONE

· · · · · · · · · ·

The self-check-in embargo had been in place for eight days when a woman with multiple haversacks presented herself at the Aer Lingus counter and accidentally began the greatest love story of Cora Hendricks's life. A story that was all the more appealing because Cora didn't have to be its star. At this point in time, in matters of the heart, she could just about handle a supporting role.

It was the last day of July and she had been with the airline less than a month. Barely enough time to get her feet under the check-in counter before the embargo threw all of Heathrow Airport into disarray. She was making her way through a never-ending line of increasingly agitated passengers, and doing her best to act like she had everything under control, when the luggage-laden woman approached and placed a small recording device on Cora's desk.

'It's for my podcast.' She flicked a switch at the side of the microphone and let her tangle of bags drop to the pristine airport floor. 'Don't worry. No one will hear you. I've been recording these things for almost a year and I never manage more than three listeners.' The woman buried her head in an overburdened tote bag and rummaged for her passport. 'And she says she's not, but I know my mother is one of them ... Found it!'

Cora took the dog-eared passport and began to enter the woman's details into her computer. 'What's your podcast about?'

'It's a book travel show. I'd always said to myself, "Trish: you need to travel more and you need to read more." So then when my boyfriend broke up with me – totally over it, don't cry for me Argentina – I decided to see it as an opportunity. Get out there and do what I always said I would.'

'Travel and read?'

'Precisely. And I don't care if nobody's listening. I'm forever losing things and forgetting things, so it's just good to have a record. This' – she tapped the mic – 'is a sort of oral history of a liberated gal.'

'That sounds great,' said Cora, meaning it. Her old self would love to have done something similar but when Cora had been 'liberated' – to use the most euphemistic of euphemisms – she'd taken the more clichéd route and just fallen apart.

'I read a ton of books, talk about them on this, and, if they're any good, I travel to where they're set. *Just Book It* is the name of the show – if you want to be my fourth listener.'

'Seat 27B, departing through Gate B,' said Cora, leaning into the mic as she returned the woman's passport with a boarding card inside. 'So what's the book that has you going to Belfast? Some thriller?'

'This one's actually a bit of a cheat. I've been reading the Game of Thrones series since I started the podcast. My ex

4

hated fantasy so initially I picked them out of spite, but now I bloody well love them! Anyway, since Westeros isn't actually a place, I thought I'd go to Belfast. It's where they record the TV show so, you know, the nearest thing.'

'Never been into science fiction myself.'

The woman paused. 'It's fantasy.'

'Oh right.'

'No science involved.'

'I didn't realise.'

'Completely different genres.'

Cora managed to break eye contact. 'Well I'll definitely give the show a listen.'

'Thanks!' The woman picked up the recorder and shoved it and the boarding pass into one of her many haversacks. 'You'll probably be the only one!'

Sitting on the Tube six months later – six months *to the day* later – Cora recalled how she had known instantly that there was something special about the podcast woman. Her energy and attitude were exciting. Cora, who had always been intrigued by the lives of others, knew there was more. So when, an hour or so later, a crinkled copy of George RR Martin's *A Game of Thrones* landed with a thud on her counter, the check-in attendant was only slightly surprised. It had the feeling of fate.

'Belfast,' she said, raising an eyebrow at the curly haired book owner. 'I presume?'

The young man looked abashed. 'Do you get a lot of *Game of Thrones* fans flying to Northern Ireland, then? I should have known I might be one of many,' he said, handing over the necessary documentation. 'I went to New Zealand after the first The Lord of the Rings film, and the hostels were half full of British fans.'

'You went to New Zealand because of a film?'

'Well I couldn't exactly visit the Shire.'

Cora looked at the gangly man and somewhere in the blacks of his twitching eyes, everything fell into place. Her mind raced back to the podcast woman, enthusiastic and frazzled from the frayed ends of her scarf to the tips of her static hair. She looked at this man, with his awkward smile and equally carefree aesthetic. Cora scanned his fingers – no wedding ring – and glanced again at the well-thumbed tome still sitting on her desk. Of all the airports, in all the land – finally a purpose had walked into hers. 'And tell me,' she said, trying not to sound too eager. 'Would you call Game of Thrones fantasy?'

The man gave an excited laugh. 'Does Bilbo Baggins have hairy feet?'

'Em . . . yes?'

'Of course he bloody well does!'

Coming to the airport hadn't been a career move for Cora, so much as a lifeline. She had returned from two years in Berlin, crawling out of a relationship that left her heart slumped in her chest and her insides jumbled up. It felt as if someone had grabbed her core and shook so hard that everything became dislodged. Cora came home thinking she'd like to help people but all the obvious careers – nursing, social work, counselling – seemed too big, too important, and she couldn't be sure she wouldn't mess it up. She thought Aer Lingus would give her time to realign, to get her insides back in place.

How had it taken her a week to see what was right in front of her? The embargo was a gift: no more online check-ins or kiosks; now everyone had to approach the desk. Their destiny – or at least where they sat for a couple of hours of air travel – was in her hands. The potential to play Cupid was endless. This was it – *this* was her chance to help people.

Cora scanned the seating plan for the flight to Belfast and found that 27A, the seat right beside the podcast woman, was still unoccupied. Cora assigned it to the curly haired man and handed over the ticket, another question occurring to her. 'You're not travelling with a significant other or—'

The man blushed. 'I'd need to have one first, wouldn't I?'

'Perfect! You'll be in 27A. Departing through Gate B. Have a great flight!'

As the early morning Tube rattled through the suburbs of South London, occasionally rising from the darkness of the tunnel into the darkness of the winter morning, Cora felt an involuntary thrill of delight. *Happy anniversary to me.* Six months since her commute had been given a purpose. Six months since her job behind the check-in counter at Heathrow went from a reasonably well-paid distraction to a meant-to-be vocation.

Most of what she needed to know about her matchmaking candidates could be found on their flight information or through Internet searches. There was as much information about people on social media as there was on any dating site. And in repayment for free standby flights, her younger brother Cian had created a computer program that allowed her to quickly highlight all passengers whose marital status was 'single'.

The Tube pulled into Heathrow and Cora alighted with the remaining passengers. She stretched out her back, ascended the escalator, and resolved to seek out the sun when it finally showed its face. There was a bench behind the taxi rank where she liked to have her lunch and watch as complete strangers negotiated sharing cabs into the city. She liked to imagine the lives they led and the things they might talk about as they sped away together.

Cora had always thought the best thing about flying was the possibility of who might be sitting next to you. Waiting at departure gates, she would look around and think which of her fellow passengers she'd most like to be seated beside. Imagine meeting the love of your life 40,000 feet above ground. The idea was enough to make her swoon. These days, Cora was in recovery mode and such happenstance was not of personal interest. But for everyone else the possibilities were endless, and now she was in a position of power.

The staffroom was full of morning crew, brewing coffee and discarding woollen layers. Cora hadn't been outside since entering Finsbury Park station at 5 a.m. but still the cold lingered on her finger tips. She'd always had poor circulation. *Cold hands, warm heart*, Friedrich used to say, and Cora dismissed the thought of him as quickly as it had entered her head. She punched the combination into her locker and opened the metallic door just as Nancy swung out from behind it, her perfect face shattering Cora's revelry.

'Coo-coo, Cupid,' said the air hostess, one hand on the locker, the other on her narrow waist.

Nancy Moone had started with the airline at the same time as Cora and accidentally become her best friend. It's a fallacy that you can choose your friends. It's all down to geographical proximity. School chums are limited to those living in the same catchment area, and work friends are whoever happens to get the locker next to you.

'Alright, Nancy,' said Cora, kicking off her trainers and sliding her feet into the required work footwear. 'You're very chipper for this hour of the morning.'

'You would be too if you'd spent the weekend with me mam. *All my children trying for babies, all except the one with a uterus.*'

'She did not say that.'

'Well, no. But that was the gist of the entire visit. Look at my fingernails, look. Bitten away to nothing.'

Nancy had always wanted to be an air hostess. Her child hood was spent commanding her brothers to sit one behind the other on the stairs of their Liverpool home while she placed a sheet of tissue paper and a small handful of raisins on each of their knees and politely reminded them, when they were done, to store their trays in the upright position. When the Moone family went on their first sun holiday to Benidorm, twelve-year-old Nancy asked the woman who gave the safety demonstration for her autograph.

Were you to see the twenty-seven-year-old Nancy out of context and out of uniform, you'd probably still guess what she did for a living. Blonde, shapely, and always immaculately made-up, she was like one of those poster girls for the early days of air travel.

'How about your weekend? Any eligible fellas in nice designer suits? Is that what's giving you the big, dreamy smile?'

'Hardly,' said Cora, her voice muffled by the pins held between lips as she scraped back her thick dark hair.

'Soon you'll be old and grey and saggy, and you'll regret not having listened to your mate Nancy.'

'And what exactly is it you expect me to do with my pert, pigmented self in the depths of Cornwall?'

'You were at a wedding! A bit of flirting never killed anyone. You've got to shake off the cobwebs. It's not like riding a bike you know: you can forget.' Nancy, who had colonised Cora's mirror, held her mascara wand aloft. 'Use it or lose it. Trust me, Cupid, I've got your best interests at heart.'

Nancy was the kind of woman over whom men happily made fools of themselves, but the air hostess took a special interest in Cora's love life. If her friend was going to turn everyone else's romance into a project, then Nancy was going to make Cora hers.

'It's good to meet a cross-section of people,' she continued. 'God knows you won't meet anyone here; big-headed pilots and the few members of cabin crew who are men, well, they're not interested in women – no matter how modest your bosom might be.' Cora frowned and pulled at her jacket. 'You have to get out there.'

'What about that BA pilot you were seeing – Paul, was it?'

'Well that was different,' breezed Nancy. 'He was unfeasibly pretty. Anyway, that was my first and last flyboy. Best to have a bit of space between work and pleasure. Was there no one at the wedding at all?'

'Oh, I'd say about 120 guests.'

'Ha ha, Cupid. You know what I mean! No man who took your fancy? Nobody of interest? Tell me there was at least a singles table!'

There had been plenty of people of interest and all in a romantic sense, but not in the way Nancy meant. Not of interest to Cora personally. Weddings in general didn't do much for her. No matter how good friends she and the happy couple might be, Cora's interest in the bride and groom disappeared once vows had been exchanged and the bouquet thrown. As a child she had lost interest in soap-opera characters as soon as they married. Their storylines became markedly less exciting and their potential diminished. At twenty-eight, she felt much the same about real life. Ring on finger, paperwork signed equalled game over – going into sleep mode. Cora considered herself a diehard romantic and as far as she could tell weddings, with their fixed schedules and months of planning, had very little to do with romance.

There was, however, one point on which Cora and Nancy agreed: a singles table made nuptials worthwhile. Not because Cora might find herself a convivial man, but because this was the one table in the room with possibilities. On a day dedicated to tidying lives away, this was where something could still happen.

At Saturday's singles table – the bride was a friend from Cora's art history class at university – there had been eight contenders. Seven, if you excluded Cora, which she did. Cora was the facilitator.

Cora tried her best with what she had. She suggested another uni friend swap seats with her in order to talk to a pair of brothers from Walthamstow. But the men only seemed interested in giggling with one another. Another woman was an artist whose work the bride had recently curated. 'Post-impressionism,' she told Cora. 'My interest is in the spaces between the paint. That's where the truth is really being spoken.' She tried to get the artist closer to a cousin of the groom, but the cousin was a level of obnoxious that involved clicking his tongue when any woman under fifty came into his line of sight and spending the rest of the evening nodding rhythmically as if Jimi Hendrix's 'Foxy Lady' was sound-tracking his wedding experience. In the end, the only thing Cora's awkward shuffling achieved was to disorientate the waitress and leave everyone with the wrong main course.

'You have your own love life to look out for too, Cupid,' said Nancy, who had finally relinquished the locker mirror.

'So you keep saying,' replied Cora, slamming the metal door shut. 'But that's just not half as fun.'

• • • • • • • • •

The bell went, indicating the next round of check-ins. Cora and Nancy vacated the staffroom, Nancy heading for the boarding gate, and Cora towards the desks.

'Good weekend, pet?' asked Joan, heaving herself onto the stool behind a second check-in desk. The older woman, who sat beside Cora for most of the week, was back from her pre-dawn smoke break. Aer Lingus hadn't permitted staff to abandon their posts for the ingestion of nicotine in more than two decades, but Joan Ferguson paid as much attention to that as she did the requirement to produce a sick cert or to stop referring to cabin crew as 'trolley dollies'. Joan had been with the airline for thirty-three years and she was going to operate within the exact working conditions she'd signed up to until the day she retired.

'Oh you know; another wedding, another hangover.'

'But it was your anniversary, Joan! Jim get you anything nice?' Joan threw her a look. 'Jim get you *anything*?'

Joan's husband had been in the bad books since he moved a flock of pigeons into their tiny Hounslow garden two months earlier and Joan's clothes line had become a shrine to bird excrement. Having reached legal retirement age, Jim had been forced to leave the local bookmaker's where he'd worked all his life. He was devastated – torn away from the horses, the dogs, the various hot tips. Joan said he was the only man who had more money when he was out of work. The pigeons had been a leaving present from a bunch of regulars, the same lads he did the table quiz with at the Goose Tavern.

This weekend had signified the final chance Joan was giving her husband of thirty-one years to make amends. If he bought her a decent gift (a kitchen appliance from a car boot out the back of the Goose did not count), and took her for dinner in one of the two 'special occasion' restaurants in Hounslow without doing his usual martyr bit of refusing to open the menu and just telling the waiter 'whatever's cheapest', then, and only then, would she forgive him the birds and their relentless bowel movements. Naturally, Joan hadn't conveyed a word of this ultimatum to Jim.

'Useless,' began Joan, redistributing her body weight across the stool as she settled into the story. Joan loved to complain. She was a fatalist and all the happier for it.

'The bugger phones me Saturday night from the Goose asking if I'll call a Chinese in for him. On his way home, he says. Sweet and sour chicken – and see if they'll throw in some crackers. And there's me still thinking we might go out, not to Il Giardino at this point, we'd have to book – that place is a bit posh anyway and Jim still hasn't gotten his tooth fixed – but to Alistair's. So I went out back, opened all those stinkin' coops, set the birds free and headed off to Maura's. I told you about Maura? The one who beat the breast cancer only for her sister to be diagnosed? Well, anyway, I get home three hours later expecting an apology, or at least that he'd be fuming at the loss of his lovely pigeons – and there he is, Lord Muck, asleep on the sofa, sweet and sour on his lap and a can still in his hand. I go out back and there are the ruddy chickens—'

'Pigeons.'

'Pigeons. All back sittin' in their cages, just looking out at the open door.'

'I suppose they're homing pigeons.'

'I bloomin' realise that now, Cora! I went in, woke him up and gave him an earful, then stormed off to bed. Next morning he makes me egg and soldiers. Take what I can get, I suppose.' Joan blew the disappointment through pursed lips, and turned from Cora to face her first passenger of the day. 'Where are we flying to today, love?'

Joan had met Jim when she first came to Aer Lingus. She had started the same year as Cora's mother. They were best friends, or at least they had been when Cora's mother still worked for the airline. She didn't get out as much any more.

'How is Sheila?' asked Joan, as if reading her mind, the early check-in sent off with her ticket for Madrid. 'Did you see her at all this weekend?'

'I was in Cornwall all weekend but I'll pop round tonight.'

'Must get in to see her myself.'

Sheila Hendricks had been in a medical institution for several months now. Cora and her older sister Maeve visited every week and Cian, who had high-functioning autism and conveniently played the Asperger's card whenever any uncomfortable situation arose, went in occasionally. Sheila had gotten Cora the job in Aer Lingus, one of the last fully coherent things she did. She pulled some strings and the daughter was in, just as the mother was starting to fade out. Cora felt a sudden wave of guilt that she hadn't been to see her in almost a week. She really would go tonight.

She ran the passenger list for that morning's Edinburgh flight through her brother's computer program. The list included a few men in their mid-twenties – too young to have a life partner, she hoped, but old enough to be open to one. She inserted some names into Facebook. Profile pictures (selfie with girlfriend on mountain top/in front of Eiffel Tower) and relationship statuses disqualified several candidates immediately.

Then came Andrew Small: single, twenty-two, a Londoner living in Edinburgh. His photo albums showed a handsome young man with thick black hair and the 'about me' section said he was from a sink estate near where Joan lived but was currently studying politics in Scotland. Andrew Small would do nicely. Heterosexual, Cora was fairly confident, thought that was always a potential pitfall.

The first few check-ins were of little interest: a lot of older commuters and a returning, bleary-eyed stag party. A young woman approached the desk, passport ready to be handed over. Cora assessed her quickly: bright tights, dip-dyed hair, canvas backpack. A possibility.

'Work or pleasure?'

'Just a day trip. Surprising the boyfriend!'

Blackballed. Two further possibilities were disqualified – the first for being too quiet to even engage in in-flight conversation and the second for living in Leeds. Cora was aiming for undying love, so geography was a factor.

But third time lucky. Cora knew it when she saw her – the perfect stranger for Andrew Small.

'Hi,' said the young woman, tall with straight hair that fell below her shoulders and a blaze of freckles across her nose. She swallowed a yawn and laid her passport and a printout of her flight number on the counter.

'Work or pleasure?'

'Em, work,' said the girl, who wore a T-shirt with the name of a band Cora had never heard of, and skinny jeans. She smiled. 'Glad to be going home.'

Cora flicked open the passport: Rita MacDonald, Scottish, twenty-three, well-travelled.

'Well, Rita,' she said, closing the passport and handing it back with the boarding card inside. 'You'll be in 27A.'

'A window seat. Ace.'

As Rita wandered off towards the boarding gate, passport slipped into the leather bag slung over her shoulder, she was replaced by Andrew Small. He was taller than his photos suggested and the darkness of his hair made Cora want to touch it.

'Alright,' he said, and handed over his passport.

'Welcome to Aer Lingus, Andrew. Seat 27C, departure gate B – enjoy your flight.'

Andrew slouched away with that slow, wide gait favoured by young men. Personally Cora liked a man with good posture but, she reminded herself as much with relief as reprimand, this had nothing to do with *her* preferences. The check-in attendant picked up the phone and rang through to Aer Lingus Airbus A320.

'Nancy? All set? Good. I've got one coming your way.'

TWO

Rita MacDonald was twenty-three and she'd had three relationships that you could probably classify as serious. The first was Adam, her teenage boyfriend. He wasn't her first love though. Rita was pretty sure she was still waiting on that. But Adam was the first boy to meet her parents, the first boy to touch her boobs, and the first boy to make her appreciate the effect she could have on men. Then there was Aaron, her college boyfriend: first time she'd had real, official sex, first boy to write her a poem, and still her longest relationship to date. And finally Alex: first boy to say he loved her, first boy who was actually a man (twenty-nine), and first boy she'd flown across the country to break up with for a second time, because he refused to accept it until she did it in person.

Rita looked down at her boarding card, hoisted the leather bag up her arm and kept walking. When she got to Row 27, it was empty. She pulled the zip firmly closed and bundled the bag into the overhead compartment. She hadn't needed much for one night in London. This trip had been about taking care of business. She sat in the window seat, pulled down the blind, and rolled her scarf into a pillow. Eight hours Alex had insisted they spend discussing the demise of a relationship that had barely stretched to six months – and half that time they'd been living in different cities. But if he felt better, and she felt less guilty, then it was worth a sleepless night and the cost of return flights. From now on though she'd be adding 'can handle rejection' to the list of criteria for people she dated, and she needed to rethink this unintentional preference for men whose names began with 'A'.

There was a girl snoring in the window seat when Andrew Small got to Row 27. *Jammy bird*, he thought. The window seat was the only place he could ever sleep. Andrew took out his phone and composed a text message to his sister saying he'd made it on time. He was about to tell her his bad luck at landing an aisle seat but decided against it. That was the kind of thing they picked up on now.

'Only an aisle seat? Aw, Andy, hadn't they heard about your A-level results?'

They refused to call him Andrew. That was his new posh-o name. He'd always be Andy round their way. Which was fine, because he didn't have to live round their way any more. He'd gotten out. His sisters resented that Andrew didn't have kid hanging from every limb, and his dad resented that he didn't have to spend his nights taxiing around drunks. They took him going to university as a personal insult. It scared them.

But he wasn't going to just make do: he was going to make something of himself.

'Good morning, sir, welcome on board.'

Andrew looked up to see a blonde air hostess with a big smile and, he wasn't being cheeky but, big knockers. 'Alright,' he said, trying not to go red. 'Morning.'

'Could you give the young lady a poke? Just need to get that blind up and we'll have this plane in the air in a jiffy.'

Andrew wavered but the air hostess nodded her confirmation of the request. He leaned across the middle seat and shook the girl gently. She jolted awake and Andrew withdrew his arm. 'Sorry.'

'Morning, miss, welcome on board. If you could open your blind for take-off.' The air hostess pointed towards the window, and the girl pushed it up. 'Lovely. Now,' she said, clapping her hands together, 'can I get either of you a coffee? On the house. A thank-you for the assistance.'

'Nice one,' said Andrew, who had been getting into coffee since moving to Edinburgh. His flatmate had a percolator – not that he'd breathed a word of that back home.

'Too good for tea now, is it? Do you have caviar with your coffee, Andy, or does that fuck with the aroma?'

'Go on so,' said the girl in the window seat, stifling a yawn. 'I can never get back to sleep anyway,' she said to Andrew as the air hostess left.

'Sorry 'bout that.'

'It's not your fault. Planes are always a fucking nightmare to sleep on.'

'Not even a lie,' concurred Andy with a nod, who hadn't

been on a plane before he got into university and had never flown anywhere but Edinburgh.

><><><><

Rita didn't think of herself as shallow. Never. But then how was she to explain giving Alex the heave-ho? She'd told him they were just incompatible, in lots of ways: emotionally, socially—

'Sexually?'

'No! Of course not,' she'd reassured him, and she supposed it was true. Rita had enjoyed sex with Alex. And if she hadn't looked down that one time, she probably still would. But she had looked down, and she couldn't ignore what she'd seen. That little bald patch right at his crown. It was such a turn-off that there had been no point in even trying any more, and she'd gently pushed his head away.

'Just incompatible,' she'd repeated last night, as she sat in his London flat listing all the vague reasons: emotionally, socially, geographically . . . But at no point did she complete the list. At no point did she tell him that the main way in which they were incompatible was follically. In that she had hair at the back of her head, and he did not.

The air hostess returned with coffee and Rita answered her questions about where she was from and what she did. The boy beside her answered too. He was from London but at uni in Edinburgh.

'Pardon me,' said a woman from the row in front. 'I'd like a tea.'

'We're just serving this row at the moment. General in-flight service will begin when the flight is in the air and has levelled off.' Then the blonde air hostess winked at Rita and her neighbour. 'We've a soft spot round here for Row 27.'

When the air hostess left, Rita introduced herself.

The boy raised a hand in response. 'Andrew.'

'Fuck off.'

'What?'

'Sorry, no,' she said. 'Nothing.'

'What? I don't look like an Andrew? Is that it? Do not tell me I look more like an Andy.'

'No, it's not that. It's just . . .' Rita wasn't sure how to say it without implying something unintended, but fuck it. She'd spent the whole of last night watching her words. 'Every boyfriend I've ever had, their name has begun with "A". I'm like a magnet for them.'

But Andrew didn't even blink. 'How many boyfriends is that?'

'Three.'

'Three? How old are you?'

'Twenty-three. Why? Is three a lot? Are you saying I'm a slut?' She wanted to add that she'd only slept with two of them and she'd never been in love with any of them, but she wasn't going to explain herself. If he thought . . .

'Fuck no. I'd never – no. I'm impressed,' he said, and he did actually look it. 'Three is good.'

You didn't date girls round where Andrew was from. You slept with them and if you got them knocked up you might marry them, but there wasn't much in between. His sisters had both gotten pregnant a year out of school. Rebecca got married, but Janine never said who the father was. 'I'm not a grass,' she'd screamed at their dad. 'I'm not dobbing him in,' and everyone just accepted this rationale.

At first Andrew felt guilty about going to university and spent far too much of his grant money flying home every weekend to sit around with his mates and mind his sisters' kids, and slag off all the twats and tossers he'd met in Edinburgh. And that seemed to appease them a bit, because everyone just wanted Andrew to keep on being like them.

The day Andrew got his A-level results he'd gotten into a fight with his dad. 'Big man now, Andy?' his dad had said and Andy called him a jealous prick so his old man chucked a Pyrex dish at his head. That stuff had to happen, he supposed, two men in a small house. They didn't fight as much now and this weekend had been more about silence and smart comments.

'So that's what you do all day, Andy, read books and have clever thoughts? Nice work if you can get it.'

'Work? Andy wouldn't know work if it kicked him in the nuts.'

And Andrew used to tell himself that it was their choice – that his sisters and his mates chose to stay around their way, and live in the shitty estate they'd grown up in and go to the same pub every weekend, or more often. But, deep down, he knew it wasn't about choices; it was about the complete fucking lack of them. Which is why when he was offered some financial aid to study politics in Edinburgh, he hadn't thought twice.

'First in your family to go to university?' asked Rita, who looked like she was in a band or wrote poems or something like that. 'They must have been proud of you.'

'They'd be prouder if I'd scammed a house on benefits. And I'm not even lying.'

'But you managed to get a bursary, as an undergrad! Uni costs a bomb. You must be proper smart. If that was me, you wouldn't be able to shut me up.'

'It's not really something I bring up at home.'

'Well I think it's amazing.'

'Yeah?' Andrew couldn't help grinning. They weren't at home now. They weren't anywhere. They were in the air. 'I think it's fairly alright too.'

The phone rang.

'Patch it through,' said Nancy Moone, nestling the receiver between her chin and shoulder as she used her hands to stick a dry-packed toasted sandwich, ordered by a woman in Row 29, into the microwave.

The operations controller, who had a thing for Nancy and allowed her to receive mid-flight calls from Heathrow, disappeared from the line and was replaced by Cora.

'How's it going?'

'Mixed bag, Cupid. At first I thought, "Total dud!" cause

24

the girl was trying to get some shut-eye but then I swooped in with the classic—'

'Coffee on the house?'

'Worked a treat!' Complimentary drinks was Nancy's first port of call when it came to initiating conversation in Row 27. Free booze generally worked better, but it depended on the supervisor on board and not at eight o'clock in the morning. They were trying to keep a low profile after all. 'They were chatting away.'

'And then?' Cora's voice cracked down the line. 'Are they still talking?'

'Well then this nuisance of a stag party started acting up in Row 18, and I've been all distracted. And let me tell you, Row 18 is not where I want to be devoting my attentions. The bald fella from Game of Thrones is sitting up in Row 1, and I have yet to make it past the emergency exit.'

'Come on, Nancy. I need more details!'

'Hang on and I'll check.'

Nancy let the phone dangle as she grabbed the ham and cheese from the microwave, leaving that door swinging too. She sailed down the aisle, past the hungry woman in 29E and stopped at Row 27. The boy was saying something about family and the girl was nodding enthusiastically.

'Ham toastie?'

The pair stared up at her. Nancy liked how they were both tall. 'No? Sorry then. Wrong passenger.'

She turned on her kitten heels, dropped the sandwich at Row 29 without so much as slowing her pace and caught the receiver on an upward swing.

'Another success, Cupid.'

'Really? I wasn't sure she'd have the energy to engage . . .'

'Well she did. And he was yakking away, all serious like. Oh you can't beat the young folk for the serious chats.'

A series of pings came from Row 18. Nancy straightened her back and rotated her shoulders.

'Got to go, Cupid. The stag is back on the prowl.'

'Guilt,' said Andrew.

Rita nodded. 'It's the fucking worst.'

They'd discussed Edinburgh's cliques and commuting, and by the time the plane had begun its descent Rita had told him why she'd come to London for less than twelve hours. Which brought them right to guilt. Not enough hair, too much distance, because she didn't fucking feel like it; it didn't matter the reason, she just wanted to break up. But guilt had made her pay ninety quid for return flights just so Alex could make her feel lousy in person.

'I feel guilty even when I know I shouldn't,' she said. 'I just hate feeling like I might be a bad person. And then I hate that I feel that way.'

'I hear that, Rita,' said Andrew, and she felt a shiver as her name made its debut on his lips. 'I did my best to hate uni for the first two years because I thought liking it meant I was betraying everyone at home.'

'And what happened?' she asked.

'I stopped going home so much.'

'That's rough.'

'You're not even lying.'

He was smart but not conceited and he had that confident thing going on, like he knew who he was and all that, and she loved his swagger. Real London swagger.

'Guilt can be good too,' she said. 'It makes us do the right thing.'

'Like what?'

'Like when people pick up their dog shit. They do it so they won't feel guilty.'

'No they don't! They do it because you're looking. No way they pick it up when no one's around. That's public perception, not guilt. Like when I go to some public toilet and I wash my hands? That's only 'cause some other bloke's in there watching, judging me. I don't do it if nobody else is in the place.'

'Mate, that is rotten.'

'What?' Andrew was laughing too. 'It's only a piss!'

Rita scrunched up her face in disgust, but she didn't really think it was rotten. The only thing Rita was thinking was that she was into him.

She asked what bands he liked and Andrew listed a few tunes he'd heard when he was out, but he didn't really care. It was a real university question: 'What music are you into?' But it was just people trying to place you. No different from school. Though nobody in Edinburgh had ever asked what team he supported.

'I mostly listen to talk radio,' he said.

'Like what?'

'Like Radio 4.' Another thing he would not be admitting to at home.

'Wow,' said Rita. 'That's cool.'

Andrew had learned most of what he knew about women from around the estate, and he'd never had any complaints. He was pretty confident when it came to sex. And he was a good kisser; that was something he'd prided himself on since he was twelve when the girls on his street said he was the only one of his mates who didn't snog like a washing machine stuck on spin. But the problem with coming from a tribe where dating wasn't part of the culture was that he didn't have a fucking clue how to ask a girl out.

The stag party was awake and singing for its supper – or at least for a drink. One of them had spotted Nancy's name-tag and they were having a great time.

'*I'll do anything, for you, dear, anything . . .*' sang one.

'Come on, Nancy!' said another.

'*I'll even fight your Bill.*'

Having politely informed them it was 9 a.m. and so there would be no alcohol served on this flight, Nancy took her leave. She was always professional, but she was nobody's fool.

'Please, sir,' they shouted after her. 'Can I have some more!'

Nancy liked that she shared a name with the *Oliver!* heroine. She remembered going to see the musical at the Empire as a teenager and thinking the actress was proper gorgeous. Nancy usually told people she was named after Nancy Sykes. It was a lot more glamorous than being named after her Granny Moone. And this wasn't the first time she'd had that song sung at her – *I'll do anything for you, dear, anything* – only the last occasion had been at a nice holiday cottage in the Cotswolds and the crooner had been serenading her from where he stood, uncorking a bottle of rosé, at the end of the bed.

She walked past Cora's couple just as the plane was near landing. Nancy loved it when Row 27 was a success. She reached the rear alcove and positioned herself slightly to the right, so she could monitor their exit. She tried to remember every detail so she could tell Cora.

You rarely meet someone who is proper different. Most of the people in your life are the same as you. This was what occurred to Rita as they landed at Edinburgh Airport. 'Cause yeah, we all think we're weird or outcasts or whatever, but you're still just going to the same gigs and the same pubs as all the other like-minded weirdos and outcasts. But when Andrew said he liked Drake – who was far too popular for Rita – she'd actually thought, *this chap is amazing*. And she fucking loved that hair.

The plane taxied to a stop and the blonde air hostess, the one who'd given them the free coffee, passed their row again.

The intercom crackled: *disarm doors and cross-check.*

'So are you going to ask me out then or what?' she said, pretending to have difficulty with her seatbelt so she didn't have to look at him.

'Is it that you want me to?'

'Well like, I got the impression you were mad into me,' she said, trying to match his confidence.

'Yeah,' he said, grinning, and she wasn't sure if it was a question or affirmation. They stood from their seats. 'I was going to ask you'.

'Just playing the long game, were you?'

'Thought you might have reservations. What with my name being Andrew.'

'Shit yeah, forgot about that. The dreaded A.'

'Some of my mates call me by my last name, if that works better.' He took his passport from his back pocket and handed it to her. She burst out laughing.

'You're alright, Andrew Small,' she said, handing it back. 'We'll stick with your first name and see how we get on.'

They shuffled up the aisle, Rita admiring the width of Andrew's shoulders and trying to keep a stupid grin from swallowing her entire face. They reached the exit at the rear of the plane to find the blonde air hostess standing there watching them, her perfectly white teeth wide between her perfectly painted lips. 'I hope today's flight got you both exactly where you wanted to go,' she beamed.

And as Rita stepped out onto the ladder and into the bracing Edinburgh wind, she could have sworn she heard the air hostess whoop behind her.

THREE
. . . .

Cora liked to think of matchmaking as a culmination of her better attributes: imagination, a sense of romance, an interest in people. Sure, it could be viewed as the pastime of a busybody, but she had yet to be accused of such. At least not to her face.

She made her first successful match as a teenager in her bedroom in the quiet London suburb of Kew. It was shortly after her parents separated. Sheila Hendricks (née O'Reilly) had come to London from Ireland after finishing school and gotten a position with the Heathrow branch of Aer Lingus. Her plan had been to transfer back home after a couple of years but then she met Cora's Londoner father and England became her resident country, if never quite her home.

And having spent her adult life with a husband who ultimately repaid her geographical compromise with adultery, Sheila Hendricks was livid. She contemplated taking Maeve, Cora, and Cian back to Ireland, which was why she kept her married name; there was a rumour that, at Dublin Airport, single mothers were sent to work in Baggage Tracing in the basement. In the end, though,

Sheila settled for throwing him out of their London home and insisting every room be given a makeover. There were weeks of furious redecoration, with her mother singing her own version of that Peggy Lee classic: '*I'm gonna paint that man right outta my hair*'.

Cora was given free rein to 'express herself' in her bedroom's redecoration and the fifteen year old took this seriously. She painted the ceiling, every wall, the radiator, and the back of the door an appetising shade of purple. And the next morning, when the paint had dried, she sat on the floor in the middle of the room and cried. For the next however many years she would be sleeping inside a giant grape. But, when the furniture was reinstated and the woollen throws layered on the bed, the visual assault relented. In place of the old boy band posters were reproductions of paintings. Pride of place went to a framed replica of Sir John Everett Millais's *Ophelia* – the same picture that has hung in every bedroom she has occupied since. This dark-haired woman lying heartbroken in a shallow ditch was as romantic an image as Cora had ever seen. It was how the fifteen year old expected, or hoped, love would one day feel. Sheila could never understand the attraction.

'She's just so tragic,' Cora's mother had said, standing at the doorway when the redecoration was complete. 'Wouldn't you rather a heroine on your wall? Someone who's not a corpse? Joan of Arc maybe?'

'Joan of Arc was burnt at the stake at twenty-one, Mum.'

'Some other heroine, so. Your woman who kept the diary in the attic?'

The new bookcases had been embellished with a Shakespeare anthology, two Sylvia Plath collections, and James Joyce's *Dubliners*. The new books could be distinguished by their smooth spines but she'd get around to cracking them eventually.

This decor – complemented by a self-imposed uniform of Che Guevara T-shirt and choker fashioned from black shoelace – represented the woman Cora was planning to become. She liked to picture herself at university, her briary hair calmed, her cosy bedsit filled with small canvases painted by herself, earnest boys calling over for tea in the hope she'd fall in love with them, and weekend protests and marches where everyone brimmed with passion. She wasn't quite sure what causes she would advocate for, but she knew there were plenty out there. She'd be an idealist who was willing to engage; she'd be a romantic who cared.

On the day that Cora's first great match was made, the teenager was sitting on her newly decorated bed, flicking through a photo album from the previous summer's German language camp to which she was about to return. And this time Roisin, her best friend, would be coming too.

'Did you know the name Ophelia didn't exist before Shakespeare invented it,' she said to Roisin, who was sitting on the floor, leafing through Cora's modest but expanding CD collection. 'He invented lots of words: "addiction", "assassination", "eyeball".' Cora had just discovered the Bard's contributions to the English language and it was her new favourite fact. Roisin was less interested.

'Do you have their first one?' her friend asked, holding

up The White Stripes CD. Roisin Kelly was the new girl at school that year. She'd moved to Kew from Dublin (Sheila had been very excited to hear of her daughter's 'Irish friend') and her allure was amplified by the fact that Roisin owned a record player. Suddenly burning CDs didn't seem so cool, and everyone had gone hunting in their parents' attics. Roisin knew more about music than anyone at school. She identified as a Dylanologist, a neo-Curehead, and a Strokes groupie. She was a diehard muso.

'First one? Yeah, got it ages ago,' Cora breezed. 'It's probably downstairs.' She made a mental note to find out what the White Stripes's debut was and buy it at the next available opportunity. Building a music collection was impossible. The new stuff was always changing, the cool old stuff was endless, and Cora was working from a budget of Saturday night babysitting.

She slid down beside Roisin and placed the German college photo album on her knee. 'What do you think of him? Just ignore the hair.' Cora pointed to a smiling young man who wore a T-shirt signed by friends and who had added Sun-In to his spiked-up mane for the last day of camp.

'Not really my type,' said Roisin. It was the first Cora had heard of her best friend having a type.

They flicked through the rest of the album, Cora telling stories to accompany the pictures, until Roisin stopped on the penultimate page. 'What about him?'

Standing two people over from Cora in a group shot was Roger Gorman. This was the boy whose group Cora would infiltrate at that summer's German college for the sole purpose of setting him up with her friend. This was the boy Roisin would kiss at the diskothek on the last night after three agonising weeks in which she became convinced he did not know she existed. This was the boy Roisin would lose her virginity to the following summer, who she would date all the way through uni, and with whom she would thereafter move to Central London.

When Roisin and Roger split, Cora was devastated. She had hoped her first match would be her most successful, and she had the photo-album anecdote ready to go for the wedding speech. Still, Roisin's single status meant she had been looking for a flatmate the previous year at the exact time Cora needed to relocate to the Finsbury Park area to be near her mother. Now Cora lived with Roisin above a twenty-four-hour sauna on the Seven Sisters Road. The exact activities of the all-night business were dubious but the women had never once had to turn on the heating. A third flatmate, Mary, had been there longer than either of them. Cora found her in equal parts fascinating and dull. Mary was doing Weight Watchers and had lost four stone. During that time, food had become her only interest. She made elaborate, low-fat meals for one in the evening and ate them in front of an endless stream of fat-shaming television programmes. A particular twist, Cora thought, was that by day Mary was a GP.

Roisin had been dating someone new for the past month or so – another Cora coupling. The two women had gone to The Dolphin one night over Christmas. Standing on the crowded dance floor, Roisin was despairing at how difficult it was to get talking to *anyone* in a London pub. 'Where's the shite talk? Where's the drunken banter?' Roisin shouted, her flat Dublin accent distinguishable above the music. 'Look at them all, sticking to their own groups. Forget the class system, Cora, this is the great English divide right here.'

Without a word of response, Cora removed her left shoe and threw it into the middle of the dance floor. When the two women went to retrieve it, they found a bewildered man considering the boot that had smacked him square in the chest. Cora grabbed the flying footwear and walked off, leaving Roisin to explain. Since then, Cora had seen Prince Charming leaving her best friend's bedroom most Saturday mornings. The 'sole mate' was one of Cora's staple moves. She thought of it like catching the bouquet at a wedding, only with less commitment.

Cora was delighted for Roisin. She was glad something exciting was happening – and that it didn't involve her. But when, in the early hours and half-asleep, she heard Prince Charming undoing the latch to let himself out, Cora's past momentarily entered the present and the sound of the door closing jolted her awake with a churn of her stomach. And every time, even after rationalising that she was above a sauna in London and not in that four-storey walk-up in Berlin, she knew there would be no chance of going back to sleep. Cora knew it wasn't *him* leaving her, saying nothing but making enough noise so she'd hear him go, but still Friedrich flooded her mind.

Whenever Cora visited her mother, enquiries were made about Roisin. Sheila described her daughter's friend, in what was her highest compliment and generally reserved for fellow expatriates, as 'salt of the earth'.

'And is she seeing anyone?' Sheila asked that Monday evening, after Cora had made them both a cup of tea and opened a packet of Sainsbury's cookies. Her mother had been preening pot plants when Cora arrived and there was barely space on the desk for their mugs. Sheila had grown up in the countryside and had surrounded herself with greenery ever since. Cora pushed a sprawling fern to one side.

'She is,' said Cora, telling her mother the shoe saga for at least the third time. Sheila laughed and progressed to the inevitable question of her daughter's own love life.

'Nobody special to report.' The stock reply.

'You know Tom has a son about your age—'

But Cora cut her off. Tom was Sheila's friend at the research facility. He was Irish too, and had come to Luton in the 1950s to work on the building sites. His Alzheimer's was more advanced but Sheila still talked to him about Irish politics and sports.

'Mother, I am fine. Honestly. I don't need any help. I'm just taking a little break.'

'I know, I know, and I think that's very healthy. It is. But it's been more than a year now since, your, what was his name. The man who never—'

'Eight months.'

'Eight months, right. I know you had a tough time, I know, sweetie pie, I do, but *you know* all men aren't the same and we all have to get back on the, the—' Sheila rotated her hands and Cora knew the word would never come.

'I have to keep going?'

Her mother looked around. 'Already?'

Sheila had always been the one Cora turned to when things went wrong. Maeve had been more independent and Cian was in his own world. But Cora and Sheila were close. When Cora was homesick that first year of German college, her mother posted her a mobile phone (summer school contraband!) and they talked under the covers at night. Sheila had been the sounding board when Cora was trying to decide what to study at university and it had been her mother Cora had phoned in floods of tears from Germany early one morning when the heartache and brain ache of second-guessing everything finally broke her. Sheila had ensured a standby seat for her daughter that same day and Cora was at home by teatime, crying into her mother's lap, with half her belongings still in the Berlin apartment occupied by her ex-boyfriend but paid for by her.

But now her mother's mind was failing and Cora was readying herself for the day when she no longer remembered all the things she had done for her daughter. *You have to be ready*, she admonished herself. *It's time to grow up.* Cora feared telling her mother new information in case it pushed out the older, more important memories. Logically, she knew it didn't really work this way – the doctors had explained the difference between short- and long-term memory – but still she wanted to pull a woolly hat down over her mother's head to stop the dying brain cells from escaping through her ears.

Sheila's memory started to wane a year ago, the usual stuff of lost keys and forgotten pin codes. One night Maeve called over for dinner, and her mother couldn't remember how to extend the dining-room table she'd had since her wedding day. It was initially diagnosed as stress, then dementia, and eventually early onset Alzheimer's. Sheila left her home for full-time care long before the doctors said it would be necessary. 'I will not be a burden on my children,' she repeated to each of them on the day she finalised the deeds to sell the house. But Sheila also had no intention of giving up on the rest of her life and, instead of going into a home, she signed up to live in a small, supervised facility where pan-European research was being conducted into the disease. Her vocabulary and short-term memory had worsened but she never forgot the names of her children or friends, and she asked just as many questions.

Sometimes Cora thought maybe she didn't have Alzheimer's at all and she was just making space in her mind by getting rid of the inconsequentials. But every time she left the facility, Cora caught glimpses of the other residents and the all-too-evident signs of Alzheimer's; she'd seen a woman crying on her children because she couldn't remember when she last showered, and the man who used to be next door to Sheila was moved to a specialised room on the ground floor after becoming incontinent.

'Can we change the subject please?' asked Cora, taking another biscuit from the packet and breaking it in half.

'Certainly,' said her mother. 'Whatever my sweetie pie wants. Will we have another cup of tea?'

Cora got up to put on the kettle and opened the cupboard that had CUPS stamped across it in bold, black lettering.

She wondered how much longer her mother would have the kettle. Tom's had been removed from his room at Christmas. She went to the fridge to fetch the milk. There was a Post-it stuck to it and in her mother's neat scroll it said: A letter for Cora in Cutlery.

'Mum?' she said, removing the note from the door. 'Have you got a letter for me?'

'Have I? Oh, yes!' said Sheila, taking the yellow slip from her. 'That was so I didn't forget. Did you know I sometimes forget things?'

'Not funny.'

'Ah, if you didn't laugh you'd cry.' Sheila pushed herself out of her seat and repositioned the glasses that hung around her neck. She pulled open the top drawer – the one marked CUTLERY – and removed an envelope. 'Here. This one's for you. I've given Maeve hers, and I've one for your brother too.'

'What's in it?'

'It's – well, it's a letter from me to you.' Sheila retook her seat and stirred the milk into her fresh cup of tea. 'When the day comes that I don't remember your name . . .' She held up a hand to Cora. 'It makes me sick to the pit of my stomach but one day it will come, so . . .'

'Mum.'

'When that happens, I'll be gone from you. And you're to let me go then. I mean it now, Cora.' Sheila placed the mug beside the plants and curled her fingers firmly into her palms. 'Because when that part's gone, all you're left with is weak bone and wrinkled flesh. But you'll have this letter. It'll be feck all comfort, just some words on a page, but you'll have it and maybe it'll remind you who I was, and you can think of me as I really am and not as the useless lump who'll be lying in some bed in front of you, not even remembering how to wipe the drool from her chin.'

'Mum—'

'There's no more to it, Cora. Except that you're not to mock my spelling. Okay?'

'Okay.'

'Good. Now, tell me all about work.'

The room had started to spin but Cora took herself in hand. *Hold it in. Later.* She told her mother all the news from that day and the previous week, and pushed everything else to the back of her mind. She told Sheila about Joan and the pigeons, about how a former colleague of hers had announced his retirement, and how more temporary staff had been added. The rest, she compartmentalised.

'And how is that friend of yours? The wee pet who brought flowers?'

'Nancy. She's well. She had three celebrities on flights today – a record apparently. And she was telling me, you know Ray from Baggage Screening?'

'Do I?'

'Yes, Mum. You worked with him for years.'

'Are you sure?'

'At the airport, at Heathrow. Ray? Big Ray?' An unfortunate and unnecessary nickname considering there were no other Rays at Heathrow from whom he needed to be distinguished.

'I have him now. Big Ray. Why didn't you just say that?'

'I should have, you're right. Sorry, Mum. Well he's been accepted as a contestant on the next series of *Fight the Flab*. Nancy was passing through Security this afternoon and they were all celebrating with a sneaky Eccles cake – his last pudding for a while, I suppose.' Nancy had relayed this bit of news as she was finishing her shift, and Cora was familiar with the show because it was one of Mary's favourites. Seven overweight 'leaders' were given personalised diets and exercise plans. Viewers were encouraged to pick the leader with whom they most identified and to follow their regime. It had been a hit around the UK but the weekly weigh-ins, for which the contestants were forced to squeeze into swimsuits they hoped to be wearing comfortably by the end of the season, seemed inhumane to Cora. Nancy, however, was beside herself with excitement. A film crew would be at Heathrow the next day to get 'establishing shots' for Ray's 'character'.

'Well, good for Big Ray,' said Sheila, yawning in the manner she had adopted since deciding her shortened life expectancy no longer left time for tact.

'Righto, I'll go. In for the long shift again tomorrow – 6 a.m. start.'

'I haven't done one of those in a while.'

Cora gathered her coat and handbag, slipping Sheila's letter into the front pocket, and kissed her mother on the top of her head.

'Mum . . .'

'Bye, sweetie pie. And get some sleep. You look tired.'

'Bye, Mum.'

Cora closed the door behind her and walked through the main corridor. She waved to the night nurse who raised a hand in reply.

Outside, it was starting to ice over and Cora pulled a scarf from her bag. She had always liked extreme weather because it meant something was happening. But now the distinct seasons seemed to come too fast: summer, autumn, winter already. Everything was speeding up just when Cora so desperately wanted it to stay the same.

She walked the seven minutes to her flat, climbed the three flights of stairs and called goodnight to Roisin and Mary, who were immersed in repeats of *The Great British Bake Off*.

Once in bed, she took the envelope from her bag and turned it over in her hands. It was light. She hoped there wasn't a cheque. Maybe she'd never have to open it. Unlikely she knew, of course she knew, but anything was possible.

She opened the chest of drawers beside her and shoved it in, under a sketch pad and various bills. From the top of the pile, she pulled out the scoreboard. She set the multicoloured pen to green and chalked down another success for 'London to Edinburgh'. She liked to fill out the matchmaking chart slowly, getting satisfaction from each new addition. It was pretty full now, and she was pleased to note there were almost as many green entries as red or yellow. The latter denoted 'undetermined'. She pushed everything else from her mind and lay down in the dark. The green marks danced against the insides of her eyelids, and she fell asleep willing the successes to infiltrate her dreams.

FOUR

••••••••••••

'If they don't get this bloomin' thing started, I'm going back inside. Are they hoping Ray might just freeze that big arse off?'

Joan was grumbling into the neck of her fleece-lined duffel coat and Cora threw an arm around her as they huddled by the entrance to the airport.

'What *are* they doing over there?' Joan demanded. 'How many monkeys does it take to work a bloomin' camera?'

A few feet away, a four-person crew was staring into a monitor at the base of a camera stand. Every now and again one of them would move away, do a small lap of the equipment and return to collective chin-stroking. Filming was supposed to have started twenty minutes ago and if it didn't get underway soon, Cora and Joan would have to head back to their desks.

Ray padded over to them, looking a little uncomfortable with all the fuss. His mousy hair was parted to the side and gelled into place, and his uniform was pristine. He reminded Cora of a little boy on his first day of school.

'You're looking well,' she said, her arm still around Joan. 'Very handsome indeed.'

44

'She's right there, Ray. Just smashing.'

'Bit nervous if I'm honest,' he said, rubbing his hands together to stop them going numb. 'Was afraid to put on my coat in case I got too warm and started sweating through the shirt.'

In the distance behind him, Nancy was approaching at as fast a speed as her wheelie bag and shoes would allow. Even at twenty metres Cora could tell those were not regulation heels.

'Coo-coo, Ray!' Nancy drew closer and Cora registered the extra inch of hair and layer of tan. The air hostess linked Ray's arm and gave them all her biggest smile.

Cora regarded her with scepticism. 'I thought you weren't flying until three o'clock.'

'Yes well, I thought I'd get in early and wish my pal Ray the very best of luck, didn't I? How are you doing, Ray? Sorry I'm late. Is it just two cameras?'

Cora doubted if Nancy had said more than 'morning' or 'no liquids today' to Big Ray in the seven months since she'd started working at the airport. Ray, for his part, had gone a curious shade of pink and was staring with alarm at Nancy's bronzed arm. Cora hoped it wouldn't leave a stain on his pristine shirt.

Nancy nattered on about how the show worked: 'You remember Nigel? Well he worked in television and he told me . . .' Joan produced a packet of cigarettes from her pocket. It was only then that Cora noticed Charlie Barrett, the head of security for their terminal, standing behind the film crew. When she clocked him, he was looking at her; perhaps she'd felt his gaze. He nodded and returned his attention to the camera men. She watched Charlie, Charlie watched the film crew and, evidently, Nancy was watching her.

'Do you like him?'

Cora rolled her eyes.

'Because he likes you. Charlie barely says two words but when it's you, he stretches to at least six. It's kind of hot, the whole strong, dark, silent bit. And he has that Mediterranean Lothario look, don't you think? But without the shirt unbuttoned to the belly button and the "hey beautiful, I want to marry you" heckles. Obviously.'

Cora grinned. 'Obviously.' Charlie Barrett was the last person she could imagine engaging in catcalls. Charlie was polite in an old-fashioned way, chivalrous even. He held doors open for everyone and he carried a handkerchief. He fetched wheelchairs for older passengers and pushed them himself, though it wasn't his job, and he'd ask all about their kids and grandkids, even though he was terrible at small-talk. He couldn't have been more than a few years older than Cora, but he had been head of security for Terminal Two for as long as she'd known him.

'Is this a security matter? People filming *outside* the airport?'

'I don't know, Cupid. But you can ask him.'

Cora looked over to see the security guard making his way towards them. He was tall and dark and pleasantly hairy. Objectively attractive. Yet Cora had the same sensation as when she thought of anyone in a romantic sense: a sudden urge to flee.

'Morning, Cora. Nancy. Joan.'

'Don't you be coming over all charming with me, Charlie Barrett. It's your bloomin' fault we're all out here. My teeth are chattering so much they're about to dance out of my head!'

'Airport rules, I'm afraid. No filming inside the terminal.'

'But you let in that bloomin' *24 Hour Flying* or whatever the programme was called, and they were never gone from the place.'

'It's a lot stricter since the security scare. No more cameras, no open bins, and *definitely* no smoking in undesignated areas.' Joan continued to puff on her cigarette but she stopped grumbling. She had a soft spot for Charlie. All the older women did. He reminded them of how it used to be.

'Hey, Charlie. Cora wanted to ask you if the filming was a security matter.'

She'd kill Nancy.

'Just keeping an eye,' he said looking at Cora and she nodded, but Nancy wasn't done.

'Making sure they don't take advantage of Ray, is it? You two have always been close. That's dead nice of you, Charlie. Isn't it, Cora? Dead nice of him.'

'*Dead* nice,' echoed Cora, pointedly.

Charlie's walkie-talkie crackled. He took the cigarette butt from Joan and gave the girls a final nod. 'See you later.'

'Hear that?' whispered Nancy. 'The "See you" was for you. If it had just been Joan and me, we would have gotten: "Later". One word. But when you're around, you can't shut him up.'

Cora threw her eyes to heaven.

'Told you he liked you.'

Before Cora could tell her to grow up, one of the television crew was addressing the masses and Nancy was giving him her undivided attention.

'Now, folks. Thanks for bearing with us. It's just sensational to see so many of you out here. Ray must be one popular fellow – am I right, Ray, amirite?!' Ray smiled awkwardly as all eyes turned towards him. 'So we couldn't actually get any shots of Ray at work which is a shame but not to worry, not to worry. Ingenuity to the rescue! Ha ha ha. Right, so what we're going to do is get a few wide angles of Ray arriving at the airport and maybe waving to a few colleagues on his way in. Sound good? Good. Then we'll get a few shots of him checking passers-by's bags – well it is Security, amirite!? Ha ha ha. Rightio. If you can all just talk amongst yourself. *Rhubarb, rhubarb* and all that. Ray? Can you take position?'

They had filmed a few sequences of Ray walking self-consciously into the airport when Nancy started to grow dissatisfied with her background role. 'When are you going to talk to Ray's friends?' she shouted to the director, as he watched back another take.

'Fan of the show are you, darling?' he said, strolling over to her. 'We'll get those later. Few vox-pops, that sort of thing. You a good friend of Ray's, is it?'

'Is the pope a Catholic?' thrilled Nancy, stepping forward so the director might better admire her television suitability. Cora listened to her friend wax lyrical about why Ray would make a great leader, and rolled her eyes as Nancy struggled to make a friendship-defining anecdote out of how Ray had helped her to hail down a black cab after the airport authority's Christmas party.

'Bugger this for a game of soldiers,' said Joan, extinguishing her third cigarette on an undesignated bollard and heading for the automatic doors. Cora gave Ray an apologetic head tilt, followed by an encouraging thumbs up, and followed her co-worker inside.

The women had been gone almost forty minutes on what was supposed to be a fifteen-minute break. When they got back to the desks, Wesley – or Weasel, as their boss was more commonly known – was standing over the empty chairs. He tapped his tiny feet impatiently and told them it would not do. 'Just. Will. Not. Do.' Cora half mumbled an apology as the two women repositioned themselves on the stools.

'I don't care if you think you're the next Cilla Black or Judge Judy, these are work hours and the last time I checked you worked for me—'

Weasel faltered. He was never quite as brave when Joan was looking directly at him.

'. . . here. You work here.' Weasel wasn't much taller than five foot and his hair grew in awkward tufts. He had a beard that existed only under his chin and he applied ChapStick with unsettling frequency. He strolled slowly behind the check-in attendants – all women –and peered into their computers as they took passenger details.

'Pull that hair back, please, Cora. You are not at the disco now.' Cora flinched as she pushed a single loose strand behind her ear and unlocked the computer.

'Next, please!'

The passengers heading to her desk were the tail-end of a Cork check-in and the beginning of a Brussels flight. Cora had a love–hate relationship with the European Union capital. On one hand, it offered an ample supply of similarly aged, similarly attired business fliers. But, on the other hand, most of them flew with laptops and heavy documents that occupied them in the sky.

'Hello, Cora.'

'Ingrid! You alright? I didn't expect to have you with us today.'

'It was a bolt from the blue. The boss sent an email this morning saying he needed me in Brussels this afternoon, so here I am.' The Swedish woman spread her palms upwards, verifying that, indeed, here she was.

'And you're very early. If only they were all as good as you.'

Ingrid Sjöqvist was a frequent flier, and one of Cora's favourites. There was Aiden O'Connor too, but Aiden was a lot more work. Ingrid was an agricultural economist – that's what it said on her LinkedIn profile anyway. Cora didn't know *exactly* what the Swedish woman did but she knew it was a good job that involved flying around Europe doing advisory work for the European Commission and staying in nice hotels. More importantly, she knew that Ingrid slept in those hotels, under the best Egyptian cotton sheets, all on her own.

She was elfin in appearance – blonde and tall with icy, unblemished features. But any otherworldly mystique was negated by the Swede's austerely pragmatic business suits. Ingrid's speaking manner, too, did not belong to the fairies.

'My weather app informed me it would be raining cats and dogs this afternoon so I decided to leave before lunch rather than after. The traffic was also lighter.'

'Well you wouldn't want to risk it.'

'A bird in the hand is worth two in the bush.'

Ingrid's vocabulary was perfect but she spoke English with the stilted air of someone reading from cue cards. And she was alarmingly fond of idioms. Despite years living in London, Ingrid had never rid herself of those stock English-isms learned at school. Nor did she seem to notice that nobody else described raindrops as 'cats and dogs' or countered the most innocent of enquires with a reminder that 'curiosity killed the cat'.

'Well,' said Cora, taking Ingrid's passport from her. 'Now you've plenty of time for a cup of coffee.'

'And plenty of time for you to find me a good match. More than two hours, in fact. It will be a piece of cake!'

Cora didn't just like Ingrid because she was single. She liked her because she was smart. Ingrid had figured out Cora's matchmaking scheme about a month after the check-in attendant implemented it. Nobody else had ever caught on – neither passenger nor staff. A lifetime of setting people up had taught Cora it was better to play Cupid from the shadows, to release those arrows unannounced. Thankfully, Ingrid was alright with it. In fact, she was in favour of it.

'I'll find you someone, promise. Now go have a look around the shops. There's a sale in Electronics.'

Cora consulted her computer and threw an eye over the queuing passengers. Ingrid was clever, attractive, and, in that accidental European way, rather funny. All of which made it frustrating that Cora had not found her a suitable match, or at least nothing that had led to more than a couple of dates. She'd asked for hints – a preferred age range, physique, eye colour, anything – but Ingrid's answers were always vague. Curiosity and that wretched cat.

Perhaps there was a cultural barrier. Maybe that was why she hadn't clicked with anyone. For all Ingrid's years amongst the English, and her love of the most hackneyed parts of their language, perhaps something was getting lost in translation. Cora searched her passenger list by nationality – you could count on a Belgian flight for diversity – and selected a Danish man. Kristian Heffler, forty years old, residing in Copenhagen. A fellow Scandinavian. Cora could find no social media pages for Kristian but his passport information listed him as unmarried.

An hour later and Kristian approached the desk. He was handsome and a healthy few inches taller than Ingrid. Cora, who was five feet, eight inches, took height to be a preference of all long-limbed women. Kristian spoke with a friendly formality that seemed to go with Northern Europe, and Cora was equally polite when she handed him his ticket for 27B – right between the window and a willowy Swede.

FIVE

· · · · · · · · · · · · ·

LHR -> BUX 2.40 p.m.

Since Ingrid Sjöqvist started flying Aer Lingus, which she did now whenever she had a say in her travel arrangements, she had become one of those people who queues at the gate before the flight has opened. She wished she could tell all the sensible people who remained comfortably seated in the waiting area, safe in the knowledge they have an allocated seat on board, that she knows this is not the most efficient use of her time. They probably looked at her as she did the boobs standing in line around her. She knew the right term was 'Sheep', but they seemed more like nervous cattle. Upon seeing one of the herd heading for the trough, they all do the same – even though it's empty and the farmer is hours from filling it. This image of home came back to Ingrid as she queued for the Brussels flight. The slack-jawed English woman in front of her slowly chomped on a slab of gum. Ingrid had the distinct impression of a cow masticating grass.

Ingrid stood in line for a reason. She queued to stop herself scanning the other passengers – to restrain herself from guessing who Cora has put her sitting beside. She liked to keep that game for the few minutes after she was strapped into her designated seat, watching the line of eligible men shuffle down the aisle – willing the sturdier specimens to keep walking, and the meeker gentlemen to bow out of the game and into an earlier row.

Ingrid had been on to Cora's plotting within a few flights. The probability of her being seated beside unmarried, attractive men of her own age on every occasion was simply too low. Not to mention the check-in attendant's questions about relationship status and living arrangements. Those were not the kind of polite enquiries made by the English. Ingrid prided herself on being a perceptive person. *Ditt lille ljushuvud*, her father used to say. *You little clever clogs*.

She could not answer Cora's questions about 'type'. Ingrid had been so long on her own – almost twelve years – that she suspected her type was now limited to the efficiently dressed woman she saw in the elevator mirror every morning. Ingrid was fond of her own company. She found other people tiring. She'd had a couple of friends at school but she was always waiting to get home: to head down the long field and sit on the hay bales with Duran the dog curled up at her feet. Now she had acquaintances from work, and her family in Sweden of course, but she was happy by herself. Her job did not allow much time for socialising; she was always travelling, preparing briefings, becoming an overnight expert on a previously unheard of subsidy scheme. She loved the work. And there was something about the controlled conditions of these mid-week flights that made meeting new people exciting and manageable. She didn't particularly want to find The One because she didn't want the sky-high speed-dating to stop. Twice, these seating arrangements had led to ground-level dates but that was all Ingrid's schedule had allowed for. Although if Mr Right did happen to sit beside her, she assumed she'd make the effort.

Ingrid watched the Brussels commuters descend the aisle. One suit after another. Navy, grey, navy, navy. Having spent the first half of her life surrounded by cows, she was now, at thirty-six, rarely more than ten yards from a suit. 'The concrete jungle!' Ingrid's grandmother shouted every time the prodigal offspring came through the door at home. 'Back from the concrete jungle!' Ingrid hoped for someone robust, a man who knew what he was about and who would provide a flight's worth of good conversation. She had been watching the gent who stopped at her row – tall and broad, with fashionable thin-rimmed glasses, hair an appealing shade of straw and parted neatly down the middle. The man took a notebook and four large children's books from his suitcase before closing the bag and putting it in the overhead compartment. He took off his jacket, more sports than suit, brushed out the creases and carefully folded it over his arm. He waited for Ingrid to stand from her aisle seat.

'Good afternoon,' he said, placing the coat and books on the window seat and sliding into 27B. 'This flight doesn't seem so full – perhaps we won't need to sit on top of each other.'

She gave him a small smile. 'I imagine you are right.'

When everyone had taken their seat and the safety announcements had begun, the man hoisted himself out of 27B and into 27A. 'No offence intended.'

'And none taken.'

Ingrid opened the in-flight magazine on to an interview with a scraggily haired musician. Her neighbour's appearance suggested Scandinavia but his accent was less clear. She scanned him for clues but could not place him. He had opened one of the books and was making notes in the margins. They were *Tintin* annuals. She remembered them from home. The writing was in French but she was sure he wasn't. Did grown men read comics? She scanned him for further information and considered how best to begin the conversation.

Kristian Heffler was not looking forward to this afternoon's meeting. His job was language, not morality, and he was wholly uninterested in passing judgement on anything other than adverbs and synonyms. This afternoon's two-hour, eight-person discussion at his publisher's Belgian headquarters would be dominated by questions of social acceptability. He did not need to be there. The politics were nothing to do with him. Kristian wanted to be left alone to do his work, not to spend his week skipping around the continent, missing his son's school play. Censorship was above his pay grade.

Yet here he was. Squeezed into a seat on an unheard of airline, heading from a morning of mind-numbing rhetoric with London publishers to a similar round of discussions with French-language counterparts. The afternoon's meetings would be longer and more intense because the author's estate would be present.

Kristian sighed as he took up one of the offending books. He began to read the original translation, trying to distinguish any differences from the English-language version. He repeated to himself what he had said on the phone to Agnes before boarding: the problem, if you believed there to be a problem, was with the drawings, not the dialogue.

Kristian circled one vignette and put an asterisk beside it. Tintin was ordering a group of Congolese men to get to work and, yes, the racial distinction was uncomfortable. But if they made the labourers look less like golliwogs and put a smile on Tintin's face (and Kristian could probably sacrifice an exclamation mark or two) surely that would suffice. But the images were 'iconic', apparently. Words, Kristian had come to learn, were always the disposable entity.

He could feel the Swedish woman watching him. 'Work,' he said, looking up just as she looked away. 'I'm a translator.'

'Ah! I was wondering why you would be reading a children's book.'

'They're re-issuing the Tintin anthologies for the author's anniversary.'

'My brother used to read Tintin. He wanted to call our dog Snowy. Which languages do you translate?'

'English, Dutch, Danish, Swedish – *Du är Svensk, elle hur?*'

Accents and languages; they were his thing. She responded in English: 'Yes.'

'We're not technically *translating* these issues. Tintin is already so widely available, but I'm reworking any dialogue that needs reworking.' Kristian turned the page to see more pitch-black Congo natives dressed in farcical western clothes. What a waste of his time. You could remove every word of dialogue, and these would still be top-shelf picture books. 'The publishers are trying to decide whether or not to edit the books to make them more politically correct.' He dipped the book into 27B so the Swedish woman might better see.

'Oh.'

'But you must remember, this story is eighty years old. It was innocent of its time.'

'I understand.'

'I feel it my duty, my *professional duty*, to protect the language, to be as true to the author's original intention as I am capable.'

The woman nodded. 'It's very difficult.' She walked her fingers along the arm rest, watching them. 'But,' she continued. 'I suppose it is racist.' She lowered her voice but Kristian still flinched at the R word. She looked at the images once more: 'A picture paints a thousand words.'

'Racist' literature was a popular hobby horse amongst liberal Europeans – the same people, Kristian noted, who denounced censorship as a general concept. Kristian didn't think free speech was a belief within which you could pick and choose. He considered his work to be a vocation, and he served it above all others. Yet the lefties, who so 'valued' the artist, had no problem picking Kristian apart when his work didn't fit with their rather narrow set of ideals.

Kristian had been involved in a translation of an old

children's story a few years previously, in which the wealthy protagonist, jokingly, made a pet of his black gardener. It was only a few lines, and the publishers decided to keep it. Its inclusion had not been Kristian's decision – again, way beyond his pay grade and realm of giving a shit – but the vitriol he had received online led him to adopt a pseudonym for all social media. Agnes had been accosted by strangers at local cafes, told her partner was racist and a traitor to Denmark's good name, and by other mothers when dropping their son off at the nice liberal school where she and Kristian had worked so hard to get him enrolled.

He didn't tell other people how to do their jobs. He didn't drop everything to run out and protest at the teaching materials being used in schools or the level of pesticides sprayed by farmers. His mind boggled at how the masses could be so sure of such passing convictions. The whole world now operated like his Twitter feed – one homogenous opinion encouraging the next, until a consensus had been established.

'It's censorship,' he said. 'We cannot change literature because we no longer like the message. It's a historical document as much as a children's story.'

The Swedish woman gave him a sympathetic smile. Did she actually believe she knew more than him? It was this self-satisfied, politically correct bullshit that had him missing his son's starring role in *The Ugly Duckling*.

'They made some changes to Pippi Longstocking and it didn't affect the story,' she said

'Forget it.'

'No, don't forget it, I just meant—'

'I should have known better than to engage a Swedish liberal in debate.'

'Excuse me?'

'You are all falling over yourselves to show how egalitarian you are. Are you not? In Sweden? Maybe you should ban *The Merchant of Venice* for anti-Semitism and the rest of Shakespeare for not meeting your gender quotas.'

Kristian felt a deep satisfaction in how un-Swedish the woman now appeared.

'And where are you from?' she asked, the strained steadiness of her voice a delight.

'Denmark.'

'Denmark. Den-mark. Of course. Well. *Herre* Denmark. If you believe pacifism to be the same as open-mindedness, then, well, I am sorry to tell you that, that,' – Kristian watched as she began to literally spit words – 'that you are barking up the wrong tree!'

Nancy watched Row 27 from her station at the rear of the plane. The man had moved away from Cora's Swedish woman to the window seat but, if the back of his head was anything to go by, he was seriously regretting this decision. They were talking, and they were dead into it. His whole body was turned to face the woman – Ingrid: that was her name – and his shoulders were so far forward as to be back in his original seat.

Eek! Nancy loved the Row 27 flights. She liked being a tag team. Cora brought the baton out and Nancy took it over the finish line; it was just like the relay races at school. And she liked how no one else knew about it. Well like, not many people. She had told George because they were mates and he often worked the same flights so he could be a help, a second pair of eyes in the sky. That's what she had told Cora at least. Although it had yet to prove true.

Nancy used to be a decent runner. She had made the interschool team at least twice – she was sure of this because of the photographs in her mam's scrapbook. Gloria Moone kept a ringbinder of mementos from her three children's early years and occasionally, when home alone, she produced it and rang her only daughter to reminisce on their achievements – predominantly those of her sons. Each brother had triple the amount of scrapbook space Nancy had; there were clippings from the local paper about Joe Moone: Goalkeeping Prodigy, and Peter Moone's glowing school reports. 'The only student at Merseyside Grammar ever to be made head boy before his final year,' her mam would swoon down the telephone. 'And it stood to him, Nancy. It did. That's what Hansard & Hansard saw in him. They knew he was a leader.'

The scrapbook achievements ascribed to Nancy weren't really her own. The book had a couple of pictures of her in stage shows at the community hall and there was the one school report in which her teacher had raved about how organised the fourteen-year-old's jotters and pencil case were. The rest of it was just events Nancy had played a passive part in: pictures of her in cutesy clothes chosen by her mam, the lyrics from a song a friend of Peter's had written about her. But Nancy's favourite item was the autograph she had gotten from an air hostess the first time she boarded a plane. Imelda Snow was the most glamorous thing Nancy had ever seen. More impressive than a West End star. Even her dad seemed to lose his nerve. When Imelda Snow had told Joe Moone Sr to open his blind he had mumbled, 'Sorry.' Sorry?! Nancy had never heard her dad apologise for anything in his life. Halfway through the flight, Nancy built up the courage to stop Imelda and ask for her autograph.

'Isn't that cute? Joe, look,' her mam cooed. 'She's not a celebrity, darling. She's just a normal person.'

But Nancy had ignored her and thrust the sick bag and purple gel pen at the air hostess.

'With pleasure, beautiful,' Imelda said, turning the bag over and removing the pen's lid with her teeth. Her teeth were so white. Nancy wondered if your teeth had to be that white before you were allowed to fly around the world. 'Do you want to be an air hostess, precious?'

Nancy nodded her head and it was like suddenly it was true. Suddenly it was the only thing she wanted to do. Isn't that weird?

'I can tell you'll be wonderful,' said Imelda Snow, handing back the sick bag. 'Us blondes were made for the skies.'

After that, Nancy's mind was made up. Her year-eleven history teacher had instructed the class to do a project on a 'historical institution'. Nancy picked Pan Am. Her father said she hadn't understood the question, but Nancy got an A.

The project, for which she used first-hand accounts of staff aboard the luxury airline, had stayed up on the classroom wall for two months.

Two whole months: about as long as Joe Moone Jr's national league goalkeeping career. But she didn't see anyone proposing a toast to her year-eleven history project, every single bloody Christmas. Nancy placed both hands firmly on the trolley and prepared for in-flight service, making the usual pit stop at Row 27.

Ingrid finally had her breathing under control. Pompous, arrogant, racist. She admonished herself for not recognising his nationality, when he had so easily placed hers. Of course he was Danish. The Aryan looks, that pseudo-laidback air. And he was at least forty; those spectacles were an embarrassment. He'd probably always been this impressed with his own arguments. A leopard cannot change its spots, Ingrid thought sagely. Oh how she loved the English language.

'Coo-coo, Ingrid,' said the air hostess appearing, as she always did, at Row 27.

'Hello, Nancy.'

The air hostess lifted her eyebrows in the direction of Ingrid's window-seat neighbour. The Dane had gone back to scribbling the *Mein Kampf* sequel in the margins of his comics. Ingrid shook her head and mouthed a firm 'no'.

'Anything for you, sir?'

'No.' He barely lifted his head to acknowledge her. *Typical Dane*, thought Ingrid.

'Oh go on. Any friend of Ingrid's is a friend of ours. What's say we give you both a complimentary tipple.' Ingrid shook her head at Nancy, more fervently this time. Could she not read body language?

'No thank you,' said the Dane, finally looking up from his book. He smiled at Nancy.

'Oh go on,' the air hostess teased again. She produced two miniature wine bottles from the drawer. 'Live a little.' She handed them both a bottle of red, reaching over Ingrid to give the Dane a plastic glass. 'What are you reading there?'

'Tintin,' he said, turning the cover towards the air hostess. He was sitting straighter now, Ingrid noticed, and his chest was puffed out. 'I'm a literary translator.'

'Ooo,' trilled Nancy, placing the second glass on Ingrid's tray. 'You must speak a lot of languages then.'

'Nine in total and six to a professional standard.'

'Nine!'

Ingrid couldn't believe her ears. Was Nancy actually so easily impressed or was it part of the job? And if it was a bid to generate conversation between them, well then, she was flogging a dead horse.

'Yes. Danish, Swedish—'

Nancy started to poke Ingrid excitedly in the shoulder. 'Ingrid's Swedish, you know.'

'Yes. It's obvious.'

'Oh right.'

'Danish, Swedish, English, Dutch, Flemish—'

'Same thing,' Ingrid muttered, unscrewing her wine lid.

'Excuse me?'

'I said: same thing. Anyone who can speak Dutch can speak Flemish. Same thing.'

Nancy started to rattle her trolley. 'Well that all sounds very impressive.'

'French, some Greenlandic—'

Ingrid snorted.

'Which means,' the Dane continued, 'I can speak most Eskimo languages.'

'How cute,' said Nancy. 'Isn't that cute? Eskimos.'

'Inuit.'

'Sorry, Ingrid?'

'Nothing.'

Nancy departed and Ingrid concentrated on her wine. She refused to catch the Dane's eye, to acknowledge his dancing grin. They drank in silence. Ingrid thought about the briefings she had to deliver this afternoon and estimated what time she would get to bed. She sipped on her wine and slipped off her shoes. When she finally snuck a glance at the Dane, he was doodling monkeys in the margin of his book.

Kristian knew she was looking and did his best not to smirk. He'd had a nanny called Ingrid: horrible woman. He felt like a teenager again, trying to goad the A student beside him in history class. Only then it was boobs and wieners he'd been drawing on the edge of his book. He'd downed the wine in three gulps and was starting to feel relaxed. He'd sit through this afternoon's meeting, smiling and agreeable. Then he'd fly home in time to collect Agnes and their son from the school hall. Maybe Nicholas would re-enact the highlights of his performance before they all went to bed.

Ingrid's breathing was long and loud. Kristian finally looked up to find her eyeballing his doodles. He started to hum, still colouring his family of apes, adding baseball caps, pigtails, and skirts as he went. He hadn't drawn in a long time but he wasn't bad. The mammy ape was practically three-dimensional. The alcohol was making him giddy. He felt brave. Kristian raised his empty glass to Ingrid.

They were out of Touche Éclat. Again. Nancy shut the duty-free tray and made a note of it on the inventory. She could never understand why someone would put highlighter on a part of their face they wanted to conceal. Yet they were constantly out of stock. More than once she had counselled a passenger to try another—

'Gaaahhh!'

A woman's scream. Nancy peered down the aisle. Seats 27A and B were pinging manically. The shout was full of rage. The air hostess threw the clipboard on top of the trolley and powerwalked down the passageway. But when she reached Lovebird Lane, Ingrid was sitting quietly. The translator was attempting to stand in the crouched confines of a window seat, and he was the one raving: talking to himself but not in English – one of those other languages. Nancy followed his line of vision.

'Oh red wine! No, don't, you'll dry it in. You need white wine. Hang on a tick.' She hurried back to her station, pulled a miniature bottle of white from the storage cupboard – did it matter if it wasn't cold? She couldn't remember – and swiped a cloth from the shelf above her seat.

Back at Row 27, Ingrid's head was bowed while the translator continued conversing with himself.

'There. Dab this on.' Ingrid, as the middle woman, took the cloth and the translator snatched it from her immediately. 'Those plastic glasses can be slippy,' Nancy added. 'Could happen to the best of us.'

'It wasn't *my* wine.'

Nancy looked at Ingrid, and the Swede finally looked up, her eyes wide and innocent. 'It was a toast.'

'It was sabotage!'

'An accident.'

'I cannot go to a meeting looking like I've impaled my crotch!'

'No use crying over spilt milk.'

Nancy cleared her throat. 'Just keep dabbing it on. Gently, gently – yes, hold it a little longer. Dab, dab, dab.'

The dark blotches on the carpet caused a twinge of regret. Ingrid had not intended to make extra work for the cabin crew. It reminded her of the floor of the shed at home; even after Ingrid had scrubbed it out, birthing season left its mark. The Dane thundered out of his seat as soon as she stood to retrieve her bag from storage. Ingrid placed the in-flight magazine over the stain and followed his path towards the open door at the rear of the plane. But not right away. She thought it best to allow a few passengers to separate them.

She felt foolish, victorious, and a little hungry. It was a lovely sensation to shock oneself. Her behaviour had been primal. Ingrid checked her blouse and smoothed her hair, but was surprised to find everything still in place. A wolf in sheep's clothing, she thought and looked around. Nobody else could tell. Alone was not the same as lonely. She continued down the aisle.

'Not The One then, no?' said Nancy, standing by the exit with the Dane's crimson rag in her hand. The spoils of a bloody battle. Well not quite a battle, but a bit of exercise to set Ingrid up for the day. She felt good, invigorated for an afternoon of economic strategising and then maybe a steak for dinner.

'No, not The One,' said Ingrid, throwing a coat over her shoulders. 'But not to worry.' She beamed brightly at the air hostess. 'Plenty more fish in the sea.'

SIX

········

From her desk, Cora watched a young couple lean backpacks against a polished handrail as they sorted through their supplies one final time. The woman pulled a faded sunhat from her bag and balanced it on her boyfriend's head. It was mid-February but both were wearing sandals. Cora imagined them heaving those backpacks from India to Vietnam and on through to Australia. They would be back here in a year's time, sporting tans and matching harem pants.

It had always amazed Cora that somewhere so sterile could be so emotional. The arrivals hall was non-stop hugs and kisses and tears. Departures was more tentative but the emotions were still there bubbling under the service. Airports were like hospitals really, only with the odds more in favour of joy.

Cora hadn't been on a plane since her return from Germany. She barely remembered boarding at Berlin airport, except for the strange sensation that every third person she saw was Friedrich. Ludicrous, of course, because he was so singular in appearance. And because he was never going to be the one to follow, to need her, to beg.

He came into her mind less and less, or at least she had gotten better at escorting him out. But still there were things that brought him back and still she thought she saw him, in the throngs at Heathrow or in the corner shop on Seven Sisters Road or any of the other places that logic told her he had never been. They'd met at a bar four months after Cora had moved to the German capital. A colleague from the copywriting agency where she'd worked was playing a gig and Friedrich Turner knew him too, vaguely, like how he knew every musician in Berlin.

Friedrich was interested in her being English. He said he had a fascination with English literature and music and he wanted to know everything about her. She knew it was a charming act, giving her a disproportionate amount of attention, but she went along with it, basking in his intelligence and how attractive he was. That first night, before the gig was over, the two of them had slipped out and wandered the city. They had walked until five in the morning, talking all the time, and when finally the sun was coming up and Cora's feet were starting to blister under her sandal straps, still Friedrich insisted he could not go home. He was falling in love, he said. Cora laughed.

'Are you not?' he asked, linking her arm in his then. 'I could be in love by noon.'

So they went back to her apartment, ate pastries, and drank coffee. At 7 a.m. Friedrich disappeared, returning with a bottle of wine. At 9 a.m., Cora called in sick to work. They had sex thereafter and, by noon, Friedrich declared that, yes, he was irrevocably in love. He was recently separated from the woman he had married at university. 'Everything, including love, is only impressive when you are young,' he said, and Cora – who was as infatuated with the idea of Friedrich as much as the fact of him – thought it brilliant.

He was still the most beautiful boy she had ever seen. And though he was slightly older than her that was always how she saw him: as a beautiful boy. It was unimaginable that he might age, ever be frail or wrinkled. He was so sure of his own brilliance, and Cora believed in it too, that it seemed to make him immortal.

He had moved in with her within a week and the intensity never waned. That it soured was a separate matter. Jealousy oozed from both of them and, as the months went on, Friedrich frequently left the bed at night to make phone calls and thereafter sometimes left the apartment entirely. Occasionally he was phoning his ex-wife and other times – because Cora had lost all self-respect to the point of grabbing his phone and locking herself in the bathroom to check his call history – he wasn't talking to anyone at all.

'Would I know it, if I was going insane?' she'd said one night after he had woken her up to see what she was dreaming about. It was a particular affront to Friedrich when she slept and he did not, like she was keeping some experience from him. The days after such nights he became withdrawn and spoke little, as if he was punishing her by keeping something of himself locked away.

And yet, perversely, she'd loved him all the more for it. He didn't belong to anyone. Nobody, not even Cora, could ever fully have him. She had thought it inspiring, to have their level of intimacy and yet still be free. Later, however, she thought it was probably more precise than that: it wasn't that he didn't belong to anyone, he just hadn't belonged to her.

Cora heard Joan beside her, cursing at a Sudoku puzzle, and blinked herself back to attention. There were more productive, deserving things to daydream about. Cora watched as the backpacking couple threw the haversacks over their shoulders, and she returned her mind to possible holiday destinations.

'Is the Euro still weak? Or has the Greek stuff all been sorted out?'

'Sorry, pet?' said Joan, keeping her eyes on the Sudoku book half hidden under her flight roll call. Whenever Weasel wasn't rostered on, Joan brought this puzzle anthology to work – that or the Daily Mail's *Mammoth Book of Crosswords*. Jim had saved up the newspaper coupons and gotten it for her last Christmas.

'Never mind.' Cora shifted on her stool. She hummed something tuneless, and tried to focus. 'It's very quiet for a Friday, isn't it? Everyone must have decided to stay put. '*Have youse no homes to go to?*'' she said to the empty queuing area in front of her. That was what her mother used to say when Cora's school friends stayed past supper. Her mind made another break for the past, but she quickly reined it in. 'Maybe I'll go on lunch.' There was no response. 'Lunch, Joan. I said, I'm going on lunch.'

'Do, love, do.'

Annoyed to realise she had forgotten her book – Nick

Hornby's new one, and she loved Nick Hornby – Cora bypassed the staffroom for the bench by the taxi rank. The day before she had sat and watched an awkward man ask a bookish woman to share a taxi. She couldn't make out what they were saying but she could imagine. That bench was one of her favourite places in all of Heathrow. Cora put an extra jumper on under her regulation coat and headed outside. It was cold but the sun was strong and she threw her face towards it, grateful, as she always reminded herself to be, that it wasn't raining.

Cora pulled a sandwich from her bag – bought in Costa this morning, and already hard around the edges – and began to tear it into pieces as she watched the masses lining up for cabs. There was no doubling up today. It made her sad to see passengers marking out their queue territory with luggage, using suitcases like shoppers use checkout dividers. 'Good fences make good neighbours,' she murmured to herself.

'Did your mother never tell you not to play with food?' Charlie Barrett had appeared beside her, a stopwatch swinging around his neck. How was it she never saw him coming? His stealth movements must be what had propelled him up the security employment ranks so quickly.

Cora shielded her eyes from the sun as she looked up at him. 'Sheila said table manners were for the English – that her lot weren't so concerned with formalities. What's the stopwatch for?'

'I'm timing Ray. He's taken to jogging around the terminal at lunchtime. This is his third day now.'

'Is he getting faster?'

'No, but I think I'll shave a few seconds off today – just to keep his spirits up.' Charlie pointed behind Cora. 'Here comes the marathon man now.'

Ray's hair was still stuck to his head, but this time the lubricant was sweat, and his uniform had been replaced by an equally new-looking Adidas tracksuit. He gave Cora an exhausted wave as he pounded past.

'He's really taken to the regime then?'

'Yep, and the television folk can't make enough of him working at an airport. They want his slogan to be "flying in the face of fat". Not a very pleasant image though, is it? Come on, mate!' Ray hadn't gotten far and was now doubled over with his hands on his knees. 'Push it, push it! Don't let fear decide your future!' Cora looked at Charlie, and he shrugged. 'It's what they say.'

Charlie and Ray were friends. They often had lunch together and Cora had a vague memory of someone saying they were second cousins. Few work environments were as nepotistic as the airport.

Ray thudded back towards them, throwing his body forward with such force Cora feared he would end up on the Tarmac. Every inch of exposed skin was red and blotchy. Cora held out her water bottle and he fell on it.

'Time of 12.20 – that's great, mate! A whole half a minute faster than yesterday.'

'You're . . . just . . . saying—' Ray wheezed between alternating gulps of oxygen and water .'I nearly . . . keeled over . . . down . . . by—' Big inhale. 'Collection point.' He collapsed onto the bench beside Cora and limply handed her back the water.

'So it's going well then, Ray?' she enthused, discreetly wiping the sweat from the bottle's rim with her Costa napkin. He nodded, too out of breath to discuss it.

'He's got a 3K run next Wednesday night at Imperial College,' said Charlie. 'Actually, you might put this up in the Aer Lingus staffroom.' He took a flyer from his pocket and handed it to her.

Fight The Flab: Run for Fitness. Audience members should arrive at 7.30 p.m. Neon accessories and rave gear encouraged.

'Never mind the dress code, but do come. I've got notices up with BA and City. The more the merrier.'

Beside her, Ray's wheezing was getting louder, as if he might be about to choke. But he was trying to speak. 'Nnn . . . Not . . .' Gulp. 'Not Nancy.'

Cora hooted. Nancy had been plaguing Ray since the filming session, enquiring about his lunch breaks, menus, and when they were recording his 'At Home with the Leaders' section. Who knew Nancy Moone would ever cause a grown man to hide in toilet cubicles? 'Roger that,' said Cora, folding the flyer and putting it in her bag.

'Come on, mate.' Charlie patted Ray on the shoulder. 'You better hit the showers.' The security officer smiled at Cora as she waved them farewell. Cora had never understood Charlie's reputation for being quiet. He didn't take part in the rampant airport gossip – news got around this place faster than the electronic buggies – but Cora always found him warm and, if not chatty, at least friendly.

Perhaps he did like her. Charlie was a good man. He got better-looking the more you saw him and there was no fear of him going bald – but he wasn't for her. Maybe someone else though. Roisin? Mary? One of the other check-in attendants?

Back at the desk, the Sudoku book was gone and Joan was checking in a flight to Madrid. 'Three ruddy complainers I've had now, all moaning about the security restrictions,' the older woman grumbled as she grabbed some poor man's passport. 'All bloomin' Americans, of course. "Why can't I choose my seat?" this, and "I need an aisle seat" that. No, love, what you *need* is a good kick up the backside.' Joan paused, eyeing her current customer suspiciously. 'You're not a Yank, are you?'

The sallow-skinned man shook his head. He was as Spanish as the ships that discovered America. Still Joan narrowed her eyes as she handed back the document, not letting go until he gave a nervous tug.

'Nancy called,' said Joan. 'Said to tell you the Belfast duo was a no-no. Whatever that means.'

A Celtic supporter and an Irish dancing promoter. Such promise.

'She also told me to tell you . . .' Joan looked at the pad where she had jotted down the message. 'That she has switched to the Dublin flight tonight and that you are very welcome.'

Below the desk, Cora clicked her heels. Aiden O'Connor was always on the Friday night flight to Dublin and while Cora wouldn't personally have gone near him with a bargepole, the Irishman was, objectively, one of her most eligible frequent fliers. Aiden was a doctor, relatively handsome, and had the kind of lilting brogue that put Colin Farrell to shame. However, he also had all the unattractive traits that tended to go with being a not-unsightly doctor – arrogance, defensiveness, and an irritating need to always be right. If you said the ocean was blue, he'd say it was only a reflection of the sky. He also refused to divulge just about anything about himself, which was particularly frustrating when you were trying to build a dating database.

Aiden would chat about the weather, travel, current affairs. The two of them discussed films – his taste being more pretentious than hers – and Aiden, who had known Sheila for a couple of months before she retired, regularly enquired as to how her treatment was going. Even religion and politics were up for discussion. But as soon as the conversation turned personal, you were as likely to get anything out of him as you were an aeroplane from a Parisian airport during a strike.

It had taken Cora weeks to learn he was single – and not just weeks of idle chit-chat, but weeks of blatantly pointed questions.

Do you have flatmates?

Constant travel must be tough on a relationship . . .

What are your feelings on Marks & Spencer's Dine In For Two?

But the man was a fortress. He only finally let it slip when they were discussing family traditions at Christmas. He said he could barely remember his because he'd spent the last seven abroad with his girlfriend. And then he murmured 'Ex-girlfriend', more correcting himself than Cora, and refused to say another word.

She knew he'd been living in London for almost a year, and that he returned to Dublin at weekends to volunteer at the burns unit of a hospital where he used to work. What kind of doctor he was or why he flew home every week when there were plenty of charities in London – and he didn't exactly seem like the bleeding-heart type – were pieces of information he never offered up. It didn't help that Aiden O'Connor was a frustratingly common name, so Internet searches yielded little.

Cora spent the next two hours checking in various European flights and researching the women on board that evening's Dublin route. Cora tended to set Aiden up with high-earners with high-pressure jobs. She was targeting the Lean-In set – a woman who could deal with his stubbornness, maybe even take him down a notch or two. She looked for power suits in profile pictures and high-achiever hobbies on LinkedIn: marathons, geopolitics, mastering obscure languages, that sort of thing. She'd have tried him with Ingrid, if only for her own curiosity, but they never took the same flight.

Cora was in the middle of some Facebook searches when

Nancy approached the desk. The air hostess propped her elbows on the counter and cupped her chin with her palms in an affected manner. She sighed. Cora looked up and gave a reluctant grin.

'What's up?'

'Everything, nothing, the planes . . .'

Cora went back to her computer and Nancy sighed again. 'What are you doing next Wednesday night?'

'Erm, I . . .'

'Because Ray has another shoot and I really feel I should be there for him,' said Nancy stoically. 'He needs support, a bit of colour in his campaign. The director said I could really help with that, but . . .' She sighed. 'I'm just so busy. The promotion interviews are right around the corner.' Nancy let her arms fall to the counter, and rested her head on them. Cora hadn't even put the Fight the Flab flyer on the noticeboard yet; how did everybody in this place know everything so fast? She decided not to mention the barring order. No matter how much you tell them not to, people always shoot the messenger.

'And,' Nancy continued, 'as if I'm not busy enough, a Gold Circle member asked for my number on the 12.40 from Milan today. He wants to take me to dinner on Wednesday – at The Shard. I've never been. Then I also have all this study to do for the interviews and—'

'I doubt you'll miss much at filming.'

'But it's exciting, with the cameras and everything. And I don't want Ray's campaign to suffer. Everyone else will be going.' Nancy paused. 'Charlie will be there.'

'Cut it out.'

'But he likes you!'

'Even if he does like me, I don't think of him like that. I'm not interested.'

'You don't have to marry him. Maybe I could have a word—'

'No. No way, Nancy. Drop it. Alright?'

The air hostess pointed. 'Alright, fine.'

'Now,' said Cora, returning to her computer. 'Let's put that passion into something we can both agree on: this evening's Dublin flight. I've a bit more research to do, but can you remind the operations controller to patch through the call? God bless your charms, Nancy.'

Boarding for the Dublin flight was open and Cora had picked a match for Aiden – a thirty-three-year-old Dublin woman whose Twitter page, although a little inactive of late, described her as 'chief executive of a children's charity and recipient of the Grant Williams award for excellence'. Her profile picture showed an attractive woman in a navy suit with classy cleavage. She knew this because the woman was literally leaning in to the camera, which Cora took as a very good sign. Maybe they'd talk about ways to encourage medical philanthropy and all the World Health Organization's recent findings and by the end of the flight they'd have fallen in love whilst also coming up with a way to save the children. The woman would give Aiden her BlackBerry, he'd type in the name of some innovative life-saving procedure, and their hands would touch as he passed it back across the plastic armrest . . .

Cora came back to reality to find the target – the charity wonder woman – standing in front of her. She was more dishevelled than her Internet photographs and she didn't engage in much chit-chat, but she did rest a shiny BlackBerry on the counter whilst searching for her passport so Cora chose to continue regarding the glass as half full.

'Enjoy your flight!' Cora said, beaming, finalising the woman's details and handing her a ticket for 27C.

Cora threw an eye over the queue, where Dublin commuters were now mixed with those headed for Brussels and Paris, and spotted Aiden about ten people back. He was tall with broad shoulders and hands that seemed too big for someone who used them for such precise work. He didn't pay much attention to his appearance – he wore the same Irish rugby jersey most Fridays, and Cora doubted he owned more than two pairs of trousers – but he had a rugged appeal that, reluctant as she was to admit it, meant he was more attractive than not. She wondered if he went home to change before coming to the airport. He hardly wore a jersey to the hospital. What was his apartment like? Minimal décor, she presumed, nothing that required imagination . . .

'Earth to Cora.'

Aiden was standing in front of her. 'Sorry. In my own world,' she said, typing his flight details into the computer. 'How are you? Long week?'

'Same length as last week, I'm fairly sure.'

Cora bit her tongue. 'You know, I still don't know what it is you do.'

'Mmm.'

'We've been having these conversations for months now – I even know how you take your coffee – and yet your exact job continues to elude me.'

'How do you know about my coffee?'

'Because of that time you so comprehensively corrected my assumption that a flat white and latte were the same thing? I also know that you won't use microwaves because one time when you were nine, the mashed potato didn't quite heat the whole way through.'

'Ten, actually,' he said and Cora could have sworn he was stifling a grin.

'And yet, I'm missing the basics. You know what I do.'

'Mmm.'

'It's only fair.'

'My job's more complicated.'

'I'll try to get my simple check-in attendant brain around it.'

'I finally watched *When Harry Met Sally*,' he said and Cora knew it was a blatant subject change but she took the bait.

'I love that film.'

'That's why I'm telling you.'

'Did I say it before?'

'At Halloween. You were going to a party dressed as Billy Crystal and you were in the market for an oversized eighties jumper.'

Roisin had won the coin toss to be Meg Ryan. And Cora had eventually found the perfect white knit sweatshirt in a charity shop. 'You remember that?'

'It'd be hard not to. You kept going on and on. Wanted to know if I had any Halloween plans, if I'd ever gone as a duo, if I was planning to do so that year, what did I think would be the best couple's costume? So many questions. As always.'

When it was all played back to her like that, Cora wondered if perhaps she should work on her subtlety. 'I didn't think that'd be your kind of film.'

'It wasn't. But it was all that was on and I couldn't sleep. Anyway, it did confirm one thing for me.'

'That all those women you thought you'd satisfied were actually faking it?'

'That you officially have the worst taste in films. *The Way We Were*, *Moonstruck*, *10 Things I Hate About You*. All terrible.'

'Blasphemy.'

'And now this. The ending is always obvious from the start.'

'So?'

'So?' he echoed incredulously as Cora continued to stare at him innocently. 'So what's the point in watching when you know what happens? Forget it. How about I recommend a film for you to watch? Something good.'

'Not a documentary,' she said. 'I hate documentaries. It might be the only genre of film I dislike. I do not think I have ever met a documentary that I liked.'

Aiden reached over the counter for Cora's pen and scribbled the name on her notepad. A flash of a smile as a dimple appeared on his left cheek.

'It's a documentary, isn't it?'

'It's good. And it's not difficult.'

Cora rolled her eyes. She hoped he was less condescending with the women she put him sitting beside. 'I'll watch it on one condition,' she said, whipping his passport and ticket for 27B off the counter. 'You have to tell me what kind of medicine it is you do.'

'You missed your calling as a detective, did you know that, Cora Hendricks?' But she continued to hold the documents in the air. 'I don't see why it matters. I specialise in reconstructive surgery,' he said finally. 'It's not very interesting.'

'Like when people have a tragic accident, and they're left disfigured?'

'That kind of thing.'

'And one more question.'

'No. We agreed – an eye for an eye, not an eye for a complete set.'

'Why do you go home every weekend?'

'That's none of your business.'

'Come on, I'm just curious. I—'

'No. You're not curious, Cora. You're nosy. Now, can I have my passport before I miss my flight?'

His tone smarted and Cora lowered her arm as her cheeks began to burn. She was at work and he was a customer. She had momentarily forgotten herself. 'Sorry,' she mumbled but he snapped the documents away without another glance.

'See you next week.'

Cora watched him turn and walk away as the colour rose further in her face. It wasn't like she'd asked to see his payslip. It was a run-of-the-mill question, and she'd said sorry. Cora called the next passenger to her desk. She could only hope the charity woman had a thing for rudeness.

SEVEN
·················

Reconstructive surgery, that's what he'd said. He hadn't lied. That was what he'd specialised in, what he'd won several prestigious awards for, and what he'd been doing up until a year ago. He corrected himself. It was *still* what he did.

Why was Cora always picking? Couldn't she just leave it at that?

The in-flight safety demonstration began and Aiden O'Connor momentarily lost his train of thought. He'd flown so much in the past year that he could have gotten up and done it himself but, much like how those with no interest in sports still find themselves drawn to TV screens in pubs, he couldn't resist watching the routine. Aiden appreciated technique. The air steward placed an oxygen mask between his knees and pointed firmly at the emergency exits, his head tilted towards the heavens. It was the kind of pose you saw at a gig, just before fireworks exploded either side of the lead singer. This guy was good. Aiden had no time for the ones who studied the carpet whilst waiting for the intercom to guide them. Those lads did not inspire a great sense of safety.

Helping disfigured people after tragic accidents?

Aiden cringed. If you considered it a tragic accident to be born with a nose that turned up ever-so-slightly at the end and engaged to a man who thought paying to straighten it was a romantic wedding gift then, yes, he was still helping life's poor unfortunates.

But it wasn't all nose jobs and Botox, he told himself. They did good work too. Cleft palates and cleft tongues and mole removals . . .

The Fasten Seatbelts sign illuminated and Aiden pulled the cord across his waist, startling the woman beside him who was powering off her phone. He threw his head back against the seat-rest. Who was he kidding? He'd had about three worthy cases since he'd started at the clinic. He was very well paid and it was all highly prestigious, but it was getting more and more difficult to be proud of what he did. A year ago, he was restoring hope to people who were so extensively and severely burnt that they would beg him to let them die. Now his time was spent advising people how they could avoid getting older without actually having to die.

He told himself it was ambition that had brought him to London, to the clinic. He'd even concede to pride. Both were less embarrassing than admitting to a broken heart.

'I try and I try with that Irish fella but it never goes any-where,' said Nancy, herself and George standing in the rear alcove, monitoring the action. 'Maybe he has a woman in

Ireland?' Nancy had flirted with Aiden once herself. She'd complimented his jumper, stroked his arm and everything, but he hadn't shown any interest. She just assumed she'd been too subtle. 'Or do you think he could be gay?'

'Why? Because he wasn't interested in you?'

'As if!' said Nancy, thankful for anti-redness foundation.

George peered out of the alcove. 'The dude in the sports sweater? Not a chance. Anyway, I don't think it's all him. That woman doesn't look like she's at the most sociable juncture of her life. Maybe Cora's losing her touch.'

Nancy picked up the Aer Lingus procedural manual from where she'd left it on the shelf. She was two-thirds of the way through.

'Are you going to intervene?'

'I just have a few pages to read first,' said Nancy. She opened the book to the marked passage but couldn't concentrate with George hovering. She closed it again. 'Since when do you care about Cora's matchmaking anyway?'

'Since about never?' George had that annoying habit of making everything sound like a question. 'I have already expressed my views on Cora's hetero bullshit. Sorry for trying to elicit a bit of polite conversation.'

George insisted he didn't have a problem with Cora, but Nancy thought otherwise. He expended a lot of energy complaining about something he supposedly had no interest in. 'I'll just read a bit more,' she said. 'Then I'm going in.'

It hadn't been Aiden's idea to move to London. Izzy was the one who wanted a change. But now she was still at the hospital in Dublin and he was living the new chapter alone at an elite cosmetic clinic where everything, from the expensive marble to the receptionist's welcome, was cold. Aiden wasn't even that gone on make-up; he'd always preferred Izzy with none. Not that she believed him. 'Men think they don't like make-up, but what they actually mean is they don't like over-the-top make-up. We all look better with a little on,' she said. 'Even me.'

But it wasn't like Aiden didn't know when she was wearing it – the face was his speciality – and still he preferred her with none. A little make-up was how the rest of the world knew Izzy, but the clear face she wore between their bed sheets and lounging around the house on Sundays, that was just for him.

They'd been together seven years when she started to drift. He'd been working long hours – he was moving up the ranks fast so he kept climbing – and Izzy was busy too. They spent less time together but Aiden's feelings never faded. He'd presumed when it all settled down they'd start a family. He'd wanted that from the start.

'We barely see each other and yet neither of us seems to mind,' Izzy said one morning when he rolled over to find her wide awake and staring up at their lopsided lampshade, a red mark on her cheek from how she'd slept, her eyes avoiding his. 'I need a change.'

Aiden sat up. He could tell she was serious. 'Okay.'

If Izzy wanted a change, he'd make it. Aiden loved his job, but he loved her more. So when, a few days later, a head-hunter phoned from one of Harley Street's top facilities, he didn't follow his usual course and politely decline. He listened. They wanted him so much that they came to Dublin to do the interview. They understood his niggles about the work he'd be doing, but there was still room for charity work, they said, and he'd be just as appreciated by these patients as the people he treated after barbeque accidents and fires. Money didn't stop people deserving his help. He convinced himself the job offer was fate and took Izzy out for dinner to tell her the good news.

'Please tell me you're not serious. You didn't even run this by me. I don't want to go to England, Aiden!'

'You said we needed a change. Where else would I find work? You always liked London.' Aiden gave a confused laugh, but Izzy just stared at her plate. 'Come on, Izzy. I love you.'

'I said *I* needed a change. I never said "we".'

Her words came slowly, but they landed with violence. A sucker punch to his lungs. 'That was – three weeks ago. You, we've been fine since then. We're still sleeping in the same bed.'

Then it was Izzy's turn to laugh, sad and tired and as devoid of humour as his own. 'I was giving you time to adjust, to come to terms with it.' She closed her eyes. 'How could you think this is fine?' And when she opened them, it was like she didn't recognise him. 'How could you *want* this to be fine?'

He couldn't say a thing. There was no air left in him. The next day, he moved his stuff out.

George Yare had always thought that if Cora actually bothered to ask, she'd quickly realise she wasn't the only one with a strong romantic streak. Newsflash: Gays Have Hearts Too. George was as romantic as the next homosexual who'd grown up in a homogenous Middle America backwater with nothing but pure fantasy to sustain him. Having zero queer role models, in real life or on television, is the perfect breeding ground for romantic longings and a vivid imagination. Not that he'd condescend to talk to any of his high-school crushes now. And as for sticking his well-travelled tongue down their redneck throats? The thought made him gag.

The first time someone had called him 'fag' he'd been at the mall trying to find a backpack that every other kid didn't already own. Two guys from the grade above passed him and whispered it under their breath. Fag. If it had been some racist jibe he could make the link. Yeah, his skin was dark. But fag? George could never figure out what had given him away. Was it the way he stood or moved? Was it his hair? Every morning for the last six months of high school he stood before the mirror and scrutinised his appearance, trying to figure out how they had known. And then, on the morning of graduation, when his hair was looking particularly awesome, he finally thought: Fuck it. If

I look like a fag and walk like a fag and shop for a backpack like a fag, then I guess I must be a fag. As soon as the graduation gown went back to the rental, he got the fuck out of Dodge, determined to find the faggiest job, and live the faggiest, most fabulous life he could.

He'd done various things in New York, Chicago, Atlanta – though hard as he tried to be a screaming stereotype, he had zero aptitude for interior design and he just did not give a shit about anyone's hair but his own. Then he came to London and had a total of one boyfriend: Tim. Ironically, London had been too small for Tim so he'd left the city and George for New York, which was fine. The problem was meeting someone new.

George was an active member of Grindr but casual sex had gotten tired a couple of years back and he was more about dating than mating. He was looking for someone who was a good lay, sure, but also interested in a meaningful relationship. It wasn't easy. And he wasn't getting any help. 'What about meeting someone through your mates?' had been Nancy's ground-breaking contribution. But George's circle of gay friends was small, and anyone he met through that group had usually already slept with the mutual acquaintance who introduced them. And then there were the Straights, like Cora, who suggested setting him up with whatever other gay man they happened to know. He wouldn't even condescend to point out the obvious insult.

Except it *was* totally insulting. Cora was putting all her energy into matchmaking strangers, and here he was desperate to meet someone and nobody to help him out.

Like, hello? He was a willing frigging candidate.

But whatever. George would just keep on fending for himself. Going on coffee date after coffee date on the off-chance that the other person wasn't the damaged psycho they invariably ended up being. He was averaging three meet-ups a week now. How many times was he going to have to list off his career history and tell the same hilarious anecdotes about drunk celebrities on flights? It was fucking exhausting. Couldn't he just hand out some sort of dating CV? Last weekend he met up with a thirty-six-year-old Frenchman. George saw him arriving through the window of the Southbank cafe and thought, 'Oh my god, this one actually looks like his profile pics.' But then he watched the super-cute Frenchman remove his wedding ring. George went up to order a second coffee, and just never came back. Peace out. The thought of rednecks in his hometown blushing wasn't enough of a reason to tolerate that shit.

He'd met Izzy at a house party when they were both training. They'd stood in the middle of the kitchen and the magnetic energy that drew them together seemed also to create a force field that kept everyone else spinning at a distance. Aiden had no idea how long that first conversation had lasted. And when the hostess finally interrupted because Aiden's help was needed in removing some drunk from a bedroom, Izzy followed him out of the kitchen. 'I've got your back,' she whispered, sliding her hand into his.

Their first date was dinner but their second was a walk on Sandymount Strand. They kept going until their fingers were so numb they had to disentangle and retreat into respective pockets. They found a pub and when Izzy returned from the bar, her nose red raw and her eyes starting to water, Aiden felt a sudden bolt of alarm. For the first time in his life, he thought: *I'm going to marry this woman.*

'Anything for you two?'

It was the air hostess who regularly worked his flight, the blonde one with a passion for textures. She'd been very interested in his navy jumper last year. He told her it was a standard Marks & Spencer rigout but she kept going on about the fabric, catching it between her fingers. Aiden had never seen anyone so excited by cotton.

'No thank you,' said the woman in the aisle seat, opening her eyes now.

'I'll have a coffee,' said Aiden, contorting his arm so it could slip through the seatbelt and into his pocket. He handed over the coins.

The air hostess passed back a coffee, an overly packaged cutlery bag, three LHT milks, and a KitKat. 'On the house.' It was funny how Aiden never seemed to pay for anything on the flight home, but on the Sunday night trips back they were much more by the book. The air hostess turned back to the woman beside him. 'Are you sure now? Nothing at all?'

'Maybe I'll have some chocolate.'

'Do! We all need to treat ourselves from time to time.' She held out a few bars and the woman selected a Bounty. 'Travelling for business or pleasure?'

'I was visiting a friend.'

'That's nice,' the air hostess enthused. 'Do anything fun?'

'We just – not really. We were catching up, and some walks. Richmond Park.'

'Oh very nice. You been there, Aiden? Aiden is Irish but he lives in London now. Isn't that right, Aiden?'

The air hostess was smiling at him like a demented badger. She knew his name and he had forgotten hers. He stretched to see her tag. 'Haven't made it to Richmond Park yet. Nancy. Still a few places on the to-visit list.'

'Well,' said the air hostess – Nancy – pushing the trolley onwards. 'Maybe your neighbour here can give you some tourism tips?'

But the woman in the navy suit quickly bowed her head again in sleep and Aiden returned to staring out his window into a deeper navy abyss. All Aiden wanted was for *this* – him and Izzy – to be fine. Yes he had gotten distracted, but by work. There were other things he wanted to achieve but he never doubted it would all end with Izzy. All roads led to her, and he'd keep walking because she was still the destination.

'I'd say the chances of copping off are slim to none.' Nancy switched the receiver to her right ear and watched George exit the alcove. He gave her a pointed eye roll as he left.

Cora's voice crackled down the line. 'Did you offer them a drink?'

'Of course. But he's useless – I've told you that before, Cupid. And I'm not so sure about your female entry either. Bit of a zombie, isn't she?'

'Give it another shot?'

'It's hopeless.'

'Please?'

'I'll see what I can do.' Nancy hung up. Much as she loved when a Row 27 match worked out, she'd like it even more if she could get a Cora match to work out. She didn't care about her friend meeting The One; she'd just like her to meet *any* one. And Nancy thought Charlie Barrett would do nicely.

George reappeared, squeezing past her. 'Have we any cheese selections left?' he asked, rummaging in the storage unit. 'Three orders already. A very European bunch on board this evening.' George delved into the back of the drawer: 'Bingo.'

'What's this?' he said, holding up the procedural manual like he might catch something. 'You hitting the books?'

'I was thinking of going for senior cabin crew.'

'Shut up.'

'Well, just thinking.'

'Oh, Nancy, babe, yes! You'd be awesome. Much better taking orders from you than Satsuma Sarah.' Sarah Martin, the senior on board, had a tendency to overdo the fake tan.

'Usually you need to be staff for three years. I've been here almost one year. But I was four at the other place, so hopefully.'

'Ab-so-lutely. Uno momento; I'll be back.' George gave a dramatic flourish and glided down the aisle, three cheese selections in hand.

There was a lot in her favour. Aer Lingus was her second airline and she had been named employee of the month for the entire European operation in December – after only six months in the job. Nancy had been made up about that. The fella she was seeing at Christmas had bought her a Moschino handbag, which was proper gorgeous and she'd wanted one forever, but the 'Employee of the Month' certificate, framed and accompanied by a nice bottle of bubbly, had been even better.

Nancy brought the champers home to Liverpool and opened it at Christmas dinner. 'That's nice, darling,' was all her mother said when Nancy told her where it came from. Gloria Moone had no energy left after all the shrieking at her brother Joe's news that he and his wife were trying for a baby. It seemed Nancy was the only one who thought this was Too Much Information.

She'd brought the award up again, just casually like, with her other brother. But Peter killed her enthusiasm instantly: 'Come on, Nancy,' he said, raising an eyebrow. Come on what, she wanted to ask. Come on, what? Why was it she could give a moderately famous musician a nipple cripple for stroking her leg as she filled his duty-free order, but she was incapable of telling her own family to shove it?

Cora had been good about the certificate. Nancy thought she might be jealous, but of course not. She probably had no interest in it; she probably thought it was a bit silly.

The airline was just a stopgap for Cora. It was a bit of fun, a chance to play matchmaker. But Nancy took it seriously. She wanted to be senior cabin crew and she wanted it before she was twenty-eight. She loved Row 27, but she needed to be more than Cupid's spy.

Aiden hadn't wanted to lose face and he no longer had a say in losing Izzy, so he confirmed his notice at the hospital and moved alone to London. Everything in a relationship is a joint decision, until it comes to the end.

But if he gave Izzy enough time, enough space, he was sure she'd change her mind. So Aiden signed up to volunteer at the very place he used to work – where she still worked – every Saturday to help with rehabilitation. He didn't see what else he could do. His new employers were reluctant; it fulfilled their charity pledge but they could do that more cost-effectively and with less of a time sacrifice at a nearer London public hospital. It had taken some bargaining and an offer to pay for his own flights. Izzy wasn't happy either. She worked a lot less Saturdays now than when they were together and when he did manage to talk to her, she only wanted to discuss work. She'd told him a couple of weeks ago that he should stop coming back altogether.

'We're not getting back together, Aiden.'

He'd done his best to sound indignant. 'Do you think I want to spend every weekend on a plane? The clinic insists. They were the ones who sent me here.'

'Why can't they find you a burns unit in London?'

He couldn't think of a believable response. 'Diversity, I guess.'

He'd have proposed years ago except Izzy told him not to. She wanted to wait until at least one of them was working set hours. That had always been the plan: marriage, kids, and whatever was the north Dublin equivalent of a white picket fence. When had she stopped feeling the same way? And why had nobody told him?

'What is it about French fellas that you like so much anyway?'

'The accent. The clothes. And they're very romantic, very confident. Although not last weekend's one, clearly. Still pretending at thirty-six.'

'Don't think I feel that strongly about any nationality. A Scottish accent is proper nice though.'

'There's not a Frenchman – so long as he's single and out – that I wouldn't at least let blow me.'

'George!' Nancy hissed, although the passengers were still only unbuckling their seatbelts.

The doors opened and the mob made their way towards the rear of the plane.

'Have a nice day,' enthused George, as they streamed out onto the gangway.

Aiden hadn't told anyone the real reason he came home every weekend. He stayed at his brother's house, in the spare room, and gave him the same story he gave everyone else: he was fulfilling his clinic's charitable obligations.

His brother thought Izzy was too good for him.

'That's not true,' said Colm when Aiden brought it up. 'I just never saw it lasting. I didn't get it.'

Aiden shook his head. He loved her. Nothing else mattered. He brought his mind back to the beginning. Walking by the Irish Sea, feeling their way across pebbles in the dark. If he could get her to remember those nights. He needed Izzy to see that he wanted her back. That this time apart *was* a change. That things would be good again.

EIGHT

....

'Jaysus, look at these lads,' said Roisin, stopping in front of a Renaissance painting of three cheerful musicians. She read the wall panel aloud, '*A Concert by Lorenzo Costa,*' and then commented, 'Yer man in the middle is actually alright-looking. The poor fucker to the right probably wrote all the music but this dude got to go out in front.'

Cora sidled up next to her best friend and rested her head on Roisin's. There was a mild throbbing at the front of her skull. The painting's subjects, with their glossy locks and groovy velvet, did seem out of place in the fifteenth century. The frontman should have been in Led Zeppelin. 'I reckon I would have done well in the 1970s,' said Cora. 'I've a strong jaw and being tall . . . I think flares would have suited me.'

Earlier, while browsing paintings of Louis XIV's court, Roisin had identified the seventeenth century as her optimum time period. 'Now they look like people who knew how to party,' she'd said, pointing to a large fresco of decadently naked women, their ample, pinkish bodies flung wide open. Roisin was not ample, she was actually quite neat, but her Irish skin was pale and she had curves. 'I would've been quids in,' she said. 'Kings lining up to ply me with wine; I could get on board with that. And sure they wouldn't know what to think of the freckles; that would have made me a deity.'

'If you're getting in with the royalty, your children are probably going to look like that,' said Cora, pointing to the portrait hall of misshapen monarchs. 'There's no escaping inbreeding. And you would have been dead by thirty-five.'

'Ah yeah, but I would have had a good innings.'

The two women were strolling the rooms of the National Gallery on the third Thursday of February. Cora wasn't due in work until 2 p.m. – a blessing given she'd been on the whiskey the night before, hence the throbbing frontal lobe – and Roisin had the day off from her job at the local library. Roisin used to work in music publicity, but she wasn't good enough at pretending that shit songs were great. Plus, the money was terrible. The music industry's loss was Finsbury Park library's gain: their CD collection had never been so progressive – it even got a shout out in *Time Out*. When the two women first moved in together, they used to go to galleries all the time.

It had started with the Tate Britain. Cora hadn't seen Millais's *Ophelia* – the image that hung in every bedroom she had ever occupied – in real life since she was a teenager. So the Saturday she lugged her worldly possessions along the Piccadilly line and moved into Finsbury Park, she and Roisin celebrated by getting back on the Tube and going to the gallery. Roisin wasn't particularly interested in art but she enjoyed a 'good day out'. They had made their way through the Tate Britain's expansive rooms until they reached the Pre-Raphaelites and spied the drowned Ophelia lying amongst a bric-a-brac of paintings. Cora had been underwhelmed to the point of grief. The green of the reeds seemed garish, almost fluorescent, and the image was so much smaller than it should have been. Perhaps time had faded the poster she had just stuck to her new Finsbury Park bedroom wall but she preferred its muted tones. After a lifetime of falling in love with the reproduction, the original seemed a cheap imitation.

They returned to the Tate Britain twice more that first month and had been in every display room by the end. Each time they bought a postcard of a painting they had liked and hung it in the kitchen. Since then, they had been to all the rooms in all of London's major galleries, and the history of art was plastered all over their kitchen wall. Cora had a penchant for the sea and Roisin swooned for female nudes.

'It's all free,' said Cora, sweeping her arms dramatically at the echoing walls. 'So many people have lived here all their lives and never been to the national gallery. The majority, probably.'

They were sitting on a bench, staring up at a large-scale painting of a tiger and a woman cradling her baby. Cora had read the description on a previous visit and knew it was an allegory, but she couldn't remember for what.

'So, go on, tell us about last night,' said Roisin. 'I saw a glow stick in the bathroom this morning.'

'They gave us those on our way in. I just put mine on my wrist but Nancy made a headband out of two because it matched her neon leggings. She looked great actually.'

Roisin laughed. 'Where was it again?'

'The Imperial College. South Kensington. I thought it was going to be a few staged shots of Ray running, but all the contestants were there and they had a professional track set up.'

The Fight the Flab run had been more fun than expected. It ended with five whiskeys and the last Tube home and was as close to a proper night out as Cora had had in months – weddings excluded. She'd arrived at 7 p.m. to find a hall jammed with neon supporters. She spied Ray standing on a platform at the front in yet another shiny new Adidas tracksuit. Losing weight must be costing him a fortune.

To Cora's left was a large group of shirtless men. Across their convex bellies they had each written a letter in neon green body paint. Cora stood for a minute, trying to solve the ever-shifting anagram: GO ZIM, possibly? Or GO MIZ? Neither an acceptable nickname for a grown man. But behind the bustling bellies was a bunch of recognisable faces. Cora shouldered her way through the crowd towards Joan, Charlie, George, two men from security, and a woman from baggage scanning.

'I didn't know you were coming,' she said to Joan, giving her a quick embrace. The older woman's hair was in curls for the occasion.

'Thought I might get some motivation. I lost my new year's resolutions somewhere in the Quality Street tin,' said

Joan, wiggling her glow stick at Cora. 'Maybe they're taking contestants for next year.'

'Good thing you're here,' said Charlie, who was wearing his trademark dark slacks and sweater over a light-blue shirt. Having never seen him outside work before, Cora had assumed this ensemble was a uniform. She noted a strip of neon green in his trainers. Subtle, but definitely not an accident. 'Ray's family is over there.' Charlie pointed into a crowd of people she could not distinguish. 'And some other friends are around somewhere, but we're one of the smaller groups. The Newcastle and Cardiff leaders put on buses.' He made it sound as if the out-of-town contestants had cheated.

'Nancy didn't come then?'

Charlie nudged his shoulder against hers and pointed towards the stage, but Cora could see nothing. 'Right at the starting line,' said Charlie.

Cora shifted her gaze to the marked running track, and there was her friend. Dressed in neon leggings and a Fight the Flab tank top, she was holding a sign that said 'Steady' and chatting excitedly to the director from the first airport shoot.

'See the woman with the "Ready" sign? She's the Bristol contestant's wife.' The hall was getting noisier by the minute and Charlie moved closer so as to speak into Cora's ear. 'And the child with the "Go" sign is the Newcastle woman's son.'

Cora knew better than to question what qualified Nancy to be up there. She shook her head and grinned. 'Does she even know Ray's surname?'

'Butter would not melt,' said Joan, her attention still aimed at the glow stick that kept flying from her hand. 'What the hell am I supposed to do with this contraption?'

Charlie took the stick from her and drove it through the front of her hair. 'There now, Joan. You'll be turning all the boys' heads.'

The contestants were brought to the starting line where tracksuit tops were removed to reveal *Fight the Flab* T-shirts with their names printed on the reverse. Ray was not the largest of the seven. The first man – mid-fifties, a tattoo either side of his neck – stepped forward and lifted his arms into the air. He turned his back to the audience to reveal his name: GIZMO. The shirtless brigade beside Cora went ballistic. The camera panned over them but the excitement was too much and they couldn't get their bellies in order in time. When Ray's turn came to step forward, their little enclave erupted. Cora gave her loudest scream. 'Go on, Ray, my son!'

The director instructed the crowd to step into the middle of the track; the leaders were going to run around them. Then he called for an 'atmospheric hush'.

'Look!' whispered Joan, nudging Cora in the side. A glum-looking child was now holding the 'Steady' sign and Nancy was front and centre, ready to instruct the runners to 'Go'. 'She's been upgraded.'

'And rolling!'

The whistle blew and they were off. The leaders kept a good pace for the first couple of laps but soon three of them had given up in favour of walking and two more were opting for intervals. Ray, however, was still jogging and Charlie was getting excited. She'd never seen him get excited. He pushed his way to the frontline and Cora could hear him yelling, 'That's it, Ray mate, you're almost there! Invest in yourself! Own the pain!' The run wasn't meant to be a race but suddenly everyone was shouting 'Ray!' or 'Carol!', for the only other contestant still jogging, and it was like the whole room had money on the outcome. As Ray hobbled over the finish line, the room broke into cheers. The difficulty was sustaining this level of enthusiasm until the last contestant – Gizmo – finally completed the circuit twelve minutes later.

Ray was walking on air after the run. He barely noticed Nancy grabbing his arm every time the local photographer came near, nor did he seem to mind when she started answering the journalist's questions for him: 'He's in training now and he's got a great network of friends behind him. That's Moone, with an e.' The rest of them were feeling the adrenaline too and it was Cora who suggested they go to the pub.

Joan bowed out. Jim was away at a match and she was on pigeon-feeding duty. But the rest of the Heathrow contingent and Ray's two sisters headed for the pub around the corner. Nancy had water; a sure sign, thought Cora, that she had plans for later – a date, probably. Camera phones were produced for Ray's impromptu speech and the woman behind the bar took a group shot.

After three drinks, Cora could feel the alcohol. She went to the bathroom for a breather and when she came back Nancy was talking about Pan Am to the woman from baggage scanning. If Nancy were ever to go on *Mastermind*, she'd have her speciality subject sorted. 'The Pan Am air hostess I saw interviewed ended up marrying a man from her third flight. Swear to god. They were like movie stars. Every glass of champagne the passengers bought for themselves, they got one for the air hostesses too. Did you ever see the uniforms . . . ?'

At the bar, the drunker of the two security guards was buying Ray another gin. 'But seriously, mate, you're bridging the gap. All sections of the airport brought together for the sake of helping you get healthy. A pilot from British Airways asked me about it yesterday. It was like Apollo coming to Rocky.' He handed Ray a glass and raised his own pint. 'Closing the divide, mate, that's what you're doing.'

Cora took a glass of water from the barmaid and returned to the table. Nancy was now sitting beside Charlie, speaking in hushed tones. When Cora approached them, Charlie did a double-take and Nancy quickly excused herself to go to the loo.

'What was that about?'

'Nothing.'

'Can I?' said Cora, pointing to the seat beside Charlie.

He slid up the bench awkwardly. 'I got you this,' he added, placing a whiskey before her.

'Thanks.'

'Nice, ah, frock by the way.'

Cora looked down at her very old, very unremarkable dress. 'Cheers.'

'Cheers,' he said, raising his own pint. When he lowered it

again, he hoisted himself up and moved even further away. He was acting strange. 'You know you're getting old when you can't sit without groaning.'

'How old are you, Charlie? Because you talk like you're ninety.'

'Thirty-four – so I've made it further than Jesus at least. You?'

'Twenty-eight last month.'

'Happy belated birthday.'

'Thanks.'

Cora surveyed the table. Glow sticks bobbed in the dregs of pints and protruded from flower vases. She picked up a damp beermat and tried to spin it like a coin, but it was capable only of a limp tumble. Nancy returned from the bathroom, and slid in beside George at the opposite end of the table. George started talking furtively, while eyeballing Cora.

'What?'

'Nothing,' replied George, shaking his head like a martyred diva. 'We were just talking about human rights. Don't know if you'd be interested though, Cora. You know they're voting on gay marriage in Ireland soon?'

'I do,' she said. 'I hope it passes.'

'Ha!'

'What, George? What is your problem?'

'He's annoyed because you don't offer your mile-high matchmaking services to the gays,' said Nancy, on her second sparkling water. George narrowed his eyes at her, and then shot Cora a look daring her to disagree.

'There are less of them,' said Cora, who had tried to

diversify her matches and failed. 'They're trickier to spot, and it's difficult to make casual enquiries about someone's sexual orientation.'

George turned his attention to a point on the ceiling.

'It's harder, George,' Cora continued. 'And you told me before – when I tried to set you up with Naomi's brother, George, remember? – that only gays should set up other gays.'

'It's about equal opportunities, Cora,' he said, standing now. 'Nancy, would you like a drink?'

'Ta, but no. Fine with this.'

George did a power turn and glided towards the bar. Cora knew he was camping it up for her benefit. She rolled her eyes towards Nancy: 'So dramatic!'

'Well now that's discrimination too, Cupid,' mocked Nancy. 'Stereotyping.'

After a fifth whiskey and two existential arguments – whether having children is a selfish act and, shortly afterwards, whether there's any such a thing as a selfless act – Cora decided it was time for home. She looked around but Nancy was gone.

'Said she had to study,' the baggage scanning woman told her, and Cora laughed. She wondered if her friend was meeting the *Fight the Flab* director. George was in the corner now, talking to Ray's sisters who were laughing outrageously. His eyes narrowed when he caught Cora looking at them. She just shook her head.

Charlie and Ray walked with her to Kensington (Olympia) station. Charlie told them about last summer's security scare, about how the fault lay with a Slovakian airport not Heathrow, but it had shown up weaknesses in their system nonetheless.

'The Slovaks planted a sample of explosives between passengers' luggage on their end, as a test for their sniffer dogs. The dogs found the explosive but some bell-end security guard forgot to remove them,' said Charlie, animated by the drink and sudden hit of fresh air. 'The explosive stuck to this chap's bag – a Slovakian brewer, in London on business. He hadn't the foggiest about any of it, poor sod – and it wasn't detected until he was back in Heathrow a couple of days later, on his way home.'

'So then, the problem is with this other airport's security?' asked Cora, looking around to see where Ray had gotten to. He was loitering a few metres behind.

'Well that, too. But this Slovakian chap was on the plane before we knew about the substance. It was only a sample, not enough to do any damage. Still. We should have spotted it.'

Cora worried they were moving too fast for Ray, but every time she slowed down he did the same. She was starting to think he was doing it on purpose. He was trailing well behind by the time Cora and Charlie reached the station. They descended the escalator, laughing at Charlie's use of the word 'frock'.

'What's wrong with it?'

'Oh nothing. But tell me this, do you see girls wearing them at the hop?'

'Now I know you're teasing me, Cora.'

'I've just never heard you talk so much.'

'I like talking to you.'

Cora hesitated. 'Should we go back for Ray?'

'No. He's – I asked him to fall back.'

Oh fuck.

'Listen, Cora. If you wanted to go out sometime, I would like that.'

If she ran, she could make it to the other end of the tunnel in ten seconds. No bother.

'And if you didn't, that's fine too. Up to you. No pressure. And no hops.'

'Well that's a relief.'

'So up to you,' he repeated.

'Okay. I better . . .'

'Course. We're heading south anyway.' Charlie saluted her and turned back towards the escalator. 'I'll go tell Ray the coast is clear.'

'So I think he asked me out . . .'

'Yes, Sherlock, I think he did.'

The two women were still sitting in front of the allegorical painting. They had been joined by a tour group of elderly Welsh women and were wedged in a sea of blue rinses. The passers-by listening to audio guides looked like spies with walkie-talkies, and Cora watched carefully to see if their mouths moved. Her hangover paranoia was in full swing. It was one downside to having an active imagination. Another was the unwanted thoughts that pounded at her mind's door whenever even a sliver of possible interest in someone else, or from someone else, occurred. Charlie was kind – a dignified, masculine kindness that shone from him. But this only made her think of Friedrich, who abhorred the trait above all others. Kind, to him, was the antithesis of brilliant. Cora had called him 'cruel' on one occasion and he almost curtseyed with gratitude. She closed her eyes and let her head fall on to her friend's. This had been a position of comfort since they were teenagers; Roisin had always been half a foot smaller. 'It came out of nowhere. One minute we're having great fun, the next he can't come up with anything to say to me – *nice frock*? – and then he's asking me out.'

'Sounds standard to me.'

'Why'd he have to do it? Now it's awkward.'

'Eh, maybe because he likes you? Do you like him?'

'Not like that. Do you think I said something to make him think I did? At one point I did sit beside him even though there were plenty of other chairs. Maybe I should have—'

'Alright, relax,' said Roisin, who had been in Cora's hung-over company enough times to know when to indulge and when to disregard. 'I just wonder if it's that you don't want to go out with *him*, or you don't want to go out with *anyone*?'

'I don't see the difference. He's very nice but he's not for me. Maybe you'd like him?'

Roisin hooted, and the blue-haired pensioner beside her jumped. 'Classic Hendricks. Sort your own love life out, yeah? You already sorted mine.'

'You still seeing Prince Charming?'

'Sporadically. A girl's got needs and it does the job. You gotta get under someone to get over someone else – as the wise proverb goes.'

'Come on,' said Cora, standing from the bench and pulling Roisin up. 'Let's go. We should get a postcard before I head to the grindstone.'

They breezed back through the sixteenth and seventeenth-century rooms, heading for the exit. Cora felt a little awkward about going into Heathrow that evening but here now, in the company of her best friend and the great masters, she felt content. They passed a portrait of Marie Antoinette. 'How would you feel about a trip to Paris?'

Roisin stopped walking and regarded her friend. She looked like she was going to say something else but changed her mind. 'I'd feel very in favour of it, is how I'd feel. About time you used those free flights. A jolly good idea.' The last bit was said with Roisin's terrible faux English accent. It always sounded like she was voicing a Scottish Terrier in some American kids film.

'Here, Cora, don't worry about the auld love life. I've got you sorted. Look.' Roisin nodded towards a fifteenth-century portrait of a man with pudgy face, bulging eyes, and the most ridiculous of hats. 'There's a grand boyfriend for you now.'

The two friends collapsed into laughter and descended the staircase towards Trafalgar Square.

NINE

· · · · · · · · · · · · · · · ·

Cora entered the staffroom to find Joan sitting alone at one of the three plastic tables, feet resting on a second chair and crossword book open in front of her. Hardened gum was wedged to the sole of her right shoe. Joan was the only member of staff who got away with wearing flats. She'd brought in a doctor's note containing intimate details of bunions, and management never said another word.

'Weasel has been sniffing around,' said Joan. She was drinking tea from a novelty mug. The side facing Cora read: 'I Like My Coffee Like I Like My Men – Strong And Bitter'. 'Promotions and redeployment are next month and he's looking to find out who's interested in a change. Or what was it he called it? "Parties interested in moving onwards and upwards". He was practically licking himself. He has these little forms with *private and confidential* stamped on the top, and they *must* be returned to him personally.' Joan threw her eyes up to heaven.

Restructuring was earmarked for spring. Cora had forgotten. She had been here eight months already. How had that happened? 'Did he ask if you were interested?'

'Oh yes,' said Joan, hoisting herself up from a slouch to a sit. 'And I told him what I've been telling them for more than thirty years. I'm perfectly happy on my stool, ta very much. They can call it a promotion all they like, but I have no ambition to spend hours on end standing at a gate.'

Check-in was seen as a starter position. When you joined the airline as ground staff, check-in was where you went. You got a few weeks' training and were expected to learn along the way. Most recruits moved on to boarding or arrivals within a year. But not Joan. She had been sitting at check-in for the past thirty-three years and did not intend to leave that stool until the day she was presented with a gold watch – or whatever lesser gift would mark her retirement. They might consider bequeathing the stool.

When Cora started at the airline, she intended to get herself together and make a plan for the future. But then the self-check-in embargo came in and Cora thought that this might be the plan after all. Since she didn't know what she wanted for herself, she would just put her energies into other people. And it had worked. But there were still several unattached frequent fliers on her books, so she didn't really have time to worry about her own future right now. She had enough to be getting on with in the present. It was unlikely Weasel would accept matchmaking as a reason for not wanting to 'move up' in the company. In which case, she'd just have to avoid him.

Cora's university choices were made haphazardly. She chose art history not fully appreciating that it had very little to do with drawing and a lot more to do with reading about other people drawing. After graduation she still didn't know what to do so she took an internship with an art journal. The money was a pittance and the work depressing. So much more value was placed on everything that surrounded an artwork – the artist's training, their spiel, and how well they networked – than the actual piece itself. Cora's last assignment before she finally called 'bullshit' on the whole thing was a three-thousand-word interview with an emerging sensation whose greatest artistry was adding 'Inc.' to the end of his name. Joseph Mason Walter Inc. had been the darling of the Frieze art fair where his entire *oeuvre* was 'the art of no production', aka making and selling absolutely nothing – and at a rapidly growing price.

She took directionless, part-time work, thinking a career would just present itself to her. But it didn't. So she went to Berlin. Leaving England felt like a valid alternative to having a career path. When relatives asked Sheila what her wayward daughter was doing, she could say 'Cora's in Germany', and there would rarely be any follow-up questions. Being in a different geographical location qualified as doing something.

In Berlin, she worked as a copywriter for an English-language company and thought seriously about going back to university. Then she met Friedrich and the idea that she could make any important life decision *and* be in this relationship was utterly inconceivable. She'd never been in love before and it was all-consuming. Keeping up with Friedrich, or perhaps just keeping Friedrich, was a full-time occupation.

In her better moments Cora thought of Berlin as her wilderness years and that that was okay. In darker moments, it was the point at which she fucked-up her life. As Cora approached thirty she became aware that being directionless wasn't as romantic as it used to be. Your twenties were for fucking up. Soon, she feared, it would just be tragic.

Since she'd come home from Berlin, and her mother had gotten sick, it was that feeling of a giant, invisible hand grabbing her by the core and shaking and shaking until everything became dislodged. Cora's insides no longer seemed to sit right. She was constantly afraid that if she made any sudden movements, everything would come toppling down. And she could no longer rely on anyone else. So she stayed where she was and tried to realign herself. For pleasure, of course, there was always the happiness of others.

Cora left Joan to her crosswords and headed out to the floor. It was a busy Thursday evening, and there were four women already behind the Aer Lingus desks. She logged into a fifth computer and started working her way through passengers destined for Edinburgh and Madrid. Charlie passed the Aer Lingus queue and saluted Cora, holding up his stopwatch. Another lunchtime run. She waved back. He was not the sort to make things awkward. Still, she wished she could go back in time and leave the pub early so the whole thing had never happened.

'Nancy!' Cora shouted as her friend glided past her desk. The air hostess redirected her path, her blonde ponytail swinging as she came to a halt at the Aer Lingus counter. 'I never heard from you yesterday,' said Cora. 'How did Row 27 go?'

'With the Icelandic fella? That one was very interesting.'

'I thought it might be! I could just see them together, you know? Those pale complexions and sensible shoes.'

'Oh, well no,' said Nancy, who was travelling with her favourite Louis Vuitton suitcase, the Harrods tag still attached as proof of authenticity. Nancy was eager to distinguish herself from the long-haul air hostesses who picked up knock-off gear in Beijing and Marrakesh. 'I don't think the match went anywhere. She pulled out an eye mask as soon as she got on board. But the Icelandic fella was dead interesting. We had a great chat. Did you know he's a life coach?'

'Of course I knew. He specialises in careers and the woman I matched him with had recently been made unemployed. It was perfect. Hence why they were supposed to be doing the flirting, not you!'

'I wasn't flirting. We were talking about work and, like I said, the woman was asleep. Anyway, anyway,' said Nancy, shaking off Cora's protestations, 'how did the rest of the other night go? After Ray's race. Anything *interesting* happen?'

'What? No,' said Cora, flustered. 'A couple too many drinks but that was it. Now, about this evening's Dublin flight: I'm thinking a young couple for Row 27. They can be flighty but it's been a while since we've given youth a chance. What do you reckon?'

'Sure, Cupid. You line 'em up, I'll do what I can.'

The first lull came at 4 p.m. and Cora started to research passengers on the 6.20 p.m. to Dublin. It was the only outbound flight Nancy was on that day. She had selected a twenty-two-year-old Irish woman who'd flown into Heathrow that morning. Megan O'Neill. Experience had taught Cora that most young people who flew in and out of London in a day were there for job interviews. She matched Megan with Philip Mellon, a twenty-two-year-old law graduate originally from near Dublin and now interning at a London non-governmental organisation. His LinkedIn page was very impressive. Almost as soon as Cora had started using social media as a research tool, she'd changed all her own settings to private. The amount of information people divulged was staggering.

Megan was one of the first to present at the desk.

'Meg—' Cora caught herself in time, biting her tongue until she had actually opened the passport. There was no reason for her to know this woman's name. 'Megan O'Neill! Welcome to Aer Lingus. Any check-in bags?'

She wasn't as chatty as Cora had hoped: 'Did you have a nice day in London?' got a mumbled response about meeting friends – but she assigned her to 27A.

'Cora Hendricks. A word in my office?' Weasel was standing behind her, peering disapprovingly at the crusts of a half-eaten sandwich on the shelf below her desk while hugging a pile of documents to himself. His lips were flaking at the edges. In all his managerial excitement, he must have forgotten the ChapStick.

'I'm in the middle of check-in.'

'Your colleagues can look after your flight. This, however, concerns your future.'

With no excuse to stay, Cora quickly pre-assigned Philips's seat – 27B – and hoped she'd be back to catch a glimpse.

She followed Weasel to the Aer Lingus staffroom, studying his feet as she went. They moved like one of those wind-up ducks, yet all that rapid movement didn't seem to propel him any faster. In the staffroom, there was a handwritten 'reserved' sign in the centre of the furthest plastic table. Weasel's 'office', she presumed.

'Have a seat.'

He cleared his throat and tapped the collective documents against the table. 'In this business we call air travel, there's no month as important as March. As you'll no doubt be aware, March is when new recruits across the entire airline confirm who they are and decide who they want to become. I'm sure you've heard about it from your mother. It's the time when we separate the boys from the men, the wheat from the chaff, the curds from the whey, the—'

'I get it.'

'This' – he shook his beloved documents – 'is the difference between gold circle lounge and baggage tracing.'

'Right.'

'There are a lot of other areas where you might like to spend some time, get a more varied insight to how we work.'

'Indeed.'

Cora watched Weasel's chin quiver. It seemed everything trembled on the higher plane of responsibility. An uninvited image of Weasel experiencing orgasmic pleasure popped into her head. *Sweet lord*, Cora admonished her imagination: *Behave*.

Weasel was content not to receive a concrete answer, sympathising that it was a big decision. He bandied around the word 'future' for a little longer, and then handed her a form. 'It's private and confidential,' he said, reluctant to relinquish eye contact or his end of the document. 'Return it *to me*, and me only.'

Cora was back at check-in just in time to see Philip striding up to a colleague's desk. She checked the system; he was still down for his designated seat. She watched him talk to the other check-in attendant. He was smaller than his profile picture suggested and he had glasses. He was wearing the ill-fitted black jeans and white T-shirt that was uniform among young men with no interest in fashion. Cora sat back to read the slogan on his T-shirt: Straight Up For Equality.

Her mobile phone vibrated on the shelf beside her discarded sandwich. A text from Roisin:

How go things with Charlie? Has he asked for your hand in marriage yet, or does he wanna get your father's permission first? Bagsy bridesmaid.

When Cora looked back, Philip was gone.

TEN

LHR -> DUB 6.20 p.m.

As she struggled down the aisle, banging into seats as she went, Megan O'Neill thought how, for the first time, it reminded her of a church. Her pew was near the back of the plane and she held herself upright as she made her way through the teens and into the twenties – 24, 25, 26, finally. She lowered her body into the seat, a heat rising in her that had nothing to do with the coat she was still wearing, buttoned up but left untied at the waist. She sat for a minute and collected herself, before standing again to remove the jacket. She kept it on her knee, fashioned like a blanket.

Megan put her hand to her face and thought about her appearance. She wondered if it gave something away. She had kept an eagle eye out for people she knew at Dublin Airport that morning, an alibi on the tip of her tongue, but she had forgotten to do the same on the way home. What had she told that check-in lady? She scanned the plane and then something came back to her: she had given the nurse Rachel's address. She had panicked. Shit shit. What

123

if they contacted her? What if they wrote to that address and Rachel's parents opened it or, worse, what if they sent it over to Megan's house and her parents opened it? The best friends had grown up minutes from each other and, as a kid, Megan had sent a postcard meant for Rachel to her own address. She often rang her best friend's house phone when she meant to ring her own. She had precedence. Megan dug her mobile from her coat pocket and frantically began to Google, worried she would be made to turn off her phone before she had found the answer. But there it was on a message board: Postal information is for records and statistics only. Megan's last two searches had been cramping and bleeding. She deleted her search history. She wondered about all the information that was never deleted.

Philip Mellon lugged his bulging carry-on down the passageway. Why didn't they open the rear entrance for boarding? They'd be ready for take-off twice as quick. The only good thing about having to parade the whole way down the aisle was that it gave the other passengers a chance to see his T-shirt and consider its message. He used his free hand to pull down the cheap cotton, removing the creases. His bag caught against a seated woman's foot and gave a little jolt. He lifted it over her and kept lugging. He had never before brought such a packed suitcase for a weekend at home. Usually it was two pairs of boxers, a T-shirt, and some study material. Usually it all fitted in his shoulder bag. There were no clothes in this weekend's luggage and, it now occurred to him, no underwear. Never mind. It was only three nights. The suitcase was filled with posters, badges, a staple gun, Straight Up for Equality T-shirts, petitions of signatures he and other Oxford alumni had collected, and flags. The monetary value was low, but this was the most important piece of luggage on board. Philip moved another suitcase from the compartment directly above his seat so he could keep the cargo as close as possible. Well this was his allocated seat and, as such, his allocated storage space.

He looked at the girl beside him and saw the passport resting on her knee. Irish, and about his own age; she'd appreciate him sacrificing his weekend. There was so much studying to do – even after you'd gotten your law degree. People had no idea.

'Do you live in Ireland?' he asked as he sat, startling the girl to attention.

'Yes,' she said.

'I'm from Wicklow myself, but living in London now. Been over here for, what, six years? Feels like home really. I couldn't imagine going back to Ireland; it just seems so small.'

She smiled without eye contact. He judged her demeanour to be not so much rude as lazy. Apathy was a terrible disease. *Engage, woman*, he thought. It's an electrifying world. Awake from your indifference.

'But I still care about the place. I'm going home to campaign, actually. A whole weekend of it. I'll be exhausted by the end but what else can you do? The vote is nearly upon us, for marriage equality, you know?' He turned to face her and pulled at his T-shirt. She nodded her recognition. Legalising gay marriage had been the only thing debated on Irish airwaves for the past year. 'I'm a human rights lawyer,' he continued, wondering if his tone was casual enough. 'And every day we see these third-world cases cross our desk and all I can think about is what's going on in my own country. I tell my colleagues, "Ireland is home to a litany of human rights violations." That's how I describe it. I say, "I come from a third-world country."'

His voice was so loud, like a fog horn. Megan tried to end the conversation, but she couldn't because it wasn't actually a conversation. She knew his type. He was one of those people who asked unforgivably long questions after film screenings or public interviews – only there was never actually a question, just a declaration of their intelligence. She had guessed Trinity College, but the length of time he'd been in England suggested Oxbridge, which made even more sense. He probably meant well but she didn't care. Megan had willed the gods to let her sit alone on the journey home but she supposed they weren't best pleased with her. She didn't believe in God, of course, it was all a nonsense, but still she could never stop herself making little deals with an unseen power. Lately, though, these deals weren't being honoured.

She found out she was pregnant three weeks after breaking up with Darragh, and one week after they had met up again and she had collapsed on O'Connell Bridge when he would not consent to take her back. Megan had sat on the cold, grey concrete and thought of how they'd strolled to the Iveagh Gardens wrapped up in each other on a Saturday morning just two months before. She remembered worrying that she'd become half a person, someone who could only walk when the other half was there to prop her up. Then that other half had severed itself completely and she could not stand. Others would not believe it but she knew she had felt the moment when her heart broke and everything around it came tumbling down.

She did not hear from him between that evening on the bridge and the Friday morning she took the pregnancy test in the bathroom of the RTE Radio building. Seven hours after her pee had turned the stick blue, she went home from her job as a radio researcher and bought a box of granola en route. She vowed that it would be the only thing she would eat. If she had not heard from Darragh by the time she had finished the box, it meant he was never coming back. Then her mother had eaten the end of the cereal and Megan had melted into floods of tears. The deal was null and void, but she persevered. Megan promised that if she was not pregnant, she would donate to charity the €900 she had saved since getting her first proper job; she picked her four favourite pieces of clothing from her wardrobe and vowed to drop them off at the local Oxfam; she would eat no chocolate for three months. But the family planning clinic confirmed that these sacrifices had not been enough. She was pregnant.

She could never imagine eating again, least of all chocolate, and her €900 bequest now constituted the abortion fund.

She had told Rachel, and together they booked flights. Rachel had offered to go to London with her but she hadn't found work since graduation and Megan did not have the money to pay for the both of them. The night before she flew to London for the procedure, Megan stayed at Rachel's house – telling her parents she was visiting old university friends on the other side of town. She slipped out before the sun came up and before Rachel's parents noticed their overnight guest.

Megan had flown out of Dublin Airport at 6.40 a.m. that morning. When she landed at home in an hour's time, she would have to get the bus straight into the city centre to her brother's eighteenth birthday dinner. Her stomach churned as she thought of the McDonald's she had vomited up in the Heathrow bathroom.

'Just throw a quick eye on them, George, when you're taking the food cart around.'

George let out a pointed sigh and snatched the trolley from Nancy. She was still making her way through the procedural manual. 'Fine. But I'm doing it for you, not for Cora.'

He'd had another car crash of a date yesterday. This one was actually a friend of a friend, and George's *friend* swore nothing had ever happened between them – which turned out to be a total lie. George had sat for an hour in Starbucks counselling this kid who had slept with his friend months ago and then been dropped quicker than a Beyoncé album. George didn't know what to say except to tell him to get used to it. 'They tell you coming out is the hardest part,' he said, as the kid scratched at a pimple on his chin. 'But that's only where it begins.'

'Ireland has been before the HRC – that's the Human Rights Commission, the UN? – anyway, Ireland has been called up three times in as many years. It's mortifying. I feel shame, genuinely I do, to come from somewhere so backwards. Nobody listens to the oppressed. Nobody lets them speak. Straight white men make all the decisions. We tell women and homosexuals and lesbians, we tell them all what they should and shouldn't do. It never ends . . .'

Megan tried to tune him out but his nasal tone kept drilling its way into her mind. She thought about the after-care sheet she had read on the bus back to the airport, before discarding it in a bin when no one was looking. Rachel had found her a clinic that did cheaper rates for Irish citizens. That's why she had given a Dublin address. How illegal was abortion, exactly? There was no chance the authorities would stop someone at Dublin Airport. Was there? At school there'd been a rumour that they sometimes did. They said you shouldn't travel for twenty-four hours after a procedure and Megan had gotten the latest flight that she could. But she had to make that dinner. The main concern was that women would start bleeding heavily mid-air. She closed her eyes and concentrated on her body; it didn't feel like more blood than a period, but she'd never had cramps like these before.

' . . . The problem is middle Ireland. You're in Dublin and you think, "Okay, maybe this country isn't such an embarrassment" but then you go into the Midlands or, you know, basically anywhere else and it's like nobody can think for themselves. That's where we should be campaigning, probably, but we'd actually be lynched – or whatever it is they do down there. Wicklow is as far as we're going. There are a lot of older people there but they just need it explained to them that everyone should be allowed to marry . . .'

Megan no longer experienced the waves of guilt that had made her feel ill on the way to the airport this morning. The primary emotion was relief. She no longer felt bad about lying to her parents – although she had wished her mother had been there. She wished she'd been holding her hand in the waiting room and sitting with her afterwards. She wished she could have told her. Whenever Megan was at her saddest, she thought of her mother and she thought of her as 'Mammy' – a name she hadn't called her out loud for fifteen years. As she lay on the bed after the procedure, she had thought of her mammy. She had imagined seeing herself from above, flying up and up until she was so far in the sky that she could see both herself on a bed in a discreet clinic beside a council estate in Brentford and her mother at her school desk, running through times tables with ten year olds in North County Dublin.

That the doctor had been male had made it worse. She wasn't expecting a man and it made her embarrassed and ashamed. She didn't think she should feel that way but she did. Megan felt the flush in her cheeks and the tear ducts beginning to widen behind her eyes. She steadied herself. She would give her mother a big hug when she reached the restaurant tonight. And her mother would return it because she was a loving person; she just happened to have different beliefs.

'... From the trolley? Anything?'

The nasal boy and a man, standing in the aisle with a trolley. They were looking at her. 'Sorry,' said Megan. 'No thanks.'

'Are you sure? It's on the house. We just love Row 27.' The air steward said the last line loudly, turning his head towards the rear of the plane. A blonde woman was watching him.

'No thanks.'

'Well I'll have a coffee anyway, cheers, pal. Any chance of something a little foamy or is it just regular?'

'It's instant.'

'Don't worry about it, that'll do. So yes, the T-shirt . . .'

Darragh had liked coffee. Megan didn't. He had tried to get her into it but to no avail. Would she always associate coffee with him, she wondered. She was, at least, thinking of him in the past tense. Did it take getting pregnant to get over someone?

' . . . Well that's the thing, George. It is George, right? The name-tag. Anyway, I'm not gay but I believe you have the right to be. It's the same with all those things. The right to choose, you know? I'm just standing up for your rights . . .'

The boy was white noise to Megan but she watched the flight attendant's stony reaction. His face was void of emotion. 'How wonderful of you,' he said, and pushed the trolley onwards. But the boy was immune to sarcasm.

'Free drinks?' he said, as much to Megan as any of his previous statements had been. 'Irish airlines certainly have come a long way since I last flew with one. You should have taken something.'

Megan felt her stomach spasm and instinctively put her hand to it. She had found herself protecting her midriff for three weeks now. Knowing it was ridiculous hadn't been enough to make her stop. She yanked her hand away and rubbed her fingers together, as if trying to remove the magnets that drew them. She dropped her head back against the rest and feigned sleep.

The girl didn't seem to care one way or the other about the country she was still living in. Or maybe Philip was boring her. That was how it was now, though, he thought, people expressing opinions on Facebook but never in real life. He watched her, pretending to snooze. But he knew she was awake because her breathing hadn't changed. He looked past her, out the window, and saw Dublin in the distance. The bay was distinctive. He was meeting the others for some pre-campaigning pints this evening. They'd like the T-shirt – oh, and the door-to-door pins! He lifted himself slightly and pulled a badge from his back pocket: Make Up Your Own Mind. Yes, they'd all love that.

ELEVEN

No matter what way she looked at it – and Cora had considered the document from every angle now – the dominant colour on her matchmaking chart was still red. The duvet pushed down and pillows propping her up, she set the rainbow pen to failure and added more results. It had been a disappointing month.

Her frequent fliers were proving particularly irksome. It had been four flights since Ingrid had even thrown her a yellow, and Cora was starting to think of Aiden as an episode of *Sesame Street* – brought to you by the colour red, and the number zero. Cora ignored Nancy's feedback on the young pair who'd flown to Dublin last week – Megan was the girl, she forgot the boy's name – and put it down as 'undecided'. Nancy had sent George to assess the situation and, Cora reassured herself as she shaded the box yellow, George would say anything to annoy her.

She felt a flash of irritation when she looked at the red mark that represented the Icelandic match Nancy had thrown off course. There were enough men in the world without Nancy having to interfere with Row 27. How was she supposed to up the amount of green on the chart, when her only accomplice was doing her best to keep them in the red?

Cora slipped the chart back into her bedside table drawer and threw her legs out from under the covers. She stretched her toes against the warm lino. Weren't dreams supposed to be forgotten once your feet hit the floor? Yet a vague sensation of discombobulation remained.

Cora wound up the blind and looked out of her narrow bedroom window straight into the upstairs deck of the 253 bus and the eyes of a teenage girl. Cora liked to imagine Seven Sisters Road as a safari route; the red London buses were road-hardy vehicles carrying curious tourists, and she was the exotic animal. As the 253 pulled away, Cora tilted her head to the side (she was an ostrich on this particular Saturday) and the girl waved. Some mornings, halfway through dressing, Cora would remember that the blind was open. But as this was not a safari route – and they were distracted commuters, not curious tourists – it never mattered. They were always too preoccupied with their mobile phones to notice her clammy flesh.

The television made itself known before Cora had entered the kitchen and, standing at the doorway, she spied a colander and the Weight Watchers scales on the draining board. No matter what meal-for-one Mary made, she always used more dishes than the basin could contain. This morning's breakfast consisted of a carefully constructed egg white omelette, oven-roasted squash, and some form of green smoothie. Spirulina lingered in the air and the discarded egg yolks sat at the bottom of a mug – Cora's favourite mug.

'What are you watching?' Cora asked, putting her porridge in the microwave and searching for a clean cup.

'*Supersize Always Dies.*'

'That's quite the title.'

'It's where really overweight people are told how long they have before their fat kills them,' said Mary, her eyes never flickering from the screen. An obese woman stood in front of a white curtain while a man in a crisp coat attached pegs to her flab. Mary watched in rapture, sucking on her fork.

Cora added a teabag and hot water to the only clean vessel she could find. 'My mother is fifty-eight today and we're having a birthday lunch this afternoon.'

'That's nice.'

'It should be good, I think. Just a few hours – that's all she could handle really, and then perhaps I'll go to the Tate.'

Her flatmate chortled. 'You're obsessed with art galleries.'

'I'm hardly obsessed, Mary. I haven't been in weeks. Three weeks, probably.'

Cora waited for a response, but Mary didn't so much as glance at her flatmate. She didn't budge. Perhaps the fork had become lodged in her throat.

Cora took her bowl from the microwave and carried it into Roisin's bedroom. 'Mary just called me obsessed,' she said, plonking herself down beside her drowsy friend. 'With art galleries, apparently. I could have gotten the Mona Lisa tattooed on my forehead this morning for all Mary would have known. She couldn't take her eyes off those exploited creatures. But oh yes, of course: *I'm* the obsessed one.'

Roisin grinned, stretching her arms above her head.

'You'd have liked her breakfast though. She basically constructed an edible Irish flag.'

'Ah, the tricolour.' Roisin rolled over to reach for her phone and check the time. Roisin didn't eat breakfast but she lived for tea. Cora handed her the mug and started to open the curtains. Her friend sat up and watched.

'You're giving me your tea, and daylight? Sure you're as good as two women.' Roisin's grandfather had said that to her father once, when he'd presented the old man with a sandwich and immediately started to set the fire. It was now one of Roisin's principal sayings. 'You're looking well, Cora.'

'Why thank you.' She curtsied, spreading the skirt of a floral dress originally bought for a wedding. 'We're having lunch at Maeve's house for Sheila's birthday.'

'How old is she?'

'Fifty-eight today, and it's making me feel old. I thought this dress might be too young actually.'

'It's not.'

'I hope not; I've barely worn it. It's funny how a bit of colour makes you feel better – which reminds me I need to get flowers for Mum and Maeve. What time are you leaving for Brighton?'

Roisin was going to a gig that evening. Prince Charming played in a band. 'Pure shite' was how Roisin described Avoid the Slam's sound, but they got free accommodation when they gigged away from London and it allowed her to wear the 'I'm with the Drummer' T-shirt she bought years ago. The purchase had originally been ironic because, as Roisin explained at the time, 'nobody boasts about being with the drummer'.

'Leaving at three and I'll be back tomorrow, probably not till late because we have to wait for the bassist to get over his hangover before he can drive the van back. Avoid the Slam are headlining, which tells you just how god-awful a shithole the venue will be, but I've never had Brighton fish 'n' chips before.'

Cora tuned in Roisin's radio and lay across the bed. She listened to Frank Skinner comparing some soap storyline to an obscure Greek tragedy. Cora stared at the lanyard hanging from Roisin's bed post – FINSBURY PARK LIBRARY N4: STAFF – and her friend began to dress.

'I found this the other day,' said Roisin, producing a letter from her underwear drawer. 'You sent it to me from Germany right after you'd met Friedrich and letters were the only way you could express *how you truly felt.*' Roisin was the only person Cora knew capable of making mockery sound like affection. 'You switched back to emails fast enough when the shit hit the fan though.'

Cora shoved her face into the duvet and groaned. She could barely conceive of how sycophantic she'd once been, but the evidence persisted. 'Throw it away, please.'

'Some of it is quite good, Cora. Whatever about Fredi the Yeti—'

'He wasn't hairy!'

Roisin shrugged. 'Still an arsehole though, wasn't he? There are some really clever passages about museums and art and stuff. Don't know half of what you're on about, but you say it well.'

Cora pulled herself up from the bed. 'Right, I better go.' She squeezed her friend's shoulders as she headed out the door. 'Enjoy tonight, and have some chips for me.'

The flower shop in Stoke Newington was closed for a family bereavement so Cora cycled the streets, familiar only with that one florist and its morose window display of wreaths and lilies, until she came across a stall in Dalston. She was now late arriving at Maeve's red-brick, semi-detached home. She noted the fresh mauve paint on the gate and the robust geraniums that ruled her sister's modest garden. Maeve had inherited their mother's green fingers. Cora, on the other hand, could just about tell a deciduous from an evergreen. She rang the bell and heard her niece squeal with excitement. Cora imagined a mild electric current running from this buzzer to the three-year-old Primrose. She considered pressing it again, just to check.

'Come in, come in,' said Chris, ushering her inside but still holding the door ajar. Cora stooped to pass under his arm, and he gave her an awkward embrace. Maeve's husband was the quintessential bumbling Englishman. He had an endless supply of red linen trousers that made Cora picture him on a camel, colonising some region of India.

'Hello, hello,' he said, jittering as he fixed his tortoiseshell glasses. 'It's, ahem, good to see you.'

'Good to see you too, Chris,' she said, handing him the slightly cheaper bunch of flowers.

'Oh they're just – well, yes, thank you.' He cleared his throat in what was a regular tic. 'Jolly good. Everyone is in here. Just, ahem, flowers, need some water . . .' He led her through the short hallway into the bright kitchen-cum-dining room.

It was a scene of such domestic contentment that Cora's heart swelled for how much her mother would enjoy it. Sheila had yet to arrive but Maeve was bent over the oven, an apron tied around her waist and a mitten on one hand. She was chatting to a dolled-up Joan, whose prosecco glass was adorned with overlapping rings of lipstick. Cian was at the table, studiously constructing Lego while Primrose used him as a climbing frame. A banner hung above them: 'Happy Twenty-first Birthday'. The old jokes were the best.

'Cora, Cora!' shouted Primrose, flinging herself from Cian and somehow bouncing off the tiled floor. She was up and running at her aunt but stopped, shyly, just in front of her.

Cora bundled the skinny child into her arms and blew raspberries all over her stomach until Primrose, through tears of laughter, begged to be put back down. Cora embraced her sister and Joan, and took a glass of prosecco from Chris who then went back to ineffectually searching for a vase. He opened and closed the same few cupboards, patting his pockets as he went. *You're not going to find one in there, mate,* thought Cora. There were two empty vases over the sink, but she decided it best to leave him to it.

'Where's Sheila?'

'They should be here any minute,' said Maeve, glancing at the bird clock by the backdoor. A housewarming present from Sheila, it made the noise of a different bird on the hour every hour. 'The nurse is bringing her and Tom. You know Tom's son ordered a bracelet online for Sheila birthday? Tom found it wrapped up yesterday and thought it was for him. He was wearing it when the nurse did the night-time checks.'

'The red-faced chap?' asked Joan, prosecco sloshing in her glass.

'The very one. Flannel pyjamas and a string of pearls.'

The women grinned, but just for a moment. Cora watched Maeve measure out the makings of a salad dressing. Since Sheila had gone to live in the research facility, her sister had assumed a matriarchal role. She phoned Cora every week to check in and invite her to dinner.

Maeve's mobile rang. 'Hi, Trish! Are you all on your way? I've just—' She cut herself off and scooted around Cora and Joan, stepping into the back garden with the screen door left ajar.

'Trish is a nurse at the facility,' Cora informed Joan as the older woman topped up their glasses. The screen door slid back and Maeve reappeared.

'They're running a little late. Should be here within the hour.' Maeve dropped her phone on the counter and opened the fridge. 'Will you hand me the pavlova? If I can fit it in the fridge, it should keep without the fruit.'

'Is anything wrong?'

'Trish said Sheila was a little muddled this morning, but she's back on track now. She had that long session for the

141

research paper yesterday. I knew it would be too much with a party the next day but that's the thing with her being in that place; nothing is movable.'

'It's nice she can still come and go,' offered Joan.

'It's a research facility, not a home.'

'But what was she muddled about?'

'Honestly, Cora, I don't know the details.' Maeve stopped rearranging clingfilmed bowls. 'Will you pop down to the shop like the dear that you are and get some more cream – double cream?'

Closing the garden gate behind her, a shard of paint chipped off. Cora pulled her phone from her bag and texted Nancy:

Hey! Are you about later? Fancy a chat and drink? I will even venture south of the river. C x

When the Rowan Centre people-carrier finally pulled up outside the end-of-terrace house, Sheila was an hour and a half late. Cora knew something was wrong. The way other people felt the rain in their bones, she knew it in her stomach.

'Hi, Mum.' Cora stepped forward to kiss the top of her head. Sheila's hair was damp and she breathed in the shampoo. Cora offered her hand to Tom but he only looked at it. 'It's Cora, Tom. Sheila's daughter? How are you?' But he just moved closer to Trish.

Maeve followed the nurse out to the car, and Chris led Tom to the dining table. It was barely three months since

Cora had last seen the old man and the transformation made her insides lurch. Sheila and Joan positioned themselves around one end of the dining table and were immediately giggling conspiratorially.

'Get us a glass of bubbly stuff, Cora.'

'Are you sure?'

'Is it not my birthday?'

Chastened, Cora went to the kitchen and fetched her mother a champagne flute. Sheila placed the glass beside her fork and turned to wink at her friend: 'So tell me, Joan: how is Jim? Asking for me?' Joan slapped Sheila on the shoulder. It was an old tease that Jim had first had his eye on Cora's mother.

Maeve returned looking happy and relaxed. But still something stirred inside Cora. The appetiser tray got passed around and she suffocated the unease with sourdough and hummus. The food was delicious. Maeve's potato gratin was always on point. Tom became overwhelmed after the main course and retired to the sitting room to watch Sky News with the sound on mute. Maeve considered phoning Trish but the others dissuaded her.

'He'll survive another hour,' said Joan, poking at the cheese board. 'I can never remember which is which. Suppose I'll have to try them all.' Maeve slid the cheese slicer towards her but Joan was already attacking the platter with her butter knife. 'That was a top meal. You're blessed to have such a talented daughter, Sheila.'

'Maeve is so good at maths. Did you know?'

'And Cora at drawing,' Maeve added.

'You're one of the best in the country. You win all the trophies, don't you, Maeve?'

'I used to, Mum.'

Joan patted Sheila's hand. 'It's great to have daughters.' But Sheila no longer seemed to be listening. She excused herself to go to the bathroom and Chris went to stick on the kettle.

'Tea or, ahem, coffee?'

Cora could hear her mother upstairs opening and closing doors until she found the toilet. Always that feeling of insides being shook out of place. Cora sat up straight and tried to align her internal jumble.

Sheila returned with her hair brushed. She nudged Joan gently as she took her seat: 'So, has Jim been asking after me?' Coffee cups were being clattered across the table, and Joan looked around to see if anyone had heard. Cora averted her gaze.

'Oh, Sheila, you know he's always asking for you.'

The unease stirring again, torpedoing up through hummus, roast chicken, and pavlova.

'What sort of cheese is this then, Maeve?' Joan's voice louder now, her hand still on Sheila's shoulder.

'Emmental, I think.'

'They have that in the new Lidl but Jim reckons it's like chewing on a bicycle wheel. He's convinced a body couldn't digest it.'

The bird clock chimed from the kitchen and Sheila tilted her head: 'A blue tit.'

'We love that clock,' said Maeve. 'Primrose knows all

the sounds. Don't you, petal?'

Primrose, who was sitting in a booster seat between her mother and grandmother, had missed the question but squeezed her juice box at the sound of her name: 'I'm here! I'm here!'

'Oh now, look at your dress. You've got a wee stain . . .' Sheila dabbed the child's skirt with a napkin, and Maeve fetched a cloth from the sink. 'Mind now, Maeve, I've got it.' Sheila's elbow knocked the juice box over again. A tiny puddle dribbled onto the child's lap and Sheila started to wipe at it frantically.

'It's fine, Mum. Don't worry.'

'I just wasn't minding. Too much of the bubbly stuff . . .' Sheila trailed off. 'I'm sorry, Primrose, I am now, I'm sorry.' But the little girl was as delighted as before and Cora, who was on the verge of vomiting, feared it was everyone else's forgiveness her mother was entreating.

'Maeve's got it, Mum,' she said, sliding her hand across the table but Sheila snapped her own hand back.

'I'm not a child. Do not treat me like a child!'

The harsh words fired like elastic bands against the skin of Cora's outstretched arm. She pulled it back as Maeve stood and started to talk loudly. She gestured to her husband to take Sheila into the sitting room.

Cora climbed the stairs to her sister's bedroom and sat at the end of their king-sized mattress. Her niece's drawings were Blu-Tacked to the wardrobe and a pair of red linen trousers hung over the edge of a wicker basket. Maeve followed her into the room and closed the door. 'Corey . . .'

Cora turned to look at her sister and, as she opened her mouth, the pain in her stomach finally escaped. It jumped straight into her throat, flooding her head and pushing at the dam.

'She had a long day yesterday.' Maeve sat beside her at the foot of the bed, rubbing her back gently. Cora missed hugs. Suddenly she felt starved of them. She squeezed her sister as if to steady her balance. She tried to absorb some of Maeve's sturdiness and transmitted all the things she could not say. One day her mother would die and Cora would be all alone. When the fear slowed, she pulled herself apart.

'I know. It's not like I don't know. But she was fine last week. She was fine every other week.'

Maeve smiled. Concern caused her brow to furrow, just like their mother.

'Was it just the extra sessions – you know, the ones you were talking about?'

'It's a degenerative condition, Cora.'

'So this it then, the bit where it all goes quickly downhill?'

'It wasn't that bad. Look at Tom.'

'I don't want to look at Tom. Tom is the future. You can't go back, can you? People don't get worse, then better, then worse, then better. It's a one-way thing. I didn't think, I just—' Cora was about to admit that she'd never fully believed their mother was sick, but she stopped. She had a flashback to when she was ten, standing in their bathroom in Kew while her older sister told her about periods. Maeve had shown her the sanitary pads in the cupboard under the sink and Cora had been horrified to think of their mother wearing nappies. Cora shook out her arms and her sister reached for a hand.

'Why was she late today, Maeve?'

'There was a problem with the plants. She had a seedling, this delicate young thing in the blue pot, and it was flooded today. Sopping with water. Their little roots can't handle much liquid. Sheila started accusing the aides of killing her shrub. But nobody had been in her room all day.'

'So what was it then?'

'She forgot, Cora. She had watered the plant and forgot and then she did it again. It'll probably die now. The poor thing.'

'Poor Sheila.'

'We should go down,' said Maeve. 'I need to keep an eye.'

'Did she give you a . . . ?'

'A letter? Yes.'

'Did you open it?'

'No.'

'Me neither.'

'How are other things? How is the airport?'

'That's all fine.'

'Have you thought any more about going back to university?'

'Work is fine,' Cora repeated, and she pulled a tissue from a box at the side of the bed and blew her nose. 'And what, Maeve Hendricks, are these tissues intended for?' Cora arched an eyebrow and did her best to smile. 'These tissues right here beside the marital bed? Hmmm?'

Maeve grinned and took a tissue herself. 'Primrose is obsessed with people blowing their nose at the moment.

She can't understand why she has to wipe her bottom in the bathroom but daddy is allowed to wipe his nose in public. She refers to snots as "nose pee".'

Cora snorted.

'I'm raising a right lady.'

'She has a point.'

The women stood and, arm-in-arm, they descended to the hallway just in time to see a Trish-shaped shadow through the frosted glass. Maeve opened the front door.

'So, ladies, how did we get on?' Trish gave Maeve the leave form to fill out. Everything had to be recorded. Trish went into the sitting room to observe Tom and Sheila sitting side-by-side watching a report about a plane crash. Sheila was explaining how a black box operates. Cora offered Trish some tea. She politely declined and continued her markings.

As they pulled on their coats, the clock chimed again.

'A woodpecker,' said Sheila to Trish. 'I bought them that.'

'What did you buy, Sheila?'

'That with the birds, that, the wall watch.'

Sheila bowed her head so Cora could kiss the top of it. Her lips dallied on the crown. What had always been a sweet gesture – she was five foot eight to her mother's five foot three – now felt like intimidation.

Joan went to catch the Tube and Cora left not long afterwards, promising to come for tea again in a couple of weeks. Cian was watching the second Lord of the Rings film unperturbed by Maeve cleaning around him. Cora liked how her brother, at least, was always the same.

It was after 5 p.m. and the light was grey. Cora mounted her bike and braced herself for the drop from pavement to road. She cycled along the bus lane and tried to picture her mother's funeral. Her father would rear his head, with his current wife, arriving on flights Cora had arranged. There'd be a large contingent from the airport and Cian would refuse to wear a suit. Who would speak? Probably Maeve. And what would happen to the siblings if their mother wasn't around? She was the centre of all their meetings. Cora tried to think of a time she had hung out with Cian alone. But she could not.

She pulled in at a bus stop to consider her options. It was too late to go to a gallery and she was reluctant to go home. Cora thought of going to a cafe to read her book. She checked her phone again. Still no response. Nancy was useless.

TWELVE
....

LHR -> UTC 8.40 p.m.

Nancy had watched a Deepak Chopra tutorial on YouTube and was now doing manifestation visualisation at the rear of the plane. She pulled the curtain over, closed her eyes, and thought solely of what she was going to achieve; she would be confident in the interview, she would get the promotion, she would deserve the promotion, and she would one day be wealthy enough to buy an apartment outright . . .

She added the last bit last minute, and it probably didn't qualify as a higher spiritual purpose. But then again, Nancy had also read *The Secret* over the weekend, and that book didn't have such a problem with materialism. *The Secret* said you could visualise anything and it would come. You just had to repeat it to yourself over and over. It had worked with finding a parking space at Westfield shopping centre on Saturday afternoon.

Nancy pulled the curtain open as she heard passengers starting to board. She ran a cloth over her new shoes – two-and-a-half-inch heels; exactly regulation height – and rubbed her tongue across her teeth to check for lipstick. *I deserve a promotion, I deserve a promotion, I deserve a promotion.* It was Wednesday, six days until interviews. She had spent the last four days in a state of deep preparation. All that procedural information they give out during training but nobody ever reads? Well now Nancy had. She had fine-combed, highlighted, summarised on flashcards, and repeated aloud. It was more work than she had done for her A levels. She had redrafted her CV and written a personal statement about all she had learned and what she could bring to the role. She had outlined her future ambitions and included a copy of her Employee of the Month certificate. It couldn't hurt. She moved down the aisle to meet passengers halfway. She stopped at Row 16, stood tall, and engaged her core. She didn't think Deepak Chopra was a quack; it did all feel connected.

Ingrid Sjöqvist had started going to the gym. It began with a book she'd found sitting on top of the microwave at work. It was a guide to running five kilometres within three weeks. Ingrid had enjoyed buying exercise clothes and picking out the right trainers. She'd walked on a treadmill in a sports shop on Oxford Street as a young sales assistant studied how she moved. The machine could tell that she leaned on the insides of her feet, so the assistant sold her insoles too. She loved Lycra now, and gym gear was very enjoyable to wear around the house. It was like pyjamas, only it caused her to stretch rather than sleep. Ingrid was so enthusiastic when she started the programme that she skipped a week of it. Within fourteen days she'd run the full amount in thirty minutes. 'Fast as lightning,' she boasted to the doorman when she crossed her lobby finishing line. The problem with London, however, was the weather; it was always cats and dogs. So Ingrid had joined a gym. The twenty-four-hour opening suited her schedule and once she avoided peak hours (which were the same as on the Tube; how were they everywhere at once, all these people who congested London from 5 p.m. to 7 p.m.?) she always found a treadmill.

It was this recent discovery that drew Ingrid to her neighbour's wrist. It was a pleasing shade of cinnamon, yes, and the protruding veins suggested a high muscle mass, but her ice-breaker was the device encompassing it.

'Is that an activity tracker?'

The man, with dark eyes and gelled-up hair, held out his arm. 'Fitbit,' he said, offering it to her.

Ingrid touched the bracelet lightly. This man did not seem to register the lowered armrest, and the boarder it implied. Perhaps his age allowed him to ignore invisible boundaries. He was a little younger than her. His face was narrow, his body broader, and he was wearing those expensive trainers, the ones with their own stand at the sports store. Ingrid had gushed to Cora about her gym membership, and now the check-in attendant had found her a practised runner.

'I see them advertised at my gym' – what a thrill to have a gym! Like knowing to stand on the right-hand side of the escalator, it made Ingrid feel like a real Londoner – 'and I wondered if they worked. Do you take more steps when you know how many you've already taken? Or, having reached your target, do you get the Tube?'

'Nah, see, I don't use it for that. You can, yeah, but I use it for training. Speed and distance? I'm headin' out to Holland for a marathon and I'll be tracking my progress, see if I can't beat my PB.'

'PB, yes: Personal Best.' The term was written on posters all over *her gym*. 'I've just started running. I'm not doing marathons yet but I am up to seven kilometres.'

'Nice,' said the man, nodding his approval. Ingrid had always struggled to identify 'cool' as a personality trait, except to know she was not it. But this man, she thought, would qualify. 'If you can run five k, you can run ten, and so on it goes,' he said. 'You can't beat the feeling, competing with yourself – gettin' faster and stronger.'

'Oh yes. It's a very nice feeling,' she said, trying to match his enthusiasm. 'The best thing since sliced bread.'

'Sliced bread! Yeah, man!' He slapped his thigh and laughed. Ingrid thought about it. Slices of bread *were* a peculiar thing to praise. Why not fresh pasta? Or pasteurised milk? *The best thing since boil-in-the-bag rice.* She, too, started to titter.

Nancy had left her Putney apartment on just three occasions that weekend: pilates, a quick food shop, and a flashcards run to Westfield. She'd cancelled a date that had already been rescheduled after she chose Ray's TV race and some late-night revision over dinner at the Shard. But Nancy wasn't that bothered; the Italian hadn't used her name once on the phone. She suspected he'd forgotten it. She had meant to reply to text messages – her mam, and a couple from Cora – but she'd left her phone in the bathroom, allowing herself to use it only during toilet breaks. She just needed a few days to herself, to know she'd given it her all.

Nancy had volunteered to restock the trolley and do a quick inventory. They needed more CK One and Touche Éclat, while the tween perfume wasn't selling at all. They should rethink that order. She made a note of it. Ronnie was the senior on board today and her sister-in-law was head of Human Resources. Nancy was treating everything as an audition, a chance to prove herself. She straightened the perfume tray carefully. *I deserve a promotion, I deserve a promotion, I deserve a promotion.*

'But you've gotta take the knocks too, that's just part and parcel.'

'Oh I know,' said Ingrid. 'I got two blisters at the beginning, and I had to wait a day and a half before running again. I told myself, "Ingrid, that's just the way the cookie crumbles."'

'It's all about how quickly you respond. You listen to your body and react. So now, I feel my ligaments strain or my shin twinge? I cut back immediately, reduce intensity, begin treatment. Strength training and foam rolling: this is the truth. I'm telling you: forget running without them.'

Having introduced himself, Rajesh Patel was now giving Ingrid a tour of his various ailments, complete with recovery solutions. Ingrid was learning a lot. Those shins didn't feel like anything that could ever splinter, and she'd never thought of knees as being aligned. He also told her the pain at the base of her left foot was probably an inflamed plantar fascia.

'Interesting,' she said. 'It's all very interesting.'

Nancy had positioned the duty-free trolley in the centre of her alcove at the rear of the plane, so Ronnie could see all the work she was doing from the senior station by the cockpit. Nancy opened compartments with exaggerated arm movements – a little something from her time at Merseyside Community Drama – and slammed them shut with more gusto than required. But when she looked up the aisle, she found George obstructing the line of vision.

'Well she's touching his leg,' he said, bustling into the rear alcove. 'Yep. Inter-gender relations may not be my speciality but where I come from, that's the deal done. She's buying what he's selling.'

'What are you on about, George?'

'Hello? Cora's couple? Row 27.'

'Oh, right. I forgot.' Nancy looked up from where she knelt, three bottles of Barbie Bliss in hand, and tried to peer around George's legs.

'I did notice I've been doing a lot of the legwork on this lately. You finally tired of being Cora's puppet?'

'I'm not her puppet.'

'Mmm-hmm?'

Why did George have to make everything sound like a buggering question? 'I am *not* her puppet,' Nancy repeated, her jaw clenched. She winced with the pain. It had not been a good time to start whitening her teeth. She told herself to relax. 'I help with Row 27 because I like it and if I don't have time, I don't have time. So I don't know what you're banging on about. Nobody's in charge of me except me. Alright?'

Nancy's mother had finally gotten through on Monday and, after rebuking her daughter for not returning missed calls, she told Nancy she was going to be an auntie. Joe's wife was pregnant.

'Oh they'll have beautiful babies, the most beautiful babies, with his height and eyes and fast metabolism . . . Joe was the most beautiful baby – have I ever told you that, Nancy? Everyone said so. Peter was handsome too, like a real little man. You were more of a late bloomer, a lot of puppy fat to get through but, still, you made it in the end. I hope you're still exercising, Nancy? Your hips will always be the first to show. I take responsibility for that, and it only gets harder to shift. Mind you, I'm not quite ready to be a grandmother yet – the women in Sainsbury's would not believe it when I told them, even when I said he was my eldest – but you can't leave it too late. Joe is thirty now and Lorraine must be twenty-eight. How about you, Nancy? What happened to that nice pilot you were seeing? I'm too young to be a nanny but time is running out for mother of the bride. Much longer and I'll be like Fran Henshaw. I told you about that, didn't I? Her own daughter's wedding and she was wearing the same outfit as the groom's grandmother. Can you imagine? Not that you'd catch me shopping in Wallis, of course . . .'

She'd let her mother in and everything in the apartment was instantly infected. The wall of flashcards looked silly, maybe a little insane. The potential interview lipsticks, lined up on her dresser, seemed moronic. Alison Beatle's memoir was lying open on Nancy's bed. It was about her time with Pan Am in the 1960s, and how Richard Burton hit on her, even though Liz Taylor was on the same flight. Nancy flipped the cover over. The book was called *Take No Passengers*, and it was her favourite. Alison Beatle was a career inspiration. *Take no passengers*. When Gloria Moone finally took a breath, her daughter cut her off. 'I've got to go, Mum, sorry. I'll call you during the week.' She threw in a quick 'ta-rah' and hung up.

Nancy closed the duty-free drawers and mentally ran through the positives. She must remember to think positive. One: She hadn't allowed her mother to undo everything. Two: The rest of her long weekend had been productive. Three: This flight was going well. Ronnie would have to be impressed, everything was running so—

'Wait. She's touching his leg. George? Lower or upper leg? I will have no one joining the mile-high club – not on my flight, and definitely not this week.'

Ingrid had found some paper but she didn't seem to have a pen. She searched her briefcase once more, shoving tomorrow's briefing documents to one side. 'No. Sorry.'

''s alright. I'll shout for one in a minute.' Rajesh leaned out and looked down the aisle. 'No one about.'

'They'll be along,' said Ingrid. 'They always are.'

'There are three principles I always tell my clients, right? The first is consistency – which doesn't mean doing the same thing over and over, not at all, but whatever you do, identify a time when you can do it regular. I imagine you have a busy life, yeah?'

'Yes, yeah,' said Ingrid, wishing she could take notes.

'So you need to identify the time that works for you. First thing in the morning, last thing at night or maybe, yeah, lunchtime.'

'I travel a lot.'

'I hear that. Interval training, you can attack that anywhere. Twenty minutes of resistance is better than an hour running.'

'No!'

'This is the truth.'

Rajesh turned to look down the aisle again. 'Sorry, mate? Wouldn't have a pen, would you?'

The American steward stopped at their row. He smiled at Ingrid and pulled a Bic biro from his breast pocket. 'Red do?'

'Cheers. I'll be quick as you like.'

'No hurry at all,' he said, peering over Rajesh's shoulder. 'Can I ask what you're drawing?

'He's a personal trainer and he's making her a workout plan. There wasn't a groin massage in sight.'

The plane had touched down in Utrecht, and George had been sent to the rear for disembarkment. Nancy was admiring the rows of merchandise now locked away in translucent duty-free drawers. 'I'll tell Cora,' she said.

'Not sure it's blatant romance though.'

'Okay.' Nancy had written her name at the top of the stock sheet, but she wondered now if she should have added the date.

'I mean, it could be.'

Usually they just left stock sheets in the folder but Ronnie had that up at the other station.

'Nancy! Hello? She's, like, your friend. I'm just passing it on? I don't even care?'

'Alright, George, I've got it. It's not that important anyway. It's just a stupid game!'

Her colleague looked at her with mock amazement. 'Well that's a first.'

'I'm not a total divvy,' said Nancy, her ears burning. 'I *know* it's only a game.' She could almost hear her mother laughing at her silliness, and her brother raising an eyebrow: *Come on, Nancy.* She was wound up, she knew, and stressed. Her jaw was in bits. 'I'll text Cora when the plane is cleared. I didn't have time to remind the stupid controller about setting up a call.'

'Well, like I said, I don't know if it's a match or not.'

'Let's call it a match. Alright, George? I'll tell Cora to chalk it down as a success.'

'No need to get touchy.'

'I'm not getting *touchy*.'

'Right – except that you are?'

'I'll tell her to mark it a success,' Nancy said evenly.

George was somewhat appeased. 'The body language *was* strong.'

The plane was cleared with time to spare and Nancy volunteered to stay an extra twenty minutes and help with turnaround. She vacuumed the seat covers, probably a little more aggressively than necessary, and remembered to check seat buckles for stains. She even took an ice cube and hand scraper to some long-ignored chewing gum. *I deserve a promotion, I deserve a promotion, I deserve a promotion.*

THIRTEEN
● ●

'That's the thing though, isn't it?' said Joan, laboriously clicking through a passenger list. 'You go to all that effort and – what was it your flatmate lost? Four stone? Five stone?'

'Four stone.'

'Four stone. And is she skinny now?'

'Not skinny.' Cora considered. 'Just average.'

'Exactly. All that effort and you're still just average. Hardly seems worth it now, does it?'

News of Big Ray's third weigh-in was circulating the airport. He'd lost a full stone, and everyone was saying what an incredible achievement it was. Everyone except Joan. He'd walked past their check-in zone an hour previously, and Joan had watched with scepticism. 'If the plane crashed on a deserted mountain, he'd still be the first one eaten.'

Cora had seen Ray out huffing and puffing on her way home the previous night. Charlie was waving the stopwatch and shouting at him to adapt to the unexpected and set his brain to train. Charlie looked well in his sports gear, even though he wasn't doing any exercise himself, and she'd thought how she really should find someone for him. He called a 'Safe home' to Cora, and even Ray managed to raise a hand in greeting. She thought he was running faster – or at least at a more consistent pace.

'But what about health? It's not all about being skinny.'

'Health!' Joan hooted. 'That's only a wind-up. Our neighbour, now she's young mind, and her hubby bought her one of those things, what is it now, that you run on and—'

'A treadmill?'

'For Christmas! A bloomin' treadmill for Christmas. She said he was very good, and that it was concern for her health – I'm sure that's what he was concerned about right enough. Her *health*. Didn't want her getting a fat arse, more like. I'm lucky really I've got Jim. There's a man who'd give cause to examine whether two fried eggs and a lump of black pudding might count as an aphrodisiac.'

It was a Friday afternoon and they were both working the late shift. Nancy was on the 7.20 to Dublin – Aiden's flight – which meant Cora had some female passengers to research. Her friend's in-flight reports had been sporadic of late and Cora worried that she was getting distracted by other things. She hadn't heard from her properly in days. And Nancy knew she needed the information for her chart. The computer screen was starting to hurt Cora's eyes so she printed out the passenger list for the Dublin flight.

Her last couple of matches with Aiden had been a disaster. Barely talked, Nancy said. Probably the women didn't find mood swings all that charming. Or maybe he'd regaled them with the story of an award-winning documentary about

162

the world's most horrific genocide. Cora had watched his movie recommendation – begrudgingly given how their last encounter had ended, but she wasn't going to give him the satisfaction of thinking his attitude had any effect on her; she was a professional after all, dealing with high-flying grumps was her job – and she gave up before the film got to the halfway mark. She went to cinema for escapism. Relentless misery was something you got enough of in real life.

Aiden had potential, but a nice smile will only distract from the other three Ps – pride, pedantry, and pompous taste in films – for so long. Still, Cora thought as she took the warm pages from the printer tray, everyone deserved to find someone.

When Cora got back to her desk, Nancy was there gabbing away to Joan, her hair high in its trademark ponytail, and her emerald gaberdine fitted perfectly across the shoulders. It was as if the mass-produced Aer Lingus uniform had been designed specifically for her.

Before Cora could ask her friend where she'd been lately, Joan cut in.

'Cora Hendricks! You never told me Charlie Barrett asked you to go courting!'

'I didn't – he – how did you know that?'

Joan inclined her head towards Nancy, who was beaming from cheek to cheek.

'He probably used the word "courting" and all.'

'How did *you* know?' asked Cora, addressing the question to Nancy this time. 'I didn't tell you that. And I know word spreads in this place, but I didn't tell anyone.'

163

'Oh, Cupid! I'd been dying to ask. How was it? I told him not to say anything too old fashioned; it'd make him sound like a dirty old man. But you can never—'

'You told him? Did he tell you he was going to ask me out? Or, wait—' Cora had a flashback to the night of the Fight the Flab race – the unusual sight of Nancy and Charlie huddled together conspiratorially in the corner of the pub afterwards. 'Did you . . . ? No, Nancy, you didn't *tell him* to ask me out . . . Did you?'

Nancy was fit to burst with joy and pride. 'I may have given him a little nudge!'

'Oh God.'

'I could see the two of you talking away during the race – I had a great view from the starting line – and oh, Cupid, I could just tell how well you were getting on. And either he was saying a lot more to you than he would to anyone else, or he just liked breathing into your ear, but either way you two looked so close and—'

But Cora wasn't listening. It was Nancy's fault Charlie had asked her out. Nancy's fault she had one more thing to contend with when her energy was needed elsewhere. There she was, doing her best to keep everything stable, and her friend – who never thinks before doing anything – had come in and shaken everything up. She'd had a frank conversation with Nancy about this only a couple of weeks ago. *Drop it*, she'd said at the idea of her and Charlie. Nancy hadn't listened to a word – or worse she had and she'd disregarded it all. Cora could feel the anger rising from her feet.

' . . . So when we were in the pub, I thought I'd say it to him – just that it mightn't be a bad idea to ask you out. While I couldn't promise anything, you might just say yes. You should have seen his face, Cora. He was—'

But Cora didn't wait to hear the end. She *had* seen his face – and she'd felt nothing but guilt. Nancy hadn't given a second's thought to her actions – how it might affect everyone else, how Charlie hadn't asked for it – setting him up to get rejected. Cora turned from the check-in counters and started to march away. She didn't know where she was going, but—

'Cora! Wait.' She could hear Nancy's heels clattering across the tiles behind her. She waited until she was out of Joan's earshot before rounding on her friend.

'How dare you, Nancy!' She was furious. The heat coursing through her started to flood into her eyeballs. So this was blind rage. 'How absolutely dare you!'

'I don't—'

'I told you not to interfere. I expressly said I did not want you meddling, that I did not like Charlie, and that I did not want to go out with Charlie – or with anyone! We had a verbal, coherent conversation about it and I do believe I actually used the word "no"!'

'But you were just scared, Cupid. Sometimes we all need a helping hand. You know that! You're always giving that helping hand. And I just thought if you were confronted with the possibility, you'd take a leap of faith—'

'I'm not some stranger on a plane! I am your friend, who you know and whose wishes you should respect.' They were standing in the middle of the floor, passengers and staff zipping around them. Still Cora couldn't manage to lower her voice. 'And I am *not* scared! I have a lot going on right now and going out with some chap isn't my priority. As hard as that might be for you to understand.'

'What's that supposed to mean?'

'Well you're very distracted these days – skipping out early on the race, only reporting back on Row 27 matches when I remind you. And I sent you two text messages last weekend and you never even replied. We had a birthday dinner for Sheila and it was awful and I could have done with someone to talk to.'

'I know you think I divide my free time between the beds of various men—'

'I never said—'

'But I have things to do. For myself. I was studying all weekend and I didn't have time to get back to anyone. If you think you're annoyed you should have heard me mam.'

'You didn't even have time to send a text?'

'I didn't have a minute. The interviews are next week. You might not care about promotion, but—'

'*That's* what you're studying for?' said Cora, catching the derision in her voice a beat too late.

'Yes *that's* what I'm studying for.'

'Sorry, Nancy, I didn't mean – I just, I'd forgotten about them.'

'There are signs all over the staffroom,' said Nancy, sounding exasperated. 'And I told you. But of course you forgot, because you're not the one going for promotion.

That's why I've been busy. I told you I was up till four one morning, and I left Ray's neon run thing early to get some cramming in – but you just thought I'd copped off with some bloke?'

'No,' said Cora, but she couldn't quite look her in the eye. She was supposed to be the victim here, the irate one. When had the tables turned?

'You did!'

'No . . . although if I did, I'd only be going on previous form. But whatever, so long as it's not one of my matches I don't care who you spend your time with.'

Nancy sighed. 'The check-in embargo isn't for ever, Cora.'

'So?'

'So people won't keep coming to your desk. It's not real, what you're doing. What are you going to do after the summer?'

'Leave it out, Nancy. I don't need—'

'You might not care about this place, or maybe you're too good for it or whatever,' she said, talking over Cora's protestations. 'But I care about my future. I want to be senior cabin crew, and I want it this year. I need it before I'm twenty-eight.'

'You *need* it before you're twenty-eight? What? Did that number come to you in a dream?'

'I'm more than your puppet, Cora.'

'My puppet!? I know you're not *my puppet*, Nancy. What are you on about?' Cora could feel the invisible hand reaching inside her again, preparing to shake everything loose. She evened her tone and took a breath. One of them had to be rational. 'You purposely meddled in my life when I specifically told you not to. You brought Charlie into it – you basically brought him in to get rejected – and now I have to clean up the mess and you don't even realise you did anything wrong. We're supposed to be friends.'

'Are we friends, aye? You and me, Cora? Funny sort of friendship, that. Where you don't even know what I've been up to for weeks, when you don't even ask.'

'How could I ask when you don't respond to my messages?'

Nancy was shaking now – anger or upset or both. 'Why would I respond when I know you just want to talk about *your* stuff, *your* bloody matchmaking? That's not friendship. Friends don't use each other. Friends know what's important in the other person's life. Friends give a shit about someone other than themselves.'

'Well I'm glad we're on the same page.'

The two women stared at each other, fury, hurt, and confusion bouncing between them. Passengers whizzed past and Cora clocked Weasel scurrying towards them. As the manager neared, Nancy turned and trundled away, her coat sleeves halfway down her arms and a notebook starting to droop from her bag. For Nancy, this was dishevelled. Before Weasel could reach the battlefield, Cora retreated to her station. She felt like someone had tripped her up and she couldn't remember if she'd banged her head.

• • • • • • • • •

Cora knew the self-check-in embargo wouldn't last for ever. Of course she knew that. Did Nancy think she was stupid? Cora was obviously going to do something else. She just hadn't figured out what that would be exactly. But there were still months left. The embargo was in place for at least a year, isn't that what the email had said? So Cora was going to get everything else sorted before she started freaking out about a career. And what? Was creating romance for people not a worthy enough thing to do with her time? And Nancy acting like *Cora* was the selfish one?

It was typical of Nancy to bring everyone else into her melodrama. Cora should have known she'd said something to Charlie – great fun for Nancy, never mind how it makes everyone else feel. Never mind if Cora was struggling to keep her own emotions in line without having to feel responsible for someone else's. And her puppet? Where had she gotten that? No doubt all tied up in some bloke, or her mother or some other drama that Nancy had decided to take out on Cora. And now who was going to keep an eye on Aiden's flight this evening? And what about the rest of the weekend? Nancy was the one in the wrong and yet Cora – and her loveless passengers – would be the ones to suffer. Well Cora would just have to wait for Nancy to wake up and smell the coffee. Smell the coffee? Jesus. This pep-talk had her sounding like Ingrid.

The Dublin check-ins had started, mixed in with passengers heading to Berlin, and Cora had yet to choose a match for Aiden. Not that she'd have anyone on the plane to report back. What if this was the weekend she found the love of Aiden's life? She highly fucking doubted it, unless he'd had a lobotomy. But she would never know *for sure*. She thought about asking someone else on board, but Nancy would just take it as proof she was using her. Which she wasn't. She just didn't want all her work to be wasted. She looked through the rest of the cabin crew roster for the 7.20 to Dublin but there was nobody she could ask.

'Anytime, Cora, would be great.'

She looked up to see Aiden standing in front of her. 'Anytime? Well that'll be another few minutes so,' she said, and went back to scanning the list. She was in no mood for his sarcasm today.

To her surprise, he stood there quietly, waiting. When she started to get dizzy from darting her eyes back and forth furiously across the same part of the screen, she raised her head.

'You okay?' he asked, a flash of concern. She was momentarily thrown.

'Yes.'

'You annoyed about the other day?'

'What other day?' she said, sickeningly sweet smile in place.

'I suggested you might have been a little . . . I'm not sure what the word was exactly—'

'Nosy.'

'Nosy. Right. It was a long week and I had a lot on my mind. I'm not always great with words . . .'

Cora studied him carefully. 'Is that – are you apologising, Aiden O'Connor?'

'I'm merely saying I may have, slightly, overreacted. You weren't exactly being polite yourself, you—'

'I'm taking that as an apology. Don't ruin it.'

'Far be it from me to correct your definition of apology.'

'Yes,' said Cora. 'Because you *never* correct *anyone*.'

'You been talking to my ex-girlfriend?'

Cora looked at him – auburn curls recently cut and rugby jersey starting to stain around the collar. Surely he could afford a second sweatshirt? That was the second reference *ever* to him being single.

'If she has the same taste in films as you, I doubt we'd have much in common.'

'You watched it?'

'Yes, I watched the documentary, well most of it. It was excruciating. Depressing and long and relentlessly boring. And it was in black and white. Why? It was made last year!'

'Black and white? I didn't know that.'

'You recommended it!'

'Mmm,' said Aiden, taking his passport and ticket before Cora could hold them hostage. 'But I never watched it. It's meant to be awful. Terrible pretentious shite.'

'What? You never watched it? Why did you recommend it?'

'Payback,' said Aiden, sounding as absolutely chuffed with himself as he looked. 'For all those awful paint-by-numbers rom-coms you had me watching.'

Cora was agog. 'You—'

'Well, this has been fun,' he said, the dimple on his left cheek very much on show.

'You little shit!'

'Ah now, Cora, don't be like that. Here—' He swung his bag around again. 'Charity pins they were selling at the hospital. Thought it'd be perfect for someone who never seems to have her mind on the job. See you next week, daydreamer.'

Aiden strutted away from the counter – oh yes, it was very much a strut – and Cora picked up the badge he had left on her counter. It was light blue with swirly white typeface that read: Head in the Clouds.

And, despite her very best efforts, she laughed.

Cora thought of herself watching that pants documentary, growing steadily more frustrated, pulling strands from her hair and muttering to herself, 'just massacre the lot of them already', and she actually laughed out loud. She was impressed. Maybe Aiden wasn't so – Aiden! She still needed to find Aiden a match. She checked her phone to see if Nancy had grown up between Security and Departures, but there were no messages. She scrolled desperately through the dwindling number of females still to check in on the Dublin flight. And there was a school group to be seated at the rear of the plane. Just perfect.

One of the teachers was single and female. Surely that wasn't her only remaining option. Cora scanned the queue for the school group and their eligible chaperone, Georgia Hancock. But she hadn't gotten past the first few waiting faces when her stomach dropped. Three passengers from the front of the line was Friedrich Turner. And it wasn't in her imagination this time. He was actually there. Flesh, blood, perfect blond curls. And beside him was his wife.

Cora couldn't get her cheeks to relax, or her jaw to move. It was as if her face was playing musical statues. Somehow, she called the next passenger forward.

'Passport and flight number, please.'

The passenger watched her as she typed in his details, and Cora wondered if he too could hear the blood banging against the walls of her veins. She wasn't staring at this elderly customer particularly, he just happened to be in her line of vision and she was afraid to look anywhere else. Her sister used to get angry because Cora couldn't grasp the rules of hide and seek. Maeve would instruct her to hide, and Cora would just stand there with her eyes shut; if she couldn't see them, they couldn't see her. She knew the rules now, but still she squeezed her eyes shut. Get it together, just smile, your life is your own. She thought of that T.S. Eliot poem from school: Prepare a face to meet the faces that you meet. She opened her eyes, slackened her face, and smiled.

'Have a nice flight.'

Friedrich was at the top of the queue. Physical, tangible, and utterly out of place. He had nothing to do with her life here. Nobody had met him and she never discussed him. It had started to feel like she'd made him up. But there he was, clear and relaxed and letting other passengers go ahead of him. His wife's hand rested gently on his arm and she was saying something into his ear, but Friedrich was watching Cora. A family skipped ahead of him. He was letting them pass. Why was he waiting for her? 'Next please!'

Friedrich strode over, the woman who had to be the wife following. His gait was as casual and confident as ever.

He was rake-thin with broad shoulders, and he had razor cheekbones that begged romantic young women to offer up their wrists. Cora had written terrible poems to that effect. His hair was a mass of golden curls she used to say had been woven by fallen angels. Cora used to say that actual line. *To him*. And, god help her, she'd thought it profound. Friedrich used to tell her his mother had sold his hair for expensive wigs when he was a boy and Cora knew it was a lie. She knew it was a lie because everything was a lie, but she could rarely prove it. And so she'd have to sit there, nodding along to these stupid tales, feeling like a fool. The relationship had invoked intense paranoia, and for the longest time she even doubted he was German. He was cut from a different world, a nineteenth-century poet who intended to stay forever young. It was an affectation but it worked.

'A vision appears before me. Cora Hendricks. How long it has been.' He was smiling and he was relaxed and it was all so very easy. 'I'd heard you were working here. Are you well? Cora, this is my wife, Sophia Turner. I'm not sure you ever met. Sophia, this is Cora Hendricks, she used to work for Stefan.'

I used to write copy for Stefan, thought Cora, *and I used to live with your husband*. Only was he your husband then? Friedrich had said they were separated but they were both so young and she couldn't be sure of anything. Sophia was pale and delicate. So much about her suggested a shadow. She held out her hand, slim and smooth, and Cora took it. 'Nice to meet you.' A hand that had money but rarely handled it. Friedrich had never taken Cora's hand in public. It used to hurt that he was embarrassed, but now she considered he may still have been married.

'Can I have your passports, please?'

Sophia touched her husband's arm lightly, and from her handbag produced both documents. They were beautiful together. Their hair and their skin seemed to glow. Cora knew that under his soft cotton shirt were surprisingly strong arms. He was much healthier now and the clothes were neater. He dressed his age. Was he thirty yet? For all that ungraspable talk of passion and truth, it seems money was what he needed most. Everything else was already in him, and better a wealthy canvas on which to project it. Cora had given him money. She refused to calculate how much, but she'd paid for flights and food and she'd let him live with her for free. Even though he had tenure and she was freelance. She keyed in the passport information and printed out the tickets.

'But are you well, Cora?' he implored. 'Are you thriving?' His voice was warm and affected. His wife's hand still on his arm.

'Fine, thank you. Working away.'

'At the airport?'

'Yes, here.' Obviously, she wanted to say, *fucking obviously*. Friedrich used to tell her she'd do something pure and worthy and exceptional. Only he never specified what employment, exactly, would tick all those boxes.

'That's really wonderful,' he said. 'You're a picture, Cora, you really are.' And she wanted to scream at him.

'An aisle seat would be great if it is possible.' Sophia's pale speckled eyes danced across Cora's face. She leaned her head on her husband's shoulder.

There were questions, Cora realised, that only Sophia could answer. She wanted to ask if Friedrich liked her best when she was upset? If he told her she has the saddest eyes? If she ever made herself cry during sex? Cora wanted to know if sex was best when they treated each other like strangers, when there was no kissing and Sophia thought of herself as a prostitute? She wanted to know if Sophia had started to get off on that. She wanted to know she was not mad.

Friedrich and Sophia married at university and were on their second separation when Cora met him. This one was meant to lead to divorce. Or so she was told. 'Everything, including love, is only impressive when you are young.' Afterwards, she doubted whether divorce had ever been discussed. Afterwards, she questioned everything. Back in England, Cora had phoned and asked to be patched through at the music college where he worked and was taken aback to find that he existed.

'Were you holidaying in London?' she asked, hoping her words weren't too slow.

'Friedrich had a job interview.'

'Not for a university, not for London,' he said, perhaps sensing Cora's alarm. 'It's an orchestra generally based in Munich but the auditions are international. It's very prestigious and they really want me but I have to decide if I want to be the kind of person who auditions. It's so vulgar to chase fame and glory and so dangerous to let others determine our worth.'

Sophia gazed at her husband, and Cora wondered how she had not learned to spot the lies. He was scared, a little boy unwilling to lose face. He used integrity as a shield when there was a chance things wouldn't go his way. He never took chances, and he refused to be vulnerable. Life cost Friedrich nothing. Fame and glory were exactly what he wanted. He would never admit that someone, or something, did not want him.

At the end of their relationship the arguments would go on so long that Cora sometimes fell asleep. He'd wake her up in the middle of the night and demand to know how she could sleep through this. But 'this' was never anything. Arguing was too omnipresent to be so specific. It felt like a torture exercise and she couldn't understand how he never needed to sleep. She would sit on the bed, so confused and delirious that she'd start to cry, and he would go bang out some nonsense on the electric piano.

'The 7.40 to Berlin: 16A and 16B.'

'Thank you, Cora.' Friedrich reached for the tickets before she could place them on the counter, sliding his fingers over hers and holding her gaze. 'It is great to see you. You look beautiful.'

Sophia beamed at her husband's kind words and nodded her agreement.

'Great to see you,' Friedrich repeated, and that was it. Cora watched until they disappeared behind a corner, Sophia a fraction behind her husband. He did not turn once. She was gone from his mind. The lesser-known rules of hide and seek.

• • • • • • • • •

The rest of check-in passed in a haze. The school teacher was all wrong – nice, down-to-earth, and bound to spend the plane journey preoccupied by her boisterous charges – but Cora couldn't think straight, and she managed to put her beside Aiden just in time. Cora tried to keep Friedrich from her mind until the day's work was done. She would let him in on the Tube journey home. She wanted to text Nancy but didn't. She was probably in Dublin by now. Was she as inconsiderate on the other side of the Irish Sea?

Cora fought to keep the memories at bay, but she couldn't. She remembered getting drunk with Friedrich – the multiple occasions forming one bric-a-brac of memory – and how intimate it had been. She had loved love since she was a child and then she had found it. All-consuming and wounding and maddening, as if someone had painted it. Other nights she was left drinking alone and Friedrich would come home at four in the morning and tell her about the fascinating women he'd met after a gig and she would pretend not to care. He steered her toward tears so he could comfort her. But wasn't that once-in-a-lifetime love? All the emotions in extreme. Cora tore her mind back to the job at hand. A middle-aged couple checked in and the wife pointed to Aiden's badge, still sitting on her counter.

'Remember that song, Gerry?' she said, nudging her husband. '*With your head in the clouds and your heart on hold*. Who was it sang that?'

'Couldn't tell you, Margaret. Sounds like one of your records.'

Friedrich used to say his music was too 'intense' for people to appreciate, but he just wasn't very good. Cora knew this at the time but she would have denied it to the end. He said money didn't matter and she had agreed in a way, but it was always her money he was dismissing. She couldn't call him a charlatan without accepting herself as a fool.

Weasel tapped her on the shoulder. 'I never received your form, Cora.'

Cora considered his face for a moment. She yearned to push him over. Here she was, trying to stay still and keep everything together, and everyone else just kept coming at her. She hadn't even looked at the form. She'd no idea where it was. It was possible she had used it to wrap the stale crusts of a lunchtime sandwich in.

'I've misplaced it.'

'Interviews are next week, Cora. *Next week*.'

'Right. Well I don't need a form because I don't want to change. I'm fine where I am.'

'You don't want to change?'

'No.'

Weasel glanced at his clipboard. 'This won't look good.'

'Okay.'

'You won't be moving forward.'

Cora shrugged. She didn't want to move forward or in any other direction. Why was that so difficult for people to understand?

'I might be able to get you an extension,' he said, flicking through pages. 'I have the ear of a few powerful people. Think about it for a day or two. I can really see you in Boarding.'

Cora slipped down from her stool and threw an eye over the queuing area. Still empty. 'Back in a minute,' she told Weasel, skirting around him and out on to the main floor. She moved quickly toward the escalator, taking it up a floor and then calling the lift. This could not be the only choice she got to make. It had been too long now and something had to happen. She had to make something happen.

She rapped on Charlie's door and waited for him to call her in.

'I didn't think floor staff knew where the offices were. Usually we just wait to be summoned.'

'I'll go out with you.'

The brief silence was enough time to shake Cora's resolve. Her words echoed back; she sounded pretty arrogant. What if he regretted asking? What if that was why he'd been acting like nothing had happened? But no, it didn't matter; nothing ventured, nothing—

'Good.'

'Right. Good,' she echoed, relieved.

'Next Saturday?'

'As in tomorrow week?'

'Yes, if that suits?'

'Right. Good.'

She remembered it now, the feeling. This was how it felt when something happened.

FOURTEEN

....

There was a schoolboy in Aiden's seat. He was kneeling backwards so he might better converse with the girls in Row 28.

'Sorry, mate, that's my seat.'

The teenager turned to face him, a bottle of Coca-Cola Zero in his hand. 'Is it, blud?' he asked, grinning back at the girls.

'It is, yeah.'

'Alright, blud,' he said, shifting himself out of the seat, and the girls began to laugh.

'Yeah, blud,' one of them murmured as the boy moved to the row across, still grinning.

'Is it, blud?'

'No, blud.'

'Yeah, blud.'

And on it went, each nonsensical statement attracting more laughs than the last. There were approximately twelve second-level students on this flight identifiable by their bottle-green uniforms, and they had him surrounded. Couldn't Cora have put him further up the plane? If it wasn't that she always put him in Row 27, he'd have thought this was *her* payback.

181

'Ronald Archibald, get your feet off that seat!' Aiden watched a woman descend the aisle, barking orders as she got to the rear. 'And button up that blouse, Matilda Middleton. It was not that low when your parents dropped you off at the airport.' The woman stopped at Row 27 and the ferocity fell from her. She smiled at Aiden.

'Poor you,' she said, lowering herself into 27C. 'Seated beside us. If it comes to it, I think the travel budget could stretch to a medicinal whiskey.'

'It's not a good idea to refer to alcohol as medicinal.' Aiden winced. 'Jesus. Sometimes I hear myself and I know I should be given a good slap.'

'I'd help you out but they banned teachers from slapping a while back. More's the pity with this lot.'

The air hostess, Nancy, descended the aisle – telling each member of the school group to fasten their seatbelt. But she glided past Aiden without a glance, and it was left to him to realise his chair needed to be positioned upright.

'I am a sick woman, right?' said one of the teenage girls behind him. 'I didn't even appreciate it when I got it. Only when it was broken. I didn't even realise how much they spent on it. I thought like, okay three hundred quid, but no.'

'When you're trying to sell it don't say Coke. Say water,' said another.

'Yeah, say water.'

'Yeah, I'll say I spilled water. Because, basically, if I sell it online, I can only sell it for thirty quid. That's how fucked it is.'

'But like, maybe they can tell that it weren't water.'

'If they tell me, I'll just say, "Oh I didn't know." I'll get my mum to go or something, because if I go myself, they'll be like "this joker". You, like, you can't turn it on. If it's going to take loads to fix it . . .' The girl sighed. 'I just want to get a new one.'

Aiden turned his head to see if he could make out who was talking but the teacher caught him looking. He turned back. With teenagers you didn't want there to be any misunderstandings.

'The utter bull that kids talk,' said the teacher, who had obviously been listening to the plotting too. She pulled a ball of wool and a pair of needles from her bag. This woman was his age. Aiden didn't think he'd ever seen anyone under sixty knitting. 'Every day I am struck by the blind confidence of teenagers. They speak so loudly because they have no doubt, not the slightest, about what they are proclaiming,' she continued, unperturbed that she too might be overheard. 'Can you imagine? I marvel that I was ever that young.'

Aiden had enjoyed being a teenager – he was good at school, good at sports, good with women. But his brother was two years older and had been all of those things too. Aiden had always wanted to be as good as Colm. He'd been secretly proving himself to his elder brother all his life, vying for his approval. Colm had studied accountancy after school so Aiden had to get an A1 in maths and accounting in his final exams too, even though he knew he would be doing medicine. Colm had gone into a high-earning profession so Aiden had to do the same. But Colm was still beating him on one front. He had a family: great wife, two kids. Aiden didn't have that domesticity. That was supposed to be him and Izzy.

'The teenage years were grand,' he said. 'But I wouldn't want to do them over.'

'Nor I,' said the teacher. 'God, when I think of it. I remember sitting upstairs on the 11 bus, preaching to my friends about the importance of wearing matching underwear. "Men like that," I said. Ha! What did I know? I probably read it in some magazine. I was still a couple of cup sizes off discovering men had no interest in underwear, and that it was just another barrier. If I'd heard myself then, shouting my mouth off, what a berk.'

Aiden looked around to see if her charges were listening. But no.

'Don't worry,' she said, watching him out of the corner of her eye as her hands twitched and more stitches appeared across the needle. 'They have zero interest in what anyone over thirty is saying. Did you think old people were humans when you were a teenager? They wouldn't be able to wrap their heads around the fact that I sleep and eat, never mind that I wear underwear.'

'I suppose,' said Aiden.

'No supposing,' she breezed, wrists still contracting. 'Teenage self-involvement is as strong a sound barrier as you'll come across. Everyone on that bus could have heard me running my mouth about matching knickers, and I'd never have registered them.'

The last time Georgia Hancock had been on the 11 bus was coming back from an evening out in some bar near Sloane Square. She had met a couple of old school friends just after Christmas. One of them, also a teacher, was married and working in Saudi Arabia. She was expecting her first child. The other was in a five-year relationship, didn't believe in marriage, had just quit her job in the City, and was off to travel the world with her partner. When it came time to share her own news, Georgia had exaggerated a Tinder date – telling it as if it had occurred the previous week rather than three months beforehand.

'He sounds great,' one of them gushed.

'It's just smashing the different ways you can meet people these days,' said the other. 'A woman I work with met her husband through *The Guardian* Singles site. I think it's fantastic.'

'If I was single I'd totally do it.'

'Absolutely. He seems great, Georgia. It sounds like there might be a second date on the cards.'

'We'll see what comes of it,' said Georgia, knowing the only thing to come of that rendezvous was a trip to the STI Clinic and a few sleepless nights. The rash, thankfully, was thrush, not gonorrhoea. The doctor told her to lay off the alcohol and sweet stuff until it cleared up. The sugar was no problem, but it had worried her a little that she hadn't put the wine bottle down. It was just so difficult to avoid. It was fine for her loved-up friends who could happily sit in with their partner and have cups of tea. But Georgia had to make an effort to be more sociable, she had to create her own situations in which to meet people, and most of those required alcohol. Even the Stitch 'n' Bitch club, which had started as knitting and tea, had quickly progressed to knitting and wine. Now the needles didn't always make it out of the bag because that left no hand free for the wine glass.

'Freddie Wheatley! Keep your hands where I can see them. And, Hannah Upshall, I don't know what you're giggling about. God knows where his mitts have been.'

'Teachers really do have eyes everywhere,' said the chap beside her. Handsome guy, lovely reddish hair, and oh how Georgia melted for the Irish accent.

'It's the first thing they teach us at training college,' she replied. 'That and how to— Right! That's it, Freddie.' The little bugger, thought Georgia, jumping up from her seat and grabbing the Sex Ed folder as she went.

Aiden watched the row of stitches unravel. He had no idea how to stop them and he was hardly going to interrupt the woman while she poured cold water on hormonal teenagers. Aiden had a young woman in his office that morning enquiring about a jaw reduction. It was a present from her parents for her sixteenth birthday. Even with his clinical hat on, Aiden couldn't find fault with her face bar a few spots on the forehead and a reddening of the cheeks as she explained what she wanted done. He tried to convince her it was unnecessary, told her how her face could still change and it was worth waiting a few more years, but she wouldn't be deterred. She had a photograph of her ideal face shape ripped from a magazine and the consent form was folded neatly inside her homework journal.

Aiden had never been immune to guilt. He considered himself agnostic but his Catholic upbringing ran deep. When he was leaving the clinic that evening, the charity collectors had been in the foyer. Mental Health Awareness that, in his place of work, had to be some sort of irony. He'd emptied his wallet – £112.50 – and they'd insisted on digging right to the bottom of their bucket until they found him the very last badge. As soon as he saw it, he knew he'd be giving it to Cora. He pictured her as she always was, sitting at the Aer Lingus counter lost in a world of her own. He didn't know what it was about that image, but he'd left the collection stand feeling a little better.

'Nothing like a few pictures of venereal disease to help them keep their hands to themselves,' said the teacher, taking her seat and opening the folder so Aiden could see the first image.

'Jesus.' He closed his eyes. 'Is that what you teach? Sex Education?'

'Lord, no. This is just part of the overnight trip kit. I also have a first-aid box, list of parental contact numbers, and a store of paracetamol. I teach Classics. We're going to Newgrange tomorrow, and the Hill of Tara. Have you been?'

'Years ago,' said Aiden. 'Though, as I recall, the Hill of Tara is more a field than a hill.'

'It doesn't matter. It barely falls under Classics, to be

honest, but the department had money left over for an outing. It's older than Stonehenge, at least.'

'That's a pretty decent outing.'

'Public school. Plenty of money – even if this lot like to act otherwise.'

'I went abroad once during school, to France, and my parents arranged it themselves,' said Aiden. 'Otherwise I don't think we ever strayed more than thirty miles from Dublin.' Aiden listened to the girls shrieking behind him and thought again of the mortified sixteen year old sitting before him that morning. A donation wasn't enough to erase her from his mind. He'd write to the girl's parents, advise against the treatment, and hope they didn't query it with anyone else at the clinic. They weren't in the business of turning away work.

He yawned, the last few patchy nights of sleep catching up. 'Am I boring you?'

'Friday night fatigue.' Flying twice a week every week didn't help and he wasn't even sure if Izzy was working tomorrow. And if she was, what would he say? The last day that they'd been on rounds together things had been normal – so normal that she could have been any physio, comfortably discussing work and the weather as they went from bed to bed. Aiden had momentarily forgotten this was the woman he was coming home for, the woman he was going to win back. He only properly remembered when they went on break and she automatically sat at a table, waiting for him to get the coffees. He remembered how she'd always done this when they were together, and he remembered how it always annoyed him.

'I've only been to Dublin the once before,' said the teacher. 'For a hen party. I have to say I found it terribly expensive.'

'That's probably because you spent all your time in Temple Bar. Don't.'

'I'll remember that,' said the teacher.

He watched as she tried to flag down the passing air hostess. 'Miss?' But Nancy just keep on pushing her cart.

'Excuse me, miss?'

Georgia flapped her arm, but nothing. Could the air hostess not hear the desperation in her voice? Mr Mortem, the other Classics teacher, was also on supervision duty but Georgia could hear him snoring all the way in the back row. Georgia had arrived at Heathrow a good forty minutes before the students were due, in the hopes of fortifying herself with a snifter. But she had taken one look at the barmaid and been turned off. The woman, probably a couple of years younger than Georgia, had a tattoo down the side of her arm. It read: Stay Forever Young and Invincible. What age had she been when she got that? Probably seemed like a great idea on a beach in Vietnam or wherever but it was one hell of a burden to have burnt into your skin back in dreary, mortal England. How could you wake up to that every morning and not be profoundly disappointed, no matter how life had turned out?

'Have you got kids yourself?' asked the wavy-haired Irish man. She could feel him making an effort to be friendly and she appreciated it, but she wondered what it was about her that made him think he had to try.

'Not yet,' she said, watching him for signs of sympathy. 'They might not be for me, if I'm honest. I already have enough of them to deal with.' Was that—? It was. She stood swiftly and reached over the seat in front, swiping Giles Stewart's mobile phone from his hand. 'Phones off!' She powered it down and threw it into her bag. 'You?' she asked, thinking the good ones always do.

'No. Too busy with work. One day, maybe.'

'Plenty of time,' she said, relieved not to have to look at any cute photos. She had a dog, whom she loved very much, and nobody ever asked to see him. 'Are you single, then? Apologies if that's forward but I've never been one for tact.'

'No, I . . .' He took a deep breath. 'Sort of.'

'Sort of single?'

'Mmm.'

'Like you're on a break? Whose idea?'

He looked at her, thrown by the bluntness, but she just nodded at him to go on.

'It's complicated.'

She raised an eyebrow. 'It's never that complicated. I am a complete stranger and you will never me see again. You lose nothing by telling me. I may even have a perspective.' Even Georgia herself doubted this was true. She just wanted something to think about over the next forty-eight hours that wasn't hormonal teenagers.

'I'm not really one for discussing these things.'

'What man is?'

He looked at her again but she kept knitting. 'We broke up and . . . If I ever *do* see you again, I'm going to pretend I have no idea who you are and I never said any of this. Alright?'

'I was never on this plane.'

'We broke up. We were supposed to move to London together, or at least that's what I thought, but she didn't come. So I suppose, ultimately, she did the breaking. But . . . things hadn't been great before that. It's only now I can see it, actually. Almost a year later.' He shook his head in amazement and she watched the curls follow. 'We had both been working a lot. And I suppose we forgot about each other. But that happens when you've been together a while.'

Georgia said nothing, just kept on counting her stitches.

'But I'm going to get her back.'

'Why?'

'What?'

'If it wasn't so great at the end, why would you want her back? Maybe it just ran its course.'

He looked at her in disbelief. 'You don't just give up. We'd been together seven years.'

Dropped stitch. Damn. She offered nothing but the clatter of her needles.

'I thought we'd get married, have kids, everything. You don't just lose all that.'

'Is that all?'

'What? That's not enough of a reason? That you've spent years working towards something?'

'Do you love her?'

191

He laughed – not a real laugh but Georgia spotted a dimple on his cheek. Cute. His face was tired but good, it had that broad honesty that was hard to fake. 'That's a ridiculous question.'

Cast on, cast off, cast on, cast off.

'It's hard to feel the same after seven years.'

Another stitch made a leap but she picked it up just in time.

'I mean, yeah. Of course I love her. Course I do.'

Maybe Izzy had fallen out of love with him, a little. But it could not be the other way around. Aiden had to love her. Otherwise he wouldn't be coming home every weekend. Aiden could stand in front of hundreds of students and wax lyrical about his sparkling career or explain to a sixty-six-year-old man why there was no point in having a scrotum lift, and none of it fazed him. Yet talking so plainly to this stranger, he felt the unfamiliar twinge of self-doubt.

Aiden remembered the feeling of loving Izzy. Some days it was stronger than others and some Saturdays now, when they were on rounds together, he mainly felt annoyance. But that was okay. Just because you don't feel something every day doesn't mean it's not there. The teacher's knitting needles seemed to grow louder. It was distracting. Aiden rarely questioned himself. His approach, which had served him well so far, was to pick an end goal and sprint towards it – jump any hurdles placed in his way, keep the finishing line in sight. It never occurred to him to consider why it was he wanted to win the race in the first place.

Nancy came back up the aisle with the trolley, and the teacher tried to catch her attention again.

'Pardon me! Miss!' she called.

'Sorry. No time. We're landing shortly.' And Nancy disappeared. She didn't even register him.

The girls behind Aiden were putting on accents now. To him, they just sounded like stronger versions of the ones they already had. 'I'm going to go, right, and I'm gonna snog everyone in the place: gay, straight, lesbian, bi.'

'Trannies!'

'Yeah, blud. I, like, I don't even care.'

Aiden turned to the teacher, who was making serious progress on whatever it was she was knitting. 'Why do they keep calling each other "blood"?' he asked. 'Why is that so funny?'

'Haven't a clue,' said the teacher. 'Last year everyone was "rudeboy". I'm never sure if they're laughing at the street kids or trying to be like them. I doubt if they know either.' Aiden watched as she dropped her left needle and leaned over the chair once more, grabbing an iPad from the same lad and throwing it into her knitting bag beside his phone. 'And I'll take that too, Giles, thank you very much.'

Aiden heard the boy, whose skin was paler than his own, mutter to his friends: 'Nigga can't be left alone.'

'You see?' sighed the teacher. 'And his father sits in the House of Lords.'

FIFTEEN

· · · · · · · · · · · · · · · · · · · ·

'California' was on its third loop when Roisin knocked on Cora's bedroom door.

'Oh good,' she said, sticking her head around the doorframe with a hand in front of her eyes. 'I reckoned if you had the Joni Mitchell on, you must be alone. But you never know. Charlie could be into a bit of Sunday morning melancholy.' Roisin inspected the pile of clothes on Cora's floor, separating out last night's dress with her foot. 'Was that "Sire of Sorrow" I heard earlier?'

'Yep,' said Cora, still listening to the lyrics. *Reading* Rolling Stone, *reading* Vogue. Like any self-respecting romantic, Cora had been turning to Joni Mitchell for guidance since she was a teenager. The matchmaking chart, atlas, and flight plans were spread across her bed. She hadn't been able to sleep, there was too much in her head, and this was the only soothing distraction. She had discovered a correlation between flight duration and likelihood of success, and she was in the middle of confirming a theory that romantic cities didn't associate with romantic journeys.

'Jaysus, Cora. How bad was it?'

Cora looked down at the pages. It hadn't gotten any worse, because it hadn't changed at all. Without Nancy to provide information, there was nothing to add to it. But, she realised, her friend wasn't asking about the chart.

'The date?'

'Of course the bleedin' date!' said Roisin, suspiciously eyeing the chart, which at this stage was really more of a multicoloured spreadsheet. Thankfully it was also elaborate to the point of encryption. Cora shut the atlas hastily and shoved the multiplying pages back into her bedside table. The drawer was becoming difficult to close.

The date had not been bad. Objectively speaking it had gone quite well, and she told Roisin this. ('*Objectively speaking*? Jesus, Cora, you're not writing a military report on the encounter.') Charlie had wanted to cook, but eating together was pressure enough without having his bed a few yards away. Cora suggested a restaurant near her flat and Charlie, being the 1950s gentleman that he is, insisted on collecting her from Seven Sisters Road. And so he had appeared at exactly 7:30 p.m., standing under her window with his mobile phone to his ear, a lone white face among the sea of older North African men who congregated outside the cafe next door to their building.

'I'll be down in a minute,' Cora had shouted, both into the phone and through the open window.

'Rapunzel, Rapunzel, throw down your dark hair,' teased Roisin, who had been sitting out of view at the end of Cora's bed. She was fashion adviser for the evening – vetoing a playsuit because it made Cora look like she was wearing a nappy, and giving the thumbs up to a flattering 'but not too hoochy' black body con dress. 'I still think you should have met at the restaurant,' said Roisin. 'Now he knows your address, which also happens to be *my* address. What if he's the clingy type and can't take the rejection and comes back some night holding a stereo above his head or, I dunno, a hatchet?'

But Cora was glad of the walk. Charlie-on-a-date was not Charlie-from-work. He'd even swapped his navy sweater for a navy blazer. If she'd had to go straight into staring at him across a candlelit table, she would have either burst out laughing or vomited from nerves. The twelve-minute journey from her house to Season was an ice-breaker – an interlude in which they didn't have to look at each other. As they fell into pace, they talked more freely, and by the end of the stroll – when they were debating which north London soccer club had the most obnoxious fans – Cora felt almost at ease.

'This is not one of your better stories,' interrupted Roisin.

'I'm setting the scene!'

'Yeah,' said Roisin, unconvinced. 'It's a bit flat . . . Let's do it like *The Guardian*'s 'First Dates'. You be the lonely heart and I'll be the journalist. I'll get the magazine.' 'First Dates' was a weekly feature in *The Guardian* newspaper where two strangers were sent on a blind date and answered questions about it afterwards. Cora and Roisin read it every Saturday. They both said the best ones were when one participant thought they were soulmates, and the other person had a terrible time. Secretly though, Cora liked it most when they both gave the other 10 out of 10. There had even been a few 'First Date' weddings.

'Okay, got it,' said Roisin, returning to the bedroom with the previous day's magazine. 'And can we at least move on to the next track?' She bent over Cora's laptop and released the repeat button. 'Right. So. Cora Hendricks, question one: What were you hoping for?'

'That it wouldn't be so awkward I could never go back to work?'

'Cora, come on. Do it properly.'

'I am doing it properly. That is actually what I thought. Alright, alright. What was I hoping for? I hoped it would flow easily, I'd enjoy myself, and I'd prove myself wrong.'

'About what? About Charlie?'

'No, not Charlie. In general, just. About lots of stuff. Go on. Next question.'

'Okay,' said Roisin, glancing back down at the magazine. 'What were your first impressions?'

'My, this blind date looks familiar.'

'Cora!'

'I thought: I'm glad he's tall so I can wear heels. He really does get better-looking the more you know him, but I'm still not sure he's for me. Oh! And he smelled good.'

'Always important. What did you talk about?'

'That side was good. We talked about books. He studied English at uni, which I didn't know. And he loves Raymond Chandler, who I've never read. He reads more than me, which was good because it meant I learned some things. We talked about public libraries and I said you worked in one—'

'What else did you say about me?'

'Funny now, I don't remember that question being on *The Guardian*'s list. Must be new.'

Roisin stuck out her tongue.

'We talked about libraries and London's transportation system, but it wasn't boring. He told me about his family – he already has three godchildren. Said he's rejected Satan so many times he's worried he might start taking it personally. I laughed though I didn't really get it. I'm assuming it's a Catholic thing.'

'It is.'

'And he talked about growing up with his grandmother, who literally beat manners into him. Which explains a lot. And, I don't know, all the usual stuff: music, restaurants, people we have in common.'

'This is fun! Any awkward moments?'

'Well this is what I was getting to before you interrupted. Once we got to the restaurant, it was all sort of awkward. Like it was fine and the conversation never stopped but I was always aware of myself – I was sitting like people do when they know they're being watched, and I always knew what time it was.'

'That's normal,' said Roisin. 'That pain in your neck from being on high alert? It's first-date whiplash.'

'Maybe, but it wasn't butterflies. I wasn't wondering what he thought of me or if what I'd said was stupid. I didn't care. It was fine but it just felt like effort.'

Cora pulled the quilt up over her. She wanted to say that the whole thing had made her feel dead inside, but she knew Roisin would have little time for that.

When Charlie walked Cora home she decided that if he tried to kiss her, she'd let him. She didn't have a preference. In the end, he had asked for permission (of course he had) and Cora had morphed her cringe into a smile and nodded her head. As he leaned in and placed his lips over hers, his hand so tentative against her back it was hardly there, her whole body tensed. All she could think of was the last person she'd kissed, and when she compared this sensation to the eviscerating effect of Friedrich's lips and tongue and hold, it didn't even feel like they were doing the same thing.

'When he kissed me, Roisin, I had a terrible fear that maybe romance really is only good when you're young.'

'These answers are a bit heavy for "First Dates".'

Cora kicked her friend through the bed covers.

'Good table manners?'

'Like you've never seen.'

'Best thing about Charlie?'

'Kind, attentive, a good heart.'

'In "First Dates" speak, that's future husband material.'

'It's an objective opinion.'

'Would you introduce him to your friends?'

'If he'd let me set him up with them, yes.'

'Describe Charlie in three words?'

'Very nice man.'

'Did you go on somewhere afterwards?'

'Didn't you hear me coming in last night?'

'Cora!'

'The Dairy pub. For two drinks. I had gin; he had pints. I paid since he insisted on getting dinner. That enough?'

'Did you kiss?' Roisin raised her hand before Cora could object. 'Just answer it.'

'Yes. We kissed. But that was all.'

'A snog, but no ride. Grand. Marks out of ten?'

'Seven and a half. They always say seven and a half.'

'Would you meet again?'

'At work tomorrow.'

Roisin let that one slide. 'If you could change one thing about the evening, what would it be?'

'I'd have sent a woman I really liked in my place.'

Everything Charlie did made Cora think of Friedrich. Even when he held a door open or offered to pay his share – things Friedrich never did – she still found herself missing him. She knew their relationship had been unhealthy, that it had damaged her in ways she was still recovering from, but, even when she had been jilted at the rural home of some friend of Friedrich's with no way of getting back to Berlin and no idea where her boyfriend had gone or with whom, Cora had always wanted him. He was an addiction. But Cora knew that wasn't a good thing. She didn't want to be an all-or-nothing person when it came to investing in someone else. She trusted Charlie, which she could never have said about Friedrich, and it was possible the rest would follow.

Cora leaned over to check her phone. Sheila had had an accident during the week. She'd scalded herself when boiling the kettle on Wednesday evening, and Maeve was sending regular updates to Cora and Cian. The kettle had been too heavy and Sheila had let it slip. Nobody knew why she had filled it to the brim since she was only ever making a single cup of tea and she'd always been conscious of the wasted electricity that went into boiling more than you needed. But anyway she had, and the water had poured all over her left arm and hand.

The Rowan Centre rang Maeve that night and the three children had rushed in to see her in the emergency room. Second-degree burns. The doctors said the trauma was worse because Sheila's skin was so thin, and intervention had taken so long. Sheila hadn't called out or reached for the alarm. The nurse didn't know how long she'd been sitting there when they found her, but the skin had started to swell around her watch and Claddagh ring and Sheila insisted she could feel no pain.

Her mother sat dazed in the hospital bed. They had her wrapped in some sort of tin-foil coat and kept insisting she drink more liquids. But she just looked from Maeve to Cora, tremors causing water to dribble down her chin as she asked over and over again when someone was going to take her home. Cora didn't know if she meant her room at the institution or the home she'd long sold in Kew. It's the shock, a terrible shock, everyone kept repeating. Cora hadn't seen her mother like that before.

She hadn't been to see Sheila since, but she was going in today. No more excuses. She climbed around Roisin, who was now reading about a new Blur album, and went to make porridge.

In the kitchen Mary was perfecting hot chocolate – her Sunday treat. Mary was never out on Saturday nights so always rose early, constructed an elaborate breakfast, did her washing, took a bath, and made herself a mug of hot chocolate from one of those treat-wise sachets. She was carefully shaking marshmallows into a cup that sat atop her Weight Watchers scales. Cora stood beside her and observed.

'What should it be?'

'Twenty-one grams of marshmallows, so 197 altogether.'

It was at 185 now and Cora watched the numbers rise slowly as Mary dropped no more than two marshmallows in at a time. 189, 192, 195, 198. Mary frowned.

'Let me help you with that,' said Cora, skimming one off the top.

'That's made it heavier somehow!' But Mary was laughing.

Cora gave her a look of mock shock and pinched another marshmallow from the pile. 'You're very welcome,' she said as the scale fell to 196. Mary squealed again, and Cora thought how rarely she heard her flatmate laugh.

Roisin was in the hallway searching for her keys. She was off to see Prince Charming. His parents were in town for the weekend but Roisin didn't want to meet them. This perceived slight had led him to send what Roisin called 'mixed emoticons'. 'A winky face followed by parents and their kid: I ask you Cora, what the fuck is that?' But they'd reached a compromise and she was going to his place while his parents were out sightseeing. 'A spot of afternoon delight,' said Roisin, reprising her terrible English accent and disappearing into the darkness of their stairwell. 'I'll be back before the Tower of London closes.'

· · · · · · · · ·

The colour had returned to her face and there was a long gauze bandage wrapped around her left arm. A researcher, who was leaving Sheila's room as Cora arrived, said she was a little shaky and needed to eat. 'Energy is crucial during the recovery phase. She needs more calories,' he said. 'Seeing her daughter will be a treat.' The researchers tried, but they could never quite emulate the compassion that came so naturally to the care staff. None of what Cora had wanted to discuss – how to know if you like someone, how to get someone else out of your head – could be described as a treat. She thanked the researcher and revised her conversation plan.

'Sweetie pie.' Sheila was sitting in her armchair with a blanket over her knees. Her injured limb was resting on the armrest. She looked a decade older than the last time Cora had been here. In the moment it took to steady herself, Cora scanned every corner of the room that did not contain her mother. She spotted the blue flower pot, empty since the seedling had died, and an extra handrail installed by the sink. Where the kettle had once stood was an empty space. The toaster was gone.

'Hi, Mum,' she said, kissing her brightly on the top of her head. 'I brought cake.'

'Lovely,' said Sheila, but she watched nervously as Cora produced the tin containing half a lemon drizzle log. 'What's that?'

'It's lemon drizzle. It's great, trust me.'

'Lemon. Lemon.' Sheila juggled the word on her tongue. 'Grand.'

'So how are you doing?'

'Me. I— Just about to clean the floor, when you came . . .'
Her mother stood abruptly, a little shaky on her feet, and
Cora rose from her chair.

'I'll do it.'

But Sheila pulled a mop and bucket from behind the
door without any trouble. She rested her hands on the
counter. 'Where did they put the kettle? They move all of
the things.'

'I'll look for it,' said Cora. The rooms were cleaned
regularly by staff but residents on the open-access programme were allowed to keep their own products. Cora
inspected the tiles on the kitchen side of the room. 'This
floor looks immaculate, Mum. I'd say the cleaners were in
already.'

But Sheila was busy opening and closing cupboards
with her good hand. 'I need water. Water. Where did they
put . . . ?'

A care worker came through the door, knocking as she
entered. 'Sheila,' she said, her Jamaican accent dividing the
name harshly and coaxing an instant look of guilt from her
mother. 'Ya can' be cleanin' She-la. I tell ya again. Ya give me
that mop. Ya give that mop and ya sit down.' Turning to Cora,
she said: 'I clean them this morning. She ask and I clean. The
floors are clean. Ya be careful or she have another accident.'

'I will not be treated like a child in my own home,' her
mother barked, as the aide carried the bucket and mop out
of the room. 'That woman is a witch.'

'I hear ya, She-la,' the Jamaican woman shouted from
the corridor.

'I should hope so!' she shouted back. 'I was speaking loud enough!' Sheila looked at her daughter and rolled her eyes.

'Will we have some cake?' said Cora, cheerfully standing to open the cupboard marked PLATES. They told them at the hospital that Sheila was at risk of infection and she needed to eat. Cora wasn't sure cake was exactly what they meant but the hollows of her mother's cheeks told her it was better than nothing.

'What's that?' asked Sheila, as Cora put the thick slice in front of her.

'It's lemon drizzle.'

'Lemon, lemon, le-mon . . .'

Cora placed the slice in front of her.

'I'm not hungry.'

'Come on, Mum, I brought it especially.'

'No.'

'Here,' said Cora, splitting her own portion with a fork and putting a morsel in her mouth even though the last thing she felt like doing was eating. 'Mmm. See? It's delicious. Now you try.' And she put a bite on Sheila's fork. But her mother just pursed her lips.

'How about a biscuit then?' she suggested, jumping back up to search the cupboards. Had Sheila had lunch? Breakfast? 'You have to feel like eating something. Even a digestive. Here, have one.' She was trying too hard, she knew, but she couldn't stop. She didn't know when Sheila had last eaten. Cora thought of finding a nurse to ask but she didn't want to leave her alone. When had she gotten so thin? Her mother had never been thin. 'Just one, Mum. Please.'

Cora remembered the day that Maeve told them she was getting married: the three women had gone shopping and their mother was trying on boots. When she couldn't get the zip to go the whole way up her calf, Sheila had collapsed onto the shoe shop's sofa in hysterics. The daughters knelt either side of her, expressions of concern across their faces, and Sheila wiped the tears from her face. 'Do you feel okay, Mum?' Cora had asked.

With a wide grin she had told them: 'Girls, I suppose I've just got to accept that I've got Irish dancing legs.'

Six years later, and back on her knees: 'Do you feel okay, Mum?' She leaned in, careful to avoid the injured arm. 'Will you have anything? Anything at all. Anything.'

Cora could hear the hysteria in her voice. She remembered what the doctors had said – how their agitation made Sheila more flustered – and she tried to calm herself. But her mother was squirming in the chair, and when Cora held a quarter biscuit up to her, Sheila started to yelp.

'Okay, sorry, it's fine, you don't have to have any.' But Sheila was whimpering, and Cora didn't know what to do. She hadn't seen her mother cry since she was a child and it created an unknowable panic.

'My arm,' said Sheila, a high-pitched note of alarm. 'My arm, my arm . . .'

'Is it sore?' Cora looked around desperately. She thought about hitting the call button but wasn't sure this counted as an emergency.

'Someone hurt my arm.' She looked at Cora as if she were the child and she needed everything made okay again. When they were children, Sheila would kiss their injuries better. So Cora, holding back her own tears, leaned in and kissed the coarse gauze.

'There now,' she said, her mother's voice as it once was ringing in her ears. 'All better!' Cora did her best to smile but the effort was pulling her heart in two. She held her mother's right hand to stop her scratching at the bandage and hummed some nonsense to distract them both. There were no words and, eventually, the tears dried up.

'I'm sorry,' Sheila whispered, her voice incongruously young. And Cora, not knowing what to say, just squeezed her fingers tighter. Not five minutes later, Sheila nodded off to sleep.

Cora fought the urge to leave. To flee. She'd go home shortly and make coffee and give the matchmaking chart her full attention. There were so many variables to look into: age profiles, professions. She'd give it all her concentration. If she could just get her mind to focus, it would all be fine. Cora was washing the plates when Sheila woke. With her good hand, she started to fish some notes from her pocket. 'Second-degree burns,' she said, reading from a slip of paper.

'I know, Mum.' And Cora put the last fork away.

'You have to talk to your sister.'

'Who does?'

'You.'

'I do. Maeve calls me every week.'

'You have to talk to her. And you'll be grand, I know you will. You will.'

'I know I will too, Mum. I *am* grand. You're just tired. Shush, it'll be alright.'

Sheila blew her nose and when Cora chanced offering her a biscuit, she took it without comment. Her face was still red and puffy, and crumbs were falling over the glasses that hung around her neck. 'Any men?'

A burst of laughter escaped from Cora. 'I had a date last night actually. With Charlie, from the airport.'

'Is he nice?'

'Charlie, Mum! You know from' – but Cora cut herself off. 'You'd like him. He's a very nice man. Very well reared, as you might say.'

'That's good, sweetie pie.'

This was the kind of conversational treat daughters were supposed to bring their poorly mothers. 'I suppose it is good, yes. I'll keep you updated.'

SIXTEEN

••••••••••••••••••••

LHR -> BHD 3.20 p.m.

Kevin Daniel Reynolds was disappointed to find himself a row behind the tasty young thing he'd been watching in line. She looked like she might be an aspiring actress – or at least that she might aspire to it if he put the idea in her head. After a couple of minutes meditating on her legs, which spilled out into the aisle, Kevin redirected his attention to his passport. It expired in three months, and he could finally make his name official. He'd initially added the Daniel because there was another Kevin Reynolds working in the film industry. But now he liked how impressive it sounded – Kevin Daniel Reynolds: a triple threat – not to mention how much space it took up on screen. When the credits rolled, his name was always bigger than anyone else's.

The Belfast Film Festival was paying for his flights but a complimentary drink, never mind a meal, was looking unlikely. Nothing put Kevin in a bad mood quite like going home. Kevin had thrown his accent, and everything else that might connect him to Northern Ireland, overboard on the boat from Larne twenty-eight years previously. Tonight was the festival's grand opening. More 'grand' in the Irish than the British sense, he suspected.

He thought about engaging the leggy youth in conversation but the seatbelt was uncomfortable enough around his middle without having to lean forward. The woman beside him was pretending to read the in-flight magazine but he caught her eyelashes flickering as she stole glances in his direction. With a bit of make-up and some clothes that fit she could be decent. She was old enough to be his wife but for a flight home he wasn't doing too badly.

'Kevin Daniel Reynolds,' he said, making sure the sleeve of his shirt rose as he proffered his hand. She shook it, and his eighteen-carat watch caught the window light.

'Ingrid Sjöqvist,' she said instantly, as if she'd been expecting the introduction.

'Nice guy, Colin Farrell,' said Kevin, pointing towards the cover photograph of the magazine she was holding. 'Such a generous actor. He wasn't in the best of places when I knew him. I'd say, "Colin, amigo, the drugs don't work," but he couldn't hear me. It was his journey. He had to get there on his own.'

They hadn't had that exact conversation but Kevin was a second assistant on one of Colin Farrell's first films and he had fetched the actor from his trailer on three occasions. How far they'd both come since then.

'I don't have much time for the cinema,' said the blonde, flicking back to the article.

'You lucky, lucky thing. I can never get away from the place. Occupational hazard.' Kevin flashed a smile – he'd gotten his teeth done a few months previously and had to remind himself to use them – and handed her a business card.

Ingrid Sjöqvist inspected the card – Kevin Daniel Reynolds, Movie Producer – and wondered what she was supposed to do with it. This match was unlikely to prove fruitful. Which was disappointing. A couple of weeks ago, Ingrid had met Rajesh Patel who had since become her personal trainer and caused her to reach such new levels of fitness that she could now do seventeen push-ups. Then, last week, she'd gone on a date with a vet she met on a Row 27 flight to Edinburgh. They had nothing in common except a knowledge of farm animals but they had enjoyed a delicious Lebanese dinner in Soho. Third time's a charm. Or so Ingrid had hoped.

She listened as Kevin – sorry, Kevin Daniel – told some story he kept reminding her was 'very funny' and wondered why Cora had chosen this man. His girth suggested he was not particularly interested in improving his PB, Ingrid's only notable hobby, and she doubted he had much concern for the dairy summit where she'd be spending the next three days.

Ingrid could almost see her reflection in his molars. 'What genre of films do you make?'

'At the moment, we're all about showcasing forgotten gems,' he said, pulling at the cuffs of his shirt. 'We reimagine them and re-film them. We architect them for a new generation.'

'Remakes?'

'That's probably the simplest description, when English isn't your first language,' he said, lips stretched back in a version of a smile. Between his teeth and his watch, Ingrid found herself squinting. 'At the moment we're looking at *Blade Runner*. I shouldn't be telling you that – we're still in development – but you've got an honest face. A pretty one too, it's got to be said.'

'That sounds like the dictionary definition of a remake,' said Ingrid who could have confirmed this immediately as she always carried a dictionary in her bag. An item she imagined was missing from the luggage of a man who used 'architect' as a verb.

But Kevin kept grinning. 'We're going to retell the story, but in London. You look at the original film and you think, "What's the difference between that dystopian world and a shitty day in London?" Everything's grey, people fleeing the rain like it might burn their skin off. So let's give the Replicants Cockney accents. Let's have near-naked, impoverished flower sellers on every corner. Let's retell a story for the kids and let's make the death scenes spectacular.'

He looked at Ingrid like he expected her to applaud. He must have been mid-forties but she was convinced the mane he kept fondling was the result of hair plugs.

If George could change anything about his life, it wouldn't be the fact that he'd grown up in a homophobic backwater, or that his African-American parents had chosen to settle

in what was officially the fourth whitest place in America
– take a bow, Osage County, Missouri. He wouldn't even
change the fact that in a community as tiny and nosy as
theirs, his mum and dad, who already stuck out like a dark
brown thumb, had an unhealthy and very public obsession
with *The Love Boat* TV series, which both alienated them
from the rest of the miniscule non-Caucasian community
and earned him the nickname of Buoy George. All of that
was cool. In fact he *welcomed* a solid high-school experience
of ridicule and exclusion compared to what he'd had to put
up with for the past however many days. If George Yare
could change one thing about his life, he would never, ever
have said anything to Nancy about being a frigging puppet.

To be honest, he didn't even realise he *had* said it. He was
always complaining about Cora and her blatant prejudices,
but it was just talk, and he couldn't figure why Nancy had
suddenly started listening. He didn't actually think Nancy
was Cora's puppet. Duh. He'd like to see someone *try* to tell
Nancy what to do. But then Cora had said something and
Nancy had gone and said the puppet thing and Cora was
pissed and they were fighting and now Nancy was as much
fun to be beside on a flight as a 9/11 conspiracist.

'Am I bothered? I'm not bothered, George, I'm not. I
don't even see Row 27 any more. I take the passenger head
count and I go "Row 25, Row 26, Row 28" . . . That's how I
count now, George. I'm not even bothered . . .'

George was trying to spend as little time as possible in the
rear alcove. He'd volunteered to work up front with Satsuma
Sarah but she'd sent him down to get more Touche Éclat.

He grabbed the make-up from the tray and tried to keep his head down.

This was not his week. As well as the painful work environment, the men of London were getting shittier. For the third time in far too short a period, George had turned up for a daytime date with someone he'd met online only to find the dude totally wasted. George had spent forever thinking about what to wear and what they were going to do and discuss, and then the guy could barely string a sentence together. A few nights before that, he'd gone to Rupert Street with friends. He hadn't particularly felt like going out but he wasn't going to meet the love of his life sitting at home watching the sci-fi channel. So he went out and some dude started chatting him up. All muscles, protein shakes, and masculine bullshit. He had this line, where he told George he reminded him of some actor he'd never heard of. George said his favourite show was *Buffy the Vampire Slayer*, and this guy – this gay fucking guy in a gay fucking bar – called him a puff. Like, hello? Fuck that. He had no time for homonormative bullshit. George would fart rainbows if he could.

Walking the red carpet at home events made Kevin's skin crawl; he couldn't cope with the inane questions that came from the other side of the partition. *Are you glad to be home? Will you have a pint of Guinness while you're here? Will you visit the Giant's Causeway? Is Belfast still your*

favourite place in the whole world? He has shot a film in the Seychelles and they're standing there, under their embattled umbrellas, asking him that with a straight face? Christ.

'Haven't been back to dear old Belfast for a while now,' he said to the Swedish woman in the window seat. He'd forgotten her name. 'Just popping over for the film festival.'

'I'm going to an agricultural conference about milk quotas.'

'It's a privilege to be invited to give something back to my hometown,' he continued, not listening. 'It's such a humbling honour.'

Ever since she'd started this exercise business, Ingrid's libido had come into its own. She wasn't sure she'd had one before but now, when she crossed the threshold of her apartment building, sweat gathering at her hairline, she felt a flutter in her nether regions. The satisfaction she had always derived from sex was in the primal responses she could elicit from the other person. This new sensation was making her think there might be more to it.

These days anything was enough to send her off. She got a thrilling sensation just sitting at the back of a rickety London bus. But she wanted to put it to the test and the only place she was likely to find a human partner was on one of these flights.

Kevin Daniel would not be proving a mate. Even during take-off, as the plane jittered along the runway, she'd felt nothing. Her brain had already decided. Ingrid would not be sleeping with Kevin Daniel Reynolds. Not for all the tea in China.

There was lots George was willing to put up with. He managed to keep his opinions to himself when guys constantly checked their phones during dinner. He didn't even mind a little artistic licence with profile pictures. And top bunk or bottom wasn't a deal-breaker. He just wanted to get to the point where you might even consider letting some dude into your bed and not have to change the locks the next morning.

'Go back down to the rear station, George, and see if Nancy needs a hand.' Sarah paused. 'Hello, George?'

'Oh you're talking to *me*? Yeah, you see unfortunately that's not going to work for me right now? I'm pretty snowed under.'

'With what?' she said, yanking the cloth from his hand. 'Turning my trolley into a bloomin' shrine?'

George made it as far as Row 27. The heck he was going any further; Nancy was ripe to send a claw flying out of her cage. Despite his best efforts, he could never help having a peak at Cora's couples. Today's was a total plane crash. And yesterday, she'd clearly paired a lesbian with a hetero. Cora would set up the queers by accident, but not on purpose? The whole thing was totally unfair and discriminatory. George didn't *want* to be the guy

216

who called homophobia on everything? But, like, hello?
Homo-frigging-phobia.

'So what has you travelling, darling? All work, or over for a
little play?'

Ingrid hit the button on the side of her Fitbit. Twenty-
three minutes for him to ask a question, and it was one to
which she had already provided the answer. He didn't even
wait for an answer.

'Because if you wanted to attend the festival's gala opening tonight, I could organise a ticket for you.'

'I will be busy this evening.'

Still smiling, he tilted his head. 'Washing your hair?'

Ingrid wondered could he hear her at all. 'Correlating last
year's creamery figures.'

Kevin didn't need this. He rang the overhead bell, and
waited for the pretty little waitress he had clocked earlier
to appear. Another air hostess started descending the aisle:
a woman with orange skin who, Kevin noted, would never
actually be cast as an air hostess. Thankfully, the tangerine
woman stopped a few rows ahead and Kevin rang the bell
again. After a couple of minutes, the delectable blonde was
at his side.

'Hello, sweetheart,' he said, pushing up his shirt cuffs.

'Can I help you with something?'

'Well, Nancy,' he said, straining his neck to read her name and taking a survey of her décolletage while he was there. 'I was looking to get a whiskey – Jameson, if you have it.' He pulled a twenty from a wad of notes and the money clip snapped back into place.

'The in-flight service is about to begin. It'll be with you in a few minutes.'

'But I have a terrible thirst, and it's so much nicer to get it from a pretty blonde. You can keep the change.'

'I don't currently deal with this row,' said the air hostess curtly, ignoring his money. 'The service tray will be with you shortly.'

Kevin stuffed the note back in his pocket and watched the jumped-up waitress waddle away. He tried to recline his seat but the button didn't work. What sort of airline was this? The leggy girl in the row in front knocked her smartphone onto the floor and it came away from her headphones. Kevin unbuckled his seatbelt quickly and picked it up.

'Thanks,' she said, as he presented it to her. But Kevin kept a hold on the device. 'Have we worked together?' he asked. 'You're very familiar. Are you an actress?'

'No,' said the girl, going a little red.

'Or a model?'

'No!' she tittered, bringing her hand up to cover her mouth and the gleaming braces within.

A burly red-faced man appeared, standing, in 26B – the seat beside the leggy kid. Clearly jealous, he eyeballed Kevin. *Know when you've been beat, my friend.* 'Can I help you?'

'You can leave me daughter alone for one. She's sixteen. What's your name?'

'I was only talking.'

'I've heard talking and that's not fucking it. I ought to report you. What's your name?'

'That's none of your—'

'Kevin Daniel Reynolds,' interrupted the Swede as she handed the beefy man Kevin's business card.

'I've got your number now, mate,' he said, raising two fingers to his bulging eyes before directing them at Kevin Daniel. 'Don't make a fucking move.'

Kevin went to say something smart but when the father threw his bulk back into his seat and all of Row 26 shook, he decided to let it go. The Scandinavian beside him raised the magazine to her face but Kevin could tell, from how Colin Farrell was jiggling up and down, that she was having a good laugh behind it.

SEVENTEEN

• •

When Roisin got in from work – entering the flat with a 'Honey, I'm home!' – Cora was sitting on the living-room floor surrounded by neon highlighters and pages torn from an A4 pad. Her laptop was open beside her and the stapler was on its side. Roisin could not see her friend sitting amidst this stationary storm, owing to the partition wall between kitchen and living room, but she chatted to Cora as she emptied the remains of her lunch into the bin and began to wash the plastic container. Cora, meanwhile, tried to concentrate.

'Do you know where all the crazy people in London go, Cora?' she said, shouting to be heard over the running water. Cora recognised the desperate squeak of the last of the washing-up liquid being forced from the bottle.

'Well let me tell you. They go to public libraries. And why wouldn't they? It's warm and free and there are lots of cosy couches where they can have a little snooze. There's Internet access to research symptoms of imaginary medical problems – and if they can't find what they're looking for well, sure, can't they ask the library staff because what are we really except underpaid social workers – and there are free newspapers and magazines to peruse, at their leisure, and there are bathrooms to wash your socks in and the heating's always on so they'll be dry in no time. Sure isn't it a great place altogether?'

Cora heard Roisin shaking out the tea towel. 'And have I told you about the accessory *de jour* of the Finsbury Park library crazies? This season's must-have item is the plastic bag. Oh yes, you're nobody without one. The more the better. No matter how old I may get and how far I may travel, I will never again be able to hear the rustle of a plastic bag without having flashbacks to that place. I might put in for a transfer to Crouch Hill. Apparently the crazies are in small quantities up there. The steep ascent must put them off. There was a woman in today with six plastic bags. She sat in the study area and spent the whole time opening and closing them – rustle, rustle, rustle. One was full of colouring books; another had a jar of mayonnaise. She'd open the bags, take the items out, swap them around, put them back in, close the bags, and then start all over. I thought I was going to— What are you doing?'

Roisin had stepped around the partition, tea towel and lunchbox in hand, and was observing the paper trail that stretched from the TV right up to where she stood. Cora sat in the centre of it, oblivious to the highlighter accidentally streaked like warrior paint across her cheeks.

'I was going to do it in my bedroom but I'm on early shifts this week so if I sit on that bed, I know I'll fall asleep.'

'But what is it you're doing?'

Cora had thrown herself into the matchmaking chart in the past week. Now that she'd added all these other layers – nationalities, destinations, reason for travel – she could lose herself in it for hours and there was no room in her head for anything else. Whatever tried to get in, the chart just pushed it right out. A bouncer for her brain. 'I didn't have enough information,' explained Cora. 'I was just giving everything a "yes" or "no" but I've been looking at it with more detail and I can see trends. We're getting some good data through on the frequent fliers. Did you know you can tell more about a person by their past behaviour than by what they think they want? And, weirdly, the English speakers are more open to romance; look at this – the success rate for non-native English speakers is one in ten, but twenty per cent of Irish and Americans came back with a match or a maybe, while that was almost thirty per cent for English and Scottish passengers.'

Roisin kicked a page out from under her right foot and watched as her friend held up one pie chart after another.

'That made me think I need to concentrate on the Scots. It's difficult though because most of our flights are London to Dublin. So then I decided to make a little file on each match.' Cora pulled some stapled pages from under the couch. 'I've been searching social media for signs of success and actually there are two couples from back in November that I can probably change to green. This Instagram photo is hard to make out but doesn't it look like the woman he has his arm around is this woman, here – that's the doctor I set him up with. Her hair is a bit shorter but—'

'Cora.'

'I know. Five months? Of course she could have gotten it cut.'

'Cora.'

'What?'

'Look at yourself.' Roisin grabbed a metal plate from the cooker and held it up so Cora could catch her distorted reflection. 'You've been like this for days. Take a good hard look at yourself.'

'So? This is not a skincare competition. It's work.'

'This is not work. Nobody pays you to do this, nobody even asks you. You cancelled on Maeve's dinner.'

'I didn't want, I couldn't . . .' She didn't have time to explain. 'I was busy.'

'Is it Nancy? Have you talked to her? Or Sheila? You didn't tell me about the last visit.'

Nancy still wasn't talking to her and Cora was starting to feel awful about it. And she couldn't even think about her mum because that was the worst of all. 'I just want to get this right.'

'You were on an early today? Then why were you up half the night?'

'I wasn't.'

'I *saw* your light on, and I *heard* Joni.'

'Are you monitoring me, officer?'

'What were you doing?'

'Nothing.'

Roisin was looking at her now as if she was a Finsbury Park crazy. Cora had been up half the night trying to distract herself. She thought about opening her mother's letter, texting Nancy, calling Charlie. At one point she even considered phoning Friedrich. So she decided the best use of her time was to create some more passenger files.

'You're letting this take over everything. You're obsessed.'

'*Obsessed*. You sound like Mary.'

'No, Cora. You're the one who's like Mary. If she uses food to distract herself, then you're using this in the exact same way.'

Cora started to gather up her pages.

'Have you talked to Nancy?' she repeated.

'Nothing to do with it,' said Cora. Her hand stopped over a page relating to a recent match on a flight to Holland. She had jotted down the man's phone number. He was an electrician and she'd found it online. What exactly had she been planning to do with that? 'As I said, I'm on earlies so I'm just going to take these into my room.'

Roisin sighed. 'Is this about seeing Friedrich? Because you need to start getting some perspective on that too. Have you considered he might not actually be the reason for all of life's woes? Maybe it was just a relationship that didn't work out.'

Cora's grasp tightened on the pages, frustrated by how easily her friend had recast something so complex, something she knew nothing about. 'Goodnight, Roisin.'

'You need to stop thinking about everyone else's life and start concentrating on your own. These passengers are total strangers and you're verging on stalker.'

But Cora held her highlighters over her ears as she exited the room and the only audible response was the slam of her bedroom door.

EIGHTEEN

·······················

Cora had been huddled over her computer for an hour by the time Joan arrived.

'And there's me thinking I'd be the early bird,' said the older woman, halting halfway up her stool to peer over Cora's shoulder. 'What are you doing there? We don't need passenger lists for at least another hour.'

'Just getting a head start,' said Cora, moving the piece of paper on which she was jotting down private passenger details to the far side of her computer. Cora had found an ally on the 9:20 a.m. to Paris, so now she was sorting potential matches. Alison was an air hostess and an old friend of her mother's. She only worked part time but Cora had run into her that morning when she was getting off the Tube.

'How is Sheila doing?' Alison had asked.

'Good days and bad. Not so many good at the moment.'

'I am sorry to hear that. Will you tell her I was asking for her?'

Cora doubted Sheila would remember Alison, but she said she would anyway. And Alison told her that if there was anything she could do, just to ask. Now Cora hadn't meant to take advantage of her mother's illness – she hadn't even fully accepted that that was what she was doing – but when she casually enquired about Alison's flights that day and learned she was on a morning route to Paris, she couldn't help but ask if the air hostess would mind keeping an eye on two friends of hers flying in Row 27.

'What do they look like?'

'Hard to describe,' said Cora, who had yet to pick out any candidates. 'But they'll be 27A and B. They, eh, they don't know each other terribly well, you see. So if you could let me know how they get on?' And she had quickly put her number into Alison's phone before the puzzled woman could find any more holes in her story.

It had been weeks since her fight with Nancy, and Cora's working days were slowly being stripped of purpose. Cora kept lining up Row 27s, hoping Nancy would send a little report. But no. Lines of communication remained closed, so Cora was trying to determine the outcomes herself. On Monday, she'd set up Ingrid with a film producer on a flight to Belfast.

Last night Cora couldn't sleep, again, so she checked the producer's Twitter account for any signs of the Swede but all she got were pictures of him having a pint of Guinness at the new *Titanic* visitor centre.

Cora turned her screen away from Joan and started Googling candidates for Alison's Paris flight. It felt good to be back in business, even temporarily. Check-in without matchmaking hardly seemed worthwhile.

'I heard you didn't sign up for redeployment,' said Joan, stifling an early morning yawn.

'That's right. I'm going to stay right here with you.'

'You weren't interested in a promotion?'

'I thought you didn't consider them promotions, Joan.'

'Ah well, not for me, but for you it's different. You're still young.'

'I'm happy here.'

'Well good. If that's true then fair enough.'

Cora continued to type but she could tell Joan wasn't done.

'I went to visit your mother last night.'

'A-ha.' Cora had been in to see her mother once since the forced-feeding-biscuit incident and she'd felt sick the whole time. Sheila kept panicking about her arm and the scars. Her mother, who had never been interested in her appearance, had discovered a hysterical kind of vanity. She wanted to know who had done it to her. Cora, as the only person there, was the number-one suspect. She felt awful when she went to visit, and she felt awful when she didn't. Cora carefully matched a French actress with a recently divorced financier: 27A and 27B. She willed Joan to stop talking. But she didn't.

'That burn business really did a number on her, didn't it? It knocked the stuffing out of her, poor love. Have to say I got a shock when I went in. But I'm sure she'll get better. Haven't they the best doctors? Nothing to worry about at all. At all, at all, at all.' Joan cleared her throat. 'You're very distracted today, Cora, and I can't help thinking you might be daydreaming about your date with a certain Charlie Barrett.'

Cora's attention was finally dragged from the screen. 'How did you know about that?'

'Oh a little birdie told me,' said Joan, enjoying the mystery but ultimately wanting the gossip more. 'Well, not such a little birdie. A fairly hefty birdie actually. Ray told me. He fixed the strap of my handbag yesterday and, you know, I do think I'm starting to see a slimming in him, around the face.'

Charlie had phoned on Monday. Nobody calls after a first date in this day and age. But Charlie didn't do text messages. He reiterated what a nice time he'd had at dinner and Cora couldn't think of any reason not to accept his request (and it really was a request) for a second date this coming Saturday. He *was* handsome and he *was* nice.

Cora groaned. 'Does everyone know?'

'*Everyone*,' Joan said, tutting. 'Who's *everyone*, Cora? Don't be daft. I thought you'd be only dying to talk about your new relationship.'

'It's not a relationship!'

'Or whatever it is you call it nowadays. But never mind the words,' said Joan, hopping her stool closer to Cora's. 'How did it go? Go on now, you can tell old Joanie. Apparently Charlie had a great time; he was quite smitten – Charlie's word, not Ray's. He is a lovely chap. A bit of a smart arse at times but he is a catch. A bit of a dish.' She giggled. 'I'm only teasing. Oh but I was delighted when I heard you'd said yes.'

Cora spied a groggy-looking George in the distance. 'Sorry, Joan, I'll be back in a minute.'

She hopped down from her stool and ran towards him. 'Morning, George,' she said brightly, his bleary eyes judging her approach with scepticism.

'It is morning, yes,' he said, dragging sleepy dust from the corner of his left eye. 'What do you want?'

'How's Nancy?'

'She's okay,' he said, still wary. 'She's surviving without you, if that's what you're asking. Still managing to get out of bed in the morning.'

'That's good. Did she get the promotion?'

George shrugged. 'Hasn't heard yet.'

Cora looked at the floor, and waited for George to relent.

'I suppose she is a little snappier since your screaming match.'

'Does she still keep an eye on Row 27?'

'I've seen her throwing a glance that way.' He shrugged again. 'I guess we both do. Monday's set-up – the Belfast flight? – was a total bust. He was a complete a-hole.'

'The film producer,' said Cora nodding. 'He seemed a little delighted with himself alright.' She stopped herself from enquiring about other matches – better to focus on the future. 'Maybe you could report back from the lunchtime flight to Edinburgh?' she said casually. 'I see you and Nancy are on it.'

George's eyes narrowed again. 'And why would I do that?'

'Because of LOVE, George! Isn't that the best reason to do anything? It's for the greater good. And maybe it'll make Nancy see what she's missing. I've tried to contact her a few times.' This was a lie, a white lie, a greater good lie. 'But to no avail. Please. Just once.'

George raised his eyebrows and threw his eyes up after them. 'Alright, alright,' he said. 'But make it a fun one, yeah?

Make them young and pretty. You're lucky you caught me after a particularly awesome first date myself.' Cora grinned at this but he drew his hand across his mouth to let her know there would be no more details. 'Ah-bap-bap. I'll give you a quick call, very quick, when we're landing. But you have to talk to the operations controller? You'll need to sweet-talk him yourself. Your legs are alright, I guess, but you got nothing on Nancy.'

Cora threw an arm around him. Just the one, mind, she didn't want to overdo it. 'Thank you, George. Eek! Thank you, thank you.'

He gave a non-committal grumble and headed on his way.

Cora went back to her desk and worked through the early Paris check-ins. The TV actress was darker in real life. The financier's face was friendly and open. She felt positive about their chances. Cora could hear the floor polisher buzzing somewhere in the distance. There were more staff than customers walking through the departure area. A new dawn, a new day. She could make this right.

Cora returned from the operation controller and rolled her skirt back down to regulation length. She sent George a text telling him they were good to go. The greater good, she repeated to herself, saddened by the value of an exposed knee.

She ate her lunch at her desk, eager to get a head start on potential matches for George's Edinburgh flight. She was in the zone now, focused and energised. Her phone beeped and she whipped it out, hoping for Alison's debrief. It was a message from Roisin:

> Expanded World War II section opened in library today. Crazies are v. excited. Currently watching 50yo woman in neon visor sniffing a book called Reich Sons. How's work? Talked to Nancy yet?

Cora slid the phone back under her desk and continued with the Edinburgh passenger list. She found a good-looking young chap with his own YouTube channel and was about to watch him perform an original composition when her phone beeped again:

> PS. I'm just going to pretend you're not ignoring me.

> PPS. Talk. To. Nancy.

Cora plugged her earphones into her computer. It was fairly standard ballad stuff but this chap could play piano. The music swelled to its cheesy romantic crescendo and Cora scanned the floor to see if she was ignoring any customers. And there was Aiden O'Connor, heading towards her.

'It's Wednesday! Since when do you fly on a Wednesday?' she said, frantically scanning her passenger lists. 'I wasn't ready for you.'

'Ready for me?'

'Not, like, *ready for you*,' she rattled. 'Just not expecting you.'

'Right. You're always so flighty, Cora. Why is that?'

'I don't know. Why are you always so smug?' Not professional. Again. 'Sorry.'

'Is that – are you apologising, Cora Hendricks?'

He was mimicking her from last time. 'Shut up. Where are you off to today?'

'I'm not flying anywhere. My brother's visiting for a couple of days and I'm collecting him. And in answer to your other question I don't know why I'm so smug. But I'll work on it.'

Cora smiled. His hair looked particularly good this week. 'When is your brother due in?'

'Not for another forty minutes.'

'Well I never took my break. If you can keep your smart comments to yourself, you're welcome to join me.'

'I'll do my best.'

Cora came out from behind her desk. 'I know just the place, and the smug one pays.'

'There! See! The two men in suits? They're negotiating their journey.'

Cora and Aiden were sitting on her favourite bench outside Terminal Two, each with a coffee by their side and a Caffè Nero sandwich on their lap. Aiden squinted towards the taxi rank, shielding his eyes from the early April sun, as they tried to decipher conversations between the people waiting in line. For someone who initially claimed not to understand the joy in 'spying' on people, he got into it very quickly.

'Well look at that, and they seem to be getting on. Sharing cabs is the new breaking bread. Who knew?'

'The best is the approach,' said Cora, pulling a chunk from her tuna melt. 'If you can catch someone before they actually approach the other person, you can tell a lot about them: confidence, friendliness, finances.'

'Finances?'

'You can tell the people who rinsed through their savings on holiday and want to share a taxi out of financial necessity, or the ones who do it for the companionship and excitement, and then there are a few who could afford their own car – it's probably on company expenses anyway – but they're just stingy.'

'You're like Heathrow's answer to David Attenborough.'

Cora dropped her voice to a deep, RP tone. 'The overpaid cheapskate circles the friendly holidaymakers. Identifying his prey, he keeps the receipt.'

'Look at the woman near the back.'

'Where?'

'There,' said Aiden. 'Behind the one in the hijab. I bet she's about to ask that couple where they're going.'

'I can't – oh yes, I see. Yes! Look! She's doing it! Nice spot, for a novice.'

Aiden gave a mock bow.

'You're a lot less annoying outside the terminal,' she said, assuming the external setting also relinquished her from professional requirements.

'Gee. What a compliment.'

'Well you're just so stubborn. You refuse to tell me anything.'

'I'm stubborn? You're like a dog with a bone with every single question. Al Qaeda suspects get less interrogation at this airport.'

'Tell me why you fly home every weekend. I'm curious.'

'You never stop!'

'I do.'

'Mmm.'

'Sometimes I do.'

'I go to Dublin to volunteer at the hospital where I used to work.'

'I know that, but why not a hospital in London?'

'It's part of the diversity policy at the clinic where I work. It was my employers' choice, not – actually no, feck that. The truth is I fly home every weekend because I'm hoping to win back my ex-girlfriend who doesn't love me any more and who I now realise I haven't loved for a long time either, but I'm just so incapable of losing at anything that I wanted her back regardless.'

Cora looked at him.

'I don't want her back any more. Obviously.' He laughed. 'It is obvious, isn't it? Jesus. What a waste of time.'

'It's not a waste,' said Cora, carefully. 'You were doing good work – hospital work.'

'I used to do good work. Now the only worthwhile work I do *is* at the weekends.'

'But you're a doctor.'

'The last patient I had yesterday was the CEO of a shipping firm who wanted a brow lift. Why? Because his company is rebranding with a new "nice guys" image and he believes his natural face makes him look grumpy.'

'Christ.'

'I saved him five grand by sending him for an eyebrow wax instead.' Aiden buried his head in his hands. 'That's not even the most ridiculous conversation I've had this week.'

'Well, that's still . . .' Cora looked at Aiden, trying to find something worthwhile in the situation.

'It's fine. I can't think of anything either.'

'So you're a plastic surgeon?'

'The worst kind. Dublin was different. But here it's wholly cosmetic and largely unnecessary. I sell youth at an ever-inflated price. I get teenage girls into my office crippled with insecurity, clutching pictures that I try to explain are Photoshopped.'

'Did you take a truth serum this morning?'

'Better I get it all out of my system before Colm arrives. I never like to lose face, but doing so in front of my big brother would be unbearable.'

They ate their sandwiches, and Cora thought about her own family. It was nice to be beside Aiden. Much nicer than when there was a counter between them.

'Sheila had an accident a couple of weeks ago and she's been much worse since. She poured boiling water all over her arm and got this awful burn.'

'Scald,' Aiden corrected. 'You get a scald from water, not – Jesus. What is my problem? Sorry. And I'm sorry to hear about your mum.' There it was again: a kindness in his eyes. It caught her off guard. 'Alzheimer's is an awful disease.'

'She's deteriorating rapidly. She's started forgetting when we visit, even if it was just the day before.' Cora didn't add that she had started to use this to her advantage. While Aiden might be able to admit his shortcomings, she wasn't quite at that stage. 'The nurse suggested a visitor book. She can get quite mean when she forgets we've come – my mother, not the nurse. But that's not her. Sheila is the kindest woman I know. Knew.'

'She's scared.'

'I know.' Cora drew her shoulders back and exhaled loudly. 'She's so upset about the burn marks, scald marks. She has never cared about her appearance. We used to have to beg her to change out of her uniform before parent–teacher meetings but now she can break into tears just looking at the marks.'

'So have it removed – once the skin has fully healed.'

Cora shook her head. 'The institution where she lives doesn't cover unnecessary aesthetic procedures. And it's not up to us. Mum signed up to their rules.' Cora rolled the end of her crusts back and forth between her fingers until they resembled Play-Doh. 'Sometimes I believe everything will be fine, and the next minute I get so dizzy thinking about it all, I'm convinced I'm going to faint. There are too many things.' Cora swallowed hard. 'And she's the only one I want to tell.'

'You're a good person, Cora Hendricks. If you didn't already know.'

Cora gave him a suspicious look but he didn't waver. 'Thank you,' she whispered. She said nothing for a moment – listening to the rhythm of Aiden's breathing, comforted by its consistency and proximity. In a way she had known him a year; in another way she knew him not at all. Yet here was this dizzying urge to tell him more – a sudden rush of trust to the head. Cora lifted her face to the sun. 'What a day.' She told herself this was a moment worth remembering. It felt like something. When Aiden took his next sip of coffee, his hand landed back on the bench, a hair's breadth from her own.

'Airports are where all of humanity meets,' she said quietly, her whole body alert, careful not to move an inch. 'They can seem clinical but then you get together with some strangers, everyone carrying their own ambitions and secrets and plans, and you all go flying in the sky. That's quite magical really.'

'I knew you'd be a romantic. Head. In. The. Clouds,' he mocked and raised his arms when Cora pretended to hit him.

They watched the taxi queue shrink and grow, no more pairs formed and no obvious partnerships presented themselves. Aiden told her about his first time on a plane and how little French he'd learned on that language exchange. She told him about living in Germany – her first time recounting that period of her life not in relation to Friedrich – and how the only French she knew was that you don't pronounce the 'c' in Sauvignon Blanc.

'I can't help thinking my time in London has been a waste,' said Aiden. 'It was never really time spent somewhere so much as time spent away from somewhere.'

'You'll meet someone else,' said Cora, suddenly remembering her failure to find one woman in whom he might be interested.

'It's not that. I don't know why I came here. Taking this job was partly about prestige. It's embarrassing to realise how much that stuff matters. I wanted to know I was getting further up the ladder, doing as well as my brother. But what ladder? And what do I do with the extra money? Bar paying higher rent.'

'You could spring for some new clothes. Just an idea.'

'Not that the flying is all bad. I am glad I met—'

'Cora.'

A voice from behind. They spun around to see Charlie with the stopwatch around his neck. 'Hello,' he said, more to Aiden than her.

'Hi.'

'Charlie. Waiting on Ray?'

He nodded. 'Early run.'

Cora felt Aiden shift beside her. 'Aiden, this is Charlie who . . . I work with. And Charlie, this is Aiden who . . . flies with us.'

'Hello,' Charlie said again.

'Hi,' said the other parrot.

Aiden gathered his rubbish and stood. As he threw it in the bin, Charlie spoke quickly and loudly. 'Are we still on for Saturday, Cora?'

'I better . . .' Aiden trailed off as he pointed towards the terminal. 'Nice talking to you, Cora.'

Before Charlie had a chance to pee around her, his pager

beeped and he had to dash off too. 'I'll call you later,' he said, giving her a meaningful look and Cora's stomach dropped. She was left sitting alone with tepid coffee and discarded crusts. She was gathering her own litter when her phone beeped. She pulled it from her pocket expecting more nagging from Roisin but it was an unregistered number.

> Hi Cora. Your friends didn't seem to know each other but were good pals by the end I think. She is a lovely looking girl. Hope you're okay. Alison.

Cora had forgotten all about the Paris flight. Another green mark for the chart. When she got home, she'd add it in. She pulled herself up from the bench and headed in to her desk. She brought her mind back to the task at hand.

NINETEEN
....

George put the life jacket and oxygen mask back in their place. Today's safety demonstration had been one of his best. He took a celebratory strut down the aisle, surveying his people and clocking the young duo in Row 27. She was all red wispy bangs and porcelain skin, and he was something between Justin Bieber and a *One Tree Hill* heart-throb. Lots of potential. George would chop off his dick before he admitted as much but he was pretty jazzed to be back on one of Cora's flights of fancy.

Of course it helped that George had spent the previous night with the man he was going to marry and so was very much feeling the love and the greater good and whatever else Cora was selling.

'You want me to take that guitar from you?' he asked the young guy, smiling at the girl as he reached over. 'How you doing, honey?'

'No, it's alright,' said the boy, positioning the instrument in empty 27A. 'I'll leave it here if no one else comes? If that's okay?'

'Ab-so-lutely. Whatever you want. Just making sure you're comfortable. Say, anyone ever tell you you look like Justin Bieber?'

The boy blushed and the girl took a sideways glance. 'Yeah, actually. This weekend.'

'Get out of town.'

'Yeah,' said the boy. That goofy smile would break frigging hearts. 'I was playing this showcase thing and one of the label reps said I had the Bieber factor, if Bieber had grown up on a farm.'

'A musician with label reps crushing on him? Although we're not surprised, are we,' said George, raising an eyebrow at the girl. 'Looks and talent: that's a very attractive combination. Well, if I can get you two anything you just let me know. I am here to help.'

As he shimmied on up the aisle George was aware of his body, and it was practically humming. George had met the man of his dreams three days ago, and last night he'd had it confirmed. Screw Nancy and her strops. She'd been a total drag lately, sabotaging her own professionalism and everybody else's with the efforts she went to in ignoring Row 27. George's whole world had been rocked on its axis and she was going to listen to every detail.

This had not been Nancy's week, and she'd long since chucked Deepak Chopra's positive outlook crap in the recycling. It was all that quack's fault anyway, and his books had no answer for what to do when you still hadn't heard from your mate or when your mam keeps calling to tell you how your skinny your pregnant sister-in-law is, which by the way was an unhinged thing to be proud of, and there was no meditation exercise that could reverse time and make it so you hadn't made a complete fucking balls of a crucial job interview. And yes, it warranted the curse. So the last thing Nancy needed was the exact thing it seemed she was about to get: an attitude-laden George sashaying towards her with hip thrusts that would make mothers lock up their children.

'Were you talking to Cora's lot?' she asked, adopting the nonchalant tone she'd perfected the summer she played Sandy in Merseyside Community Drama's production of *Grease*. 'And what's with the walk? Never exactly a shrinking violet, George, but that swagger is bordering on indecent.'

'Nancy, babe, you can expect me to be floating on air for the foreseeable. I've met the man of my dreams, and last night he made me come like the fourth of July.'

'For the love of god, George!' beseeched Nancy, pulling over the alcove curtain.

'No, Nancy. I will not be censored and I will not be silenced. My sexual story will not be excluded.'

Nancy sighed. How George had ever gotten the impression he was being censored was utterly ridiculous. She could never shut him up.

George had heard him before he saw him. He was standing at the bar, where the cocktail line was twice as long as the line for beer. It was drag night. Anyway. George heard some guy laying into another dude, hollering how he wasn't going to 'mirror the heteronormative ideal' and that 'his anus was not a vagina with self-esteem issues', and George just full on left the Martini line. It was only liquor. This was love at first sound.

'We left after like a half hour and we just talked and talked and talked. The connection, Nancy? It was, just wow.'

'Your place or his?'

'Em, hello? I told you before I do not go there on the first date so I said goodnight and he was a total gentleman and then last night, after he emailed me several times asking when he could see me again we went for round two and got to know each other in a deeper, more intimate sense. If you know what I mean.'

'I definitely do.'

'It was totally profound. I was existing on a higher plain.'

George sighed, a swoony sigh. Maybe it was the adrenaline from operating on little sleep, or maybe it was the thrill of finding someone you actually wanted to stay up talking to all night, but George was feeling the love. He untangled a pair of earphones from the mound on the top shelf and glided back down to Row 27.

'How's everybody doing here?'

The junior popstar and Irish colleen looked up at him with their adorable little smiles.

'You both like music, right?' He looked at the girl and

she nodded quickly, as if she'd missed a cue. 'Well super. Because we've got a new in-flight playlist that we're trying out, and I wonder if you might give it a listen and let us know what you think? Now we don't usually have this facility for short haul but I've switched it on for you guys. I'm afraid that means I've only the one set of earphones. You don't mind sharing, do you? An earphone each. Super—'

'I've got my own set, if it helps?'

'No, Bieber boy, it does not help. So just put them away.'

The boy shoved the white cord back in his pocket.

'So great.' George smiled again. 'You guys just plug that in there, that's it, and have a listen. Share opinions, go ahead, don't be shy. I'll be back to get the consensus.'

What exactly did a favourite colour have to do with how suitable Nancy was for senior cabin crew anyway?

'An ice-breaker,' the woman on the interview panel had said. 'To get the ball rolling.'

Ask her about procedural structures or company history or the step-by-step process for dealing with an emergency landing. Ask her about the mechanical make-up of the front propellers. It was all at the tip of her tongue. But they wanted to know her favourite colour.

'Em . . .'

She couldn't think. She used to say pink. When she was seven. But she wasn't going to give them any reason to think she was an airhead. She could say green, like their uniforms and Aer Lingus's colour in general. But green was also the colour of envy. Not a good shade on someone looking to be promoted above her colleagues.

'Really, Nancy, any colour at all. Whatever you like.'

It was one of those trick questions, she knew, where the answer represented something, like a personality type or an intelligence level. She racked her mind for the right response.

'First thing that pops into your head. Seriously now. Anything.'

And then, from somewhere in that spongey part of your brain that stores the home phone numbers of old school mates and lyrics to radio songs you don't even like, something came back to her.

'Well,' she said, sitting up tall and ensuring to make eye contact. 'There isn't really any such thing as colour. Or sound or texture, not in the natural world. It's all about context and perception.' She could hear Deepak in her mind, guiding her in his pursuit of empowerment and her pursuit of getting this job. She'd had his Rabbit Hole series on repeat for a week straight and now it was the only sound in her head. 'We all say a rose is red, but actually what it is is, we all have a nervous system and that gets these frequencies from electromagnetic radiation, right, and then we give that *experience* the name "red".'

For a moment none of the interviewers said anything. 'Is that, are you saying "red", then?'

But there was another bit. 'Perception is a passive act, or no, wait, it's *not* a passive act, it's—' What was it? She'd started thinking about what she was saying and it made no

sense. *For the love of god, Nancy, don't think! Just repeat.*
'Hang on, just give me a minute. Perception is not a passive act, it's—'

'Tell you what,' said the woman, the same one who'd asked the stupid question to begin with. 'How about we just put down "undecided". That alright? Good. Now would you like a drink of water? Nice and slowly. That's it.'

And that was it. Nancy answered all the follow-up, *job-related*, questions succinctly. She wowed them with her historical knowledge of Aer Lingus's expansion and changes in hiring procedures. But there was no coming back from being the kind of person who denies the existence of colour.

The rejection letter mightn't have been such a blow if it wasn't for the fight with Cora. Falling out with a friend always made everything else seem worse. It was like trying to build a house on rocky foundations. Nancy felt bad about the Charlie thing – she'd thought she was doing something nice for her friend by setting them up. Nancy wanted to make up but she didn't know how and she was starting to worry Cora wasn't interested.

She took a deep breath and peered out from her station at the rear alcove. George was back at Row 27. Was he trying to annoy her? She shut the curtain quickly, before he caught her looking.

'Don't think so, Cora,' said George, speaking into the receiver as the plane began its descent. Nancy stood beside him, pretending not to listen. 'Things were going well but then someone insulted Bob Dylan. And, well, now there's a guitar case between them.'

Cora sighed down the line. 'Too young. I've got to make age a permanent factor in my analytics.'

'You're doing analytics now?'

'I'm making things more efficient.'

George gave Nancy an incredulous look but the air hostess was still pretending not to eavesdrop.

'Did you happen to detect any political leanings?' Cora continued. 'Or signs of religious beliefs? Or anything else I might be able to use?'

'Not so much, no,' he said, twisting the cord around his finger. 'Shockingly for a seventy-minute journey with strangers, their fundamental belief systems never came up.'

TWENTY

· · · · · · · · · · · · · · · ·

Cora lay on her bed, staring up at the water cracks on the ceiling. She usually saw them as an outline of London but, positioned with her head at the foot of the bed, they looked more like a poppy. She was tired but too wound up to nap. Her body lay on the only part of the bed not taken up with papers and maps and the chart.

Her bed in Berlin was the only one over which the Ophelia print had not hung. It gave Friedrich the creeps, so she'd moved it into the hallway. She looked at it now, on the opposite wall. Everything was altered from this angle.

Friedrich was just a relationship that hadn't worked out. It sounded so simple. How could it sound so simple? Could she think of everything like that? She writhed around her bed and imagined each shift giving her a new perspective. She was glad Roisin couldn't see her because now she really did look like a woman possessed. As the map of London became a poppy that became a puddle, she considered things differently. *Friedrich was just a relationship that hadn't worked out. Her mother was sick but she was alive. And she loved her. Sheila would always love her.* Cora continued to shift around on the mattress. *She would never be this young again. There was plenty of time. She had options. The world could still be her oyster.*

There was a knock on her door.

'Come in.'

'What are you doing?'

Cora didn't take her eyes off the ceiling. 'Getting some perspective.'

'Glad to hear it,' said Roisin, sitting beside her. 'Aren't you supposed to have a date this evening? Dinner at Charlie's?'

'That's taken care of.'

'How?'

'I cancelled.'

'Cora!'

Cora had phoned Charlie that morning, apologising profusely for the short notice. And when he suggested rescheduling, she told him she didn't think that would work either. Cora told herself she wanted today to concentrate on matchmaking, but she also knew there would never be a time when she got butterflies thinking of Charlie Barrett. She gripped the phone tightly, heard his slow swallow down the line and pictured his Adam's apple rising as she said it really wasn't him, it was her. She'd pinched the skin on her forearm when he asked solemnly if she was certain and she said that she was. He said he thought she was making a decision 'about us' too quickly, and she shut her eyes at the phrase. He said he thought it could be something good and that she should give it another couple of dates but she said her decision was final and that she was sorry and she heard him sigh and then, proving how fair and kind a man he was, Charlie told her he wouldn't argue so and promised there'd be no awkwardness at work. There was a silence that he probably hoped she would fill by changing her mind but she didn't and she just said she was sorry and goodbye and sorry again. When she hung up she felt remorse and unease, but mainly she felt release.

'Honestly, Roisin, it was the right thing to do.'

Her flatmate was leafing through the spreadsheets scattered across the bed. 'This has to stop.'

'It's just a hobby.'

'Cora.'

'Giving people a bit of happiness, how can that be a bad thing? It's all for the greater—'

'If you say "the greater good" I swear to god I'll throw this stuff out the window and send you flying after. It's a distraction. What are you going to do after the summer? When the embargo lifts? Have you even thought about that?'

'I don't want to go out with Charlie, is that so—'

'I don't give a shite about Charlie!'

'. . . or anyone else. I don't even want to think about it. I want to do this. Surely it's a good thing to be thinking about other people's happiness?'

'The trouble is, Cora, you're so busy writing everyone else's happy ending that you've forgotten all about your own. Jesus, you're not even the protagonist of your own story. You're a supporting character, and that makes me sad.'

Cora felt hot tears prickling at her eyes but she blinked them away. 'I'd be happy if I could just get this right.'

'But this – *other people* – it's not enough.'

Cora turned her gaze back to the ceiling. There was nothing as useless as self-pity. After a minute or so, Roisin stood. 'You need to call Nancy.'

'I know.'

'And not because you need her to be your spy.'

'I know.'

'And you need to draw a line under Friedrich.'

'That's got nothing . . . I have—'

'Cora, I see you,' said Roisin, her hand on the door handle. 'And I know you far too well.'

Another twenty minutes of water crack gazing, and Cora pulled herself upright. She opened the bottom cupboard of her bedside cabinet, scooped everything off her bed and dropped it in. Except the original chart. She returned that to the top drawer. Everything in moderation. Then she reached for her phone and began to type:

I'm sorry. I miss you. Meet for a drink tonight? C x

How exactly did people go about figuring out what it was they wanted to do with their lives? It was the kind of thing her mother would know. Not the one who was rapidly disappearing up the road at the Rowan Centre, the one whose failing memory had dragged the rest of her down too, but the mother who was built on courage and strength and protective love, the one who taught Cora how to be a person. The check-in embargo would come to an end in a few months. Cora always knew that, of course, but she was starting to accept it. And that was enough adulting for now.

Her phone pinged and she scrambled upright again, dizzy from the sudden rush of blood to her head. Nancy.

Cupid! I'm sorry too!!! I'll come to you. Zone 2 is the new Zone 1! See you at seven. Xoxo

Throwing herself back onto the bed, Cora kicked her legs into the air and whooped. She had called her Cupid.

Nancy arrived at quarter-past seven with a bottle of wine under each arm and a head zipping with apologies.

'Oh, Cora, I'm so sorry. I should never have poked my nose in where it wasn't wanted. And I should have been able to apologise instead of getting so bloody stroppy and I know you care, of course you do, but I was just so preoccupied with work and it didn't matter anyway and then my mam was doing me head in and I was a right cow and . . .'

When she finally made it to the kitchen, she placed both bottles on the table and threw her arms around Cora. 'Oh I did miss you.'

'I'm sorry too.' Cora laughed, patting Nancy on the back. 'I was a shit but I was too pig-headed to admit it. I've always been so terribly stubborn – someone pointed it out to me this week and it's true. The Charlie thing wasn't such a big deal. I should have phoned you ages ago.'

Nancy admonished herself for being a meddler and selfish, and Cora insisted she had been inconsiderate and derisive, and there were a few more hugs and apologies and by the time the corkscrew was found and the lukewarm white wine popped, everything was pretty much back to normal.

'Cheers,' said Cora, raising her glass. 'To friendship.'

'To friendship and catching up,' gushed Nancy, rushing to clink glasses. 'There have been so many things, Cupid! George is seeing some lad and my brother is having a baby and then there were the job interviews that I royally cocked up.'

Cora opened a large bag of crisps and divided the contents into two bowls. She handed one to Nancy, who placed it beside her on the couch, and took the other one with her as she repositioned herself on the floor.

'So you didn't get the promotion?'

'No I didn't and I was proper gutted.' She explained how she had done an excellent first interview but she'd botched the second one because of some self-help guru's mumbo-jumbo that Nancy could no longer understand. 'I literally brainwashed myself, Cora,' she said, grabbing a fist of crisps. 'I still hear his voice when I fall asleep.'

'I'm sorry, Nancy.'

'Fuck them,' she said. If the strengthening of Nancy's Liverpool accent wasn't proof the wine was working, that was. 'They said it was down to experience and that I was a shoo-in for next year but who knows, maybe I'll be gone by then.'

'Ah now, Nancy. You love being an air hostess.'

'Yes, well, maybe I'll move to a different airline.'

'Any airline would be lucky to have you.'

'Thanks, Cupid.'

Cora filled her own glass and pushed the bottle across the floor towards Nancy. The television was set to some music channel. Cora switched it off and started to rummage through Roisin's vinyl collection. 'White Stripes or Arcade Fire?'

'Em, Arcade Fire,' said Nancy, and her shoulders began to sway as the needle lowered onto the record.

'I had Friedrich check in for a flight a couple of weeks ago.'

'The German Lothario?' said Nancy, a handful of crisps paused before her face.

'I don't know about Lothario but yes, him. He was flying back to Berlin – with his wife.'

The crisps had rendered Nancy's mouth momentarily out of service but her eyes widened into a non-verbal 'No!'

'Oh yes.'

'The same wife?' she asked, chewing quickly. 'The one he got back with while you were living together?'

'There's only one wife, Nancy. At least as far as I know. He waited for my counter to be free. Can you believe that? And afterwards I thought maybe he was punishing me. That whatever reason he'd come up with to travel with his wife to London was actually just to parade his life in front of me. Isn't that insane? I know it is. I always end up sounding insane around him. But if you knew him.'

'You loved him,' said Nancy, and Cora was grateful for her sincerity. She had loved him.

'The night I told him I loved him we were walking by the Spree. He'd said it from the first night we met – standard Friedrich, all big gestures, so ultimately none of them meant anything – but I refused. Then when I did finally say it, by the river, the sky just opened. As if I had cast a spell with those three words the heavens erupted, and we ran for cover. The hailstones were so big I got a bruise on the back of my calf. I swear to God. I know it sounds like a movie, too unbelievable for a movie almost, but that's just how it happened.'

'That's so romantic.'

'That's what I thought, that the gods must have been on our side and it was something special. But only recently has it occurred to me that, actually, where exactly in the legends of the gods are thunder and lightning and hailstones ever a sign of something *good*?' Cora reached for the wine and emptied the last of it into their glasses. 'Anyway, I think it was positive that I saw him. It was anticlimactic, in a good way, and I'm thinking about it differently now.' In the hour before Nancy had called over, Cora had been scanning job sites just to see what might be possible. The market wasn't half as bleak as it had been the year she'd completed her arts degree. 'And I went on a date with Charlie.'

'I heard! I didn't want to say anything in case you thought I was gloating or something. Which I'm not! But I have been dying to ask.'

'Where did you hear it?'

'From Roger, you know the ginger fella who drives the luggage truck?'

'Where did he hear it? Never mind. We went out once, but that was it and that will be it.'

'I'm just glad you went out with *someone*, Cupid. Was there a kiss?'

Cora nodded.

'How was it? I can't imagine snogging Charlie.'

'It was . . . very polite. Very . . . English.' They both grinned.

Cora told her about the date, and she relayed the details of her earlier phone call. Nancy said she had taken the honourable route. When Nancy ended things with a man, she generally sent a text.

'I was out with a City Jet pilot during the week.'

'I thought you said no more pilots!'

'Yeah but he was dead handsome.'

'Fair enough.' Cora stood to fetch the second bottle of wine.

'But it's not going to work out. He's smaller than me when I wear me favourite heels. Which mightn't be the end of the world 'cept when I pointed it out he goes, "Well it's all the same when we're lying down." On a first date! Who says that? It's just inappropriate.'

Cora laughed. She felt great, and drunk. Nancy told her about a restaurateur before the pilot, but that had been it. The interview preparations had greatly reduced her friend's romantic activities. Cora's mind wandered to Aiden as she remembered his arm against hers, and in her drunken state she considered saying something but ignored the impulse.

Nancy brought up Row 27, much to the delight of Cora who hadn't wanted to broach the subject, lest Nancy think it was why she had extended the olive branch. Nancy told her about the flights Ingrid had been on, although Cora had gotten most of that from Ingrid herself. Then Nancy mentioned Aiden's recent journeys, and Cora shivered at the mention of him. She asked follow-up questions even though she found herself with no interest in the outcome of Aiden's matches. She just wanted to say his name.

'I think I like Aiden.' And that was it. It was out.

Nancy had been lying across the couch attempting to balance her glass on her stomach but now quickly pulled herself to attention. 'As in: like him, like him?'

'He's proud and stubborn and very annoying but he's also smart and kind, and good. I can tell that he's good. And I think about him. Like, a lot. And not only when he says something irritating and I'm trying to come up with a comeback for next time. Although that too.' Cora watched as her friend tried to get her head around this.

'Well then, first things first: stop putting him in Row 27. I know it's been a while, Cupid, but flirting doesn't usually extend to setting the fella you like up with a pile of other girls.'

'Don't you go interfering, Nancy.'

Nancy raised her hands. 'I've learned my lesson. Just a bit of friendly advice. A crush, Cupid! This is exciting.'

'Okay. No more. If I say anything else, I'll scare myself off. Tell me other things. What about that classy couple I set up last week? The ones going to the opera festival? That has to have been a success.'

Nancy relayed all the Row 27 stories she'd been storing up and Cora, who was apparently giving into every urge this evening, got up and went to get the matchmaking chart. After a moment's hesitation, she left the additional paperwork in the bottom drawer. Things needed to return to a healthy level of fixation.

'The mysterious chart!' cooed Nancy, when Cora returned and spread it across the floor. 'Is that me?' she squealed, pointing to a blonde caricature in an Aer Lingus uniform. 'That's dead good, that is! You can really draw. And look! There I am too, and there!'

'All my best matches involve you.'

'Aw, Cupid! I'm gonna cry!'

Cora explained the chart to Nancy, and Nancy told her about George and the new guy he was seeing. 'A messiah in the sack, apparently,' she said, descending into fits of giggles that somewhat ruined her punchline: 'The second coming.' They had just started discussing Ray – who, having lost two and a half stone, was the most 'followed' contestant on *Flight the Flab* and had already been offered an endorsement deal for slimming supplements – when Roisin came in the door.

'Roisin!' exclaimed Cora, clambering up to meet her.

'Row, row, row your boat,' sang Nancy, back in a horizontal position on the couch. 'Row-sheen . . . Is that Gaelic? I never asked.'

'Well hello, Nancy,' said Roisin, throwing her bag down beside the air hostess. 'Yes, it means Little Rose. How are you two? Hammered, I see.'

'Quite drunk, yes,' said Cora. 'Though we've run out of booze.'

'Aww. Have we?'

'Lucky I got here when I did then,' said Roisin, magically producing a bottle of whiskey from her bag.

'Hurrah! We're saved!' Nancy raised her arms triumphantly.

'Where were you?' asked Cora. 'Are you drunk? It's better if we're all in this together.'

'Out with yer man,' she replied, now flicking through her records. 'A house party at his mate's but it was shite so I bailed. I've got my period anyway and he's weird about sex whilst menstruating so if I'm just going to be sleeping, I'd rather do it on my own. I'll swap you a share of whiskey for me getting to choose the tunes.'

'Deal,' said Cora, pulling tumblers from the cupboard. 'We even have the right kind of glass.'

'You're so classy, Cupid!'

'What is this thing doing out again?'

'Don't worry, Roisin, it's just the old chart. No obsessive details involved. Honest.'

'Hmmm,' said Roisin, kicking it under the couch. 'Where's Mary?'

'At her parents.'

'Pity.'

They'd only gotten drunk once with Mary, right when Cora moved in. It was also the only time Cora had heard her housemate express an interest in anyone. Some new guy at work, but he'd never been mentioned again. Mary didn't have the same closeness Roisin and Cora did, and she hardly ever had friends to visit. Having a marshmallow swiped from the brim of her hot chocolate was the most intimate interaction she had ever seen Mary have. Why had Cora never tried to do something about that?

Roisin, who had always had impressive DJ intuition, stuck on Fleetwood Mac's *Rumours* and the three women were instantly crooning along. By the time the slide guitar kicked in on 'Dreams', they were on their feet, throwing shapes and singing, their whiskey still untouched on the counter.

'*Thunder only happens when it's raining,*' sang Cora.

'*Players only love you when they're playing,*' sympathised Nancy, hands over her heart as she articulated towards her friend. '*Women they will come and they will go!*'

The dramatic pronunciation briefly gave way to unsure mumbles but they soon regrouped: '. . . *you'll know! You'll know. You will know.*'

'Are we going to go to Paris, Roisin,' shouted Cora, even though the music had faded down between tracks.

'Why not? You just say when.'

'Paris! Oh I love Paris! Can I come?'

'Absolutely,' said Cora, grabbing Nancy's hands and doing some version of the twist. 'We'll all go to Paris. Maybe we could go for a summer!'

'That sounds great, Cupid! We could all learn French!'

'Yes! And we could eat baguette and cheese for dinner every day.'

'Yes!'

Roisin, in her greater state of sobriety and reason, had bowed out of the conversation and was waiting for the record to end so she could flip it over.

'They say you should go to Paris in the spring but why is that? The winter's probably too cold but surely it's just as good when—' With that, Cora finally tripped over her own legs, landing on the floor and deciding she better leave the whiskey for tonight if she ever wanted the room to stop spinning.

The three women travelled via Cat Stevens and Van Morrison to arrive, lying about the living room in various stages of exhaustion, at the final destination of Joni Mitchell.

'At least you know what you want, Nancy,' said Cora after a long period of silence in which she may or may not have fallen asleep. 'If I was dismissive of your career – I really didn't mean to be. I'm a terrible person.'

'Don't say that, Cupid!'

'But what I'm saying is you know what you want and you're going for it. I'm just lying on the floor listening to the same songs I did when I was fifteen. But like, that's because Joni knows. She just *knows*. Like that bit! *All romantics meet the same fate someday, cynical and bored and boring someone somewhere in some dark café,*' sang Cora, failing to quite keep up with the tongue-twister lyrics. 'I mean, that's it exactly. She's so right.'

'I *knew* what I wanted, Cora. But I didn't get it. Now I don't know. I haven't the foggiest.'

'You'll get it next time. You're on a path, is what I'm saying.'

'But I wanted it this year, I wanted it before I turned twenty-eight.'

'What is with you and turning twenty-eight? It's not that different from twenty-seven.'

'Never mind.'

'What?'

'No.'

'Go on.'

'You'll laugh.'

'I won't.'

Nancy pushed herself upwards from her reclaimed position on the couch. 'Twenty-eight was the cut-off age for women who wanted to be air hostesses with Pan Am. I know times have changed and women's rights and all that and I don't adhere to the weight restrictions that Pan Am had – you know they had monthly weigh-ins to ensure none of the air hostesses went above 125 pounds? I mean, that's never going to happen.' Cora tried to calculate her own weight but her brain was too mushy to break stones down into pounds. 'I don't believe in any of that stuff,' continued Nancy. 'But I always thought of the age thing as the cut-off. It was like they were saying, "You're old at twenty-eight." And I always sort of thought that was true.'

'I'm thirty!' shouted Roisin from where she lay on the floor by the records but Nancy ignored her.

'I just thought I'd be in a better position, something as good as the Pan Am girls, by twenty-eight. But I'm not. Now, I'll turn twenty-eight and I'll be no better off than I was when I started out. That was four years ago! And my brother is having a baby and me mam keeps going on about how "tiny" his wife's bump is. How is that a good thing?' said Nancy, her hair falling out of its ponytail as she reached for a glass of water on the floor. 'His wife is twenty-seven and she's one of those perfect women. You can't even hate her because she works for it. She puts it all up on Instagram and she's so good, motivating everyone else to follow her workout videos and, like, hashtag clean living. She's one of those women who seriously calls avocado "avo" and you don't even laugh.'

'What?' asked Roisin. 'Like she's on pet-name terms with vegetables? That's fucking ridiculous. When really skinny women get pregnant they just look like those starving Ethiopian children with the swollen bellies.'

'Roisin Kelly!' spluttered Cora. 'That's a dreadful thing to say!' But Nancy was already laughing and Roisin just shrugged.

'That's part of why I loved the matchmaking. This will give you a right laugh, Cora, but I always thought that the fact that it was Row 27 was a sign. Twenty-seven. Like twenty-seven was the year I'd change my life, and maybe change other people's too.'

'If the whole air hostess thing doesn't work out for you, Nancy, you've got a future in Miss World competitions.'

'Sod off, Roisin.'

'I'm deadly serious!'

Cora rolled over to face Nancy: 'I chose 27 by accident and then kept it because it was near where you sit at the rear of the plane.'

'I know but, still, like with you and the thunder and hailstones, I always thought it was a sign. Like something great would come from it.'

'You, Nancy Moone, are goodness personified. I wish my heart was as big as yours.'

'It is Cora!' effused Nancy. 'You're the big-hearted one.'

'No you are! I feel like Paris . . . I'm just like Paris.' Cora was indulging the melancholia now, as the hazy epiphany came to her. 'So cold and old and settled in its ways. That's me – me and Paris . . .' Cora was making an analogy with a song but she couldn't remember the lyrics or what song she was talking about or what her point was exactly. She'd need to go to bed soon.

'I'm the one who's thirty!' said Roisin again, turning towards her drunk flatmate. 'You're not cold or old. Get a grip. Both of you. Would someone so cold be so obsessed with the happiness of others?'

'Well that's one way of looking at it,' said Cora, glad for this positive angle on her recent behaviour, which even in a state of inebriation she could acknowledge had ventured into derangement.

The women lay in silence. The only noise was the needle leaving the vinyl, and then the record spinning of its own accord.

When Cora awoke it was 6 a.m. The sun was starting to come up and Roisin had retreated to bed. She threw a rug over Nancy and went to her own room.

• • • • • • • • •

In the morning, Cora and Nancy had toast together and hatched a plan. It was Sunday and they were both on lates. They were hungover and tired, but their renewed comradeship invigorated them and they agreed that the 5.20 p.m. to Barcelona would be their come back show.

TWENTY-ONE
....

LHR -> BCN 5.20 p.m.

Jeffrey Williams pulled the in-flight menu from the seat pocket in front of him as soon as he had adjusted the seatbelt in 27C. He had eaten out with his daughter on enough occasions to be sceptical of her food choices. The restaurants she chose always specialised in 'small plates'. Maybe all London restaurants were serving small plates these days. He didn't know. She seemed to think it was exciting to bring him to new, trendy places. But every time he ended up wishing he'd eaten at home, where he knew what he was going to get. And there was beetroot in everything now. He hadn't liked it as a boy, and he still didn't like it at sixty-four. His daughter had tried the small plates trick when she was visiting him one weekend. He would be polite in restaurants, but he was not going to eat tiny portions of pink vegetables in his own home. And now they were going to Spain, the home of small plates. Tapas, they called them.

He flicked through the menu. He'd been hoping for a stew or meat and two veg, something substantial. It was all Italian dishes and cheese plates. Wasn't this an Irish airline?

He settled on lasagne. Jeffrey was glad the check-in lady had been able to seat him and his daughter separately. She'd just be on at him about cholesterol and what was that other one? The bread one? That was the latest. Decades of gobbling up the jerk chicken sandwiches her mother put in her lunchbox and now she didn't eat bread. He'd never heard anything so ridiculous. Well, he was a free man, at least for another two hours, and the menu offered sides of garlic bread.

Never in her entire life, not even when flying transatlantic, had Leonora Talty been at an airport with so much time to spare. They were going to Barcelona, not Beijing. But the head of the retirement group had insisted they congregate at Heathrow at two o'clock. And then – partly because they had three and a half hours to use up, and partly because their group was one-third metal – it had actually taken them that long to get through Security. The woman with the pacemaker and Zimmer frame set the speed. No one wanted a heart attack to ruin the whole trip.

Leonora didn't have anything against the elderly but she did not want to spend her four days in Barcelona seeking out tourist attractions with wheelchair access and eating dinner at five o'clock. She would be like them one day but not yet. Up until last year, she was on yard duty three lunchtimes a week, chasing after children who disobeyed the 'walk don't run' rule. She was only fifty-eight for heaven's sake. When she told people she had taken early retirement, she stressed the *early* part.

Two of her buddies were in the retirement group. That was the downside of starting your family and career early; you got your life back with a few decades to spare, but most of your pals were older. Anyway, Kay and Carmel were in the retirement group and they had insisted she come along. 'The three amigos,' Kay had said. But now, for some reason, they were seated up the front of the plane with the rest of the pensioners while Leonora was Billy-No-Amigos all the way down in Row 27.

'Excuse me now,' she said to the grey-haired, ebony-skinned man seated on the outside of her row. 'It's a nuisance, isn't it, when the inside person gets here later?'

'I'm always early,' he said, rising from his seat. He was an impressive height – six foot, maybe more – and that really was an excellent head of hair. It was an indulgence, she supposed, to still have a thing for hair at this age. Johnny had been bald as a coot when he died and she hadn't been any less attracted to him, but she would forever cherish that photograph from their wedding day: the two flower girls sitting on his flare-clad legs, braiding either side of his luscious mane.

'Well isn't that a bad match,' she said laughing, feeling her way into the window seat. 'You're always early and I'm afraid I'm always late.'

Jeffrey flagged down a robust-looking flight attendant who was aggressively shutting those high-up storage units. 'Would it be possible to order some food?' he asked.

'Not until we're in the air, dear,' she said, shutting the compartment above his head. 'There's no in-flight service until after take-off.'

Jeffrey hadn't flown since his honeymoon. Air travel was a lot cheaper now but, as with everything else, there were a lot more rules. It had been almost forty years so he was a little sketchy on the details (had that air hostess just called him 'dear'?) but he didn't recall all that fuss with the bag scanners and shoes when he and Jackie had flown to Rome. There were drinks upon boarding the plane then too. Or maybe they had bought those later. All that Al Qaeda, Osama Bin Laden fallout had definitely left its mark, and then there was Heathrow's own security threat last year. That'd nearly put him off the trip. This was Jeffrey's fourth time flying in his entire life. Otherwise there was just the return trip to Rome, and that multi-parted one-way journey from Tobago in 1968.

Jeffrey felt his gut heave at the disappointment of not being fed. 'When did air travel get so complicated,' he muttered.

'Oh I know,' said the woman in the window seat. 'I'm travelling in a retirement group – early retirement, mind. Very early. Try getting through Security with the metal plate gang. Then you'll know all about it.'

'I have a metal plate.'

The woman looked horrified. 'Sorry, oh lord. I didn't think – you seem far too young.'

'I'm sixty-four.'

'You're not!'

'I am.'

'I thought you were younger than me,' she said.

'Well you know what they say, black don't crack.'

The woman was utterly shocked now; her pale, defined cheeks suddenly flushed. He could tell she'd been thinking the same thing. 'I'm only joking,' he said, enjoying himself.

'You're not sixty-four?'

'Oh I am. But I don't have a metal plate. Not yet anyway. Jeffrey Williams,' he said, offering her a handshake.

She laughed, relief spreading across her face. It was a long face, framed by short, free-roaming grey hair. She looked a bit like that woman . . . what was her name. The one that sang with Bob Dylan. He used to have her records.

'Leonora Talty,' she said, her soft, spindly fingers encompassing his coarse skin. 'Or Clear, I suppose. Leonora Clear.'

Black don't crack. Christ. Where had she even heard that? Thank the lord she hadn't said it aloud. He looked great all the same. And no doubt he'd managed it without the aid of pots and potions. Six years older than her and yet had anyone all day to do a wrinkle count, she was sure he would come out triumphant.

'I have a neighbour called Talty,' he said. 'In Kilburn?'

'I wouldn't know that side of the family as well. That's my married name – my late husband. Their lot came from Bath but that's all I know. They weren't close.'

'Sorry to hear about your husband.'

'Thank you.'

'How did he die? If you don't mind me asking?'

Almost two years on and Leonora still balked at this question. She supposed if the answer had been cancer or a stroke or a road traffic accident she wouldn't have minded it as much. When Johnny had decided to go out the back garden and hang himself from the tree, knowing she'd find him when she got home from school, had he thought that as well as leaving her all alone in the world with two sons still not fully reared, he'd be leaving her with the responsibility of explaining his actions to complete strangers? 'Cancer,' she said.

'The same for my wife,' he said. 'Pancreatic cancer, four years ago.'

'I'm sorry.'

He nodded.

Leonora grabbed the arm of her chair as the plane took off and looked at the in-flight magazine poking out from the seat pocket in front of her. She pulled it out, flicking past the cover interview with Colin Farrell. An article on Barcelona, well that was fortunate, and they recommended Montjuïc Park. Some of the younger teachers at school had gone to Barcelona a few years ago and they had raved about the park. Although this article said there were a lot of steps. Leonora couldn't imagine that lot climbing stairs out of choice. She had been blue in the face trying to get them to sign up for the after-school aerobics class. There was a local instructor willing to come by the school if she could get the numbers together but the younger ones were terribly lazy.

One of them – Denise – drove the single kilometre journey from her house to work every day. Leonora missed them though. She missed the whole buzz of work. People said she was right to retire after what happened with Johnny but she thought it was a mistake. She knew it was. Too much had gone too quickly.

'I've never been to Spain,' said Jeffrey. He had always felt less exposed in offering information than asking questions. 'The trip was my daughter's idea, but I bought a guide book and all those Gaudi buildings do look interesting. It won't be the worst, hopefully.'

He watched Leonora smile. Joan Baez: that was the singer she reminded him of. 'That's the spirit,' she said. 'You're on holidays with your daughter, then? Or is she living over there?'

'She lives about five miles from me in Kilburn. For my sins. She's up the front of the plane.' He leaned in to Leonora, lowering his voice. 'I asked the lady at the check-in desk if she could put us sitting separately.'

'You brat,' she teased, both of them laughing.

'Ah. She's a great girl, but she mothers me. She's gotten worse since her mum passed away. Establishing herself as the show-runner.'

'I wish my sons would take that kind of initiative.'

'It's always the girls.'

'That's probably true.'

Jeffrey also had a son, and he was sorry to say that he had yet to amount to much. At the moment he was off in Turkey teaching English. He had phoned Jeffrey to say he'd be back in the summer. And you'll be very welcome at home, Jeffrey had said, but only for a week. He wouldn't be setting up camp this time. His son was thirty-four now and he needed to stand on his own two feet. Tough love – the very thing he could have done with years ago but Jackie was a soft touch. Jeffrey wasn't even allowed to give the children a little smack on the bottom when they were young. Jackie would brandish the wooden spoon but the kids soon learned it was an empty threat. Anyway, Jeffrey's daughter said he was seeing someone now, so maybe that'd sort him out.

'I was in Spain once before,' said Leonora. 'A sun holiday when my children were small. But I've never been to Barcelona. Have you seen this?' She pushed the magazine towards him. 'Montjuïc. It's supposed to be gorgeous.'

'A lot of steps, isn't there?' he said. 'It looks nice. So long as it doesn't rain.'

'Paris would be lovely too,' she said, turning the pages of the magazine. 'Look at that now. I've never seen a bad picture of Sacré-Cœur Basilica.'

'That'll be your next trip.'

She guffawed at this. 'I'm a pensioner. Only fifty-eight mind; early retirement.' He nodded. Early, he got it. He'd have known anyway. 'But still,' she said. 'I'm what they call "time rich, cash poor". That's what my son says about himself. He's an actor, or he'd like to be anyway. He's quite terrible really.'

'I read an article recently about how companies are missing a trick by not targeting the over-fifties. We're a neglected market, it said. Apparently older people hold all the disposable income.'

'Maybe some of them do, but it's probably not the ones who have two grown sons still living at home.'

'Boys.' Jeffrey shook his head.

'The pits.'

'Chuck them out.'

'I keep threatening to,' she said, closing the magazine. 'They fool themselves, or maybe they think they're fooling me, that they're there to look after me in my bereavement. As if one of the steps in the grieving process is to constantly be making dinners.'

'You're a fool.'

'I know,' she said. 'And that's the worst of it.'

Then the food trolley pulled up and Jeffrey heard his stomach rumble.

'Oh, Cupid, it is a thing of beauty!'

'I knew it! When he came up early and asked to be seated away from his daughter, I just absolutely knew it!'

'How did you know he wasn't married?'

'"Take pity on a poor widower," he said to me. "Give me a couple of hours' peace." A charmer. Very handsome, don't you think?'

'A total Denzel,' said Nancy. 'And she's pretty too.'

'Details, please!'

'Well,' said Nancy, giddy with such a triumphant return to matchmaking. 'They have been chatting since they got on board – yap, yap, yap. I heard some talk of holidays and flying and the usual, and I didn't fancy interrupting them. So then I brought the trolley down and he asked for the lasagne – she said she hadn't had cheese in an age – and then, guess what. Go on, guess.'

'What Nancy, come on!'

'He bought her one too! Paid for both. Ordered two garlic breads as well but she drew the line at that. And then, just as I was leaving, she calls me back and she goes, "What are your holidays without a glass of the god's nectar?" and they both start laughing and bam! "Two glasses of red please." She meant wine, Cora! They're dead cute, old people. Like they can be proper cute.'

'Young people,' Jeffrey consoled. 'They want to be something different every week.'

'Exactly,' said Leonora, wiping a string of cheese from her mouth. 'And by the time he actually settles on a career, how's his CV going to look? Six months here, six months there. Who'd hire that? He'll be a liability. I complain about them to my daughter sometimes – she lives in Manchester, just had a baby—'

'A grandmother. Congratulations.'

'Thank you. She's the eldest so I complain to her and she

says, she's joking mind, but she always says: "You should have stopped after me."'

'That sounds like something my daughter would say, only she wouldn't be joking. She's around my place every few days, putting stuff where it doesn't belong and giving me updates on her useless brother.'

'You're lucky to have her so nearby,' said Leonora.

'Maybe.'

Leonora and her daughter were close. It was funny because, had they been peers, they never would have been friends. Sarah was too innocent, too much of a worrier, but she made an excellent daughter. Sarah had been back in London to help with the financial mess – she had found multiple accounts that Johnny had never told Leonora about. Sarah's worries extended to her mother. She tried to set her up on a dating website, but Leonora had heard reports in the staffroom of the sorry state of dating when you were over fifty. Men her age were soliciting women in their thirties. She'd looked at one of the websites and saw that men were actually stating this two-decade age gap as a preference. Leonora was several degrees of dignity off settling for an eighty year old.

'Do you miss your wife?' The question left her mouth before she'd realised.

Jeffrey nodded. 'I do.' He did silent gravitas very well. 'Less and less, though, is the truth. But I can never get used to the silence when I come into the house. It's such a loud silence. I have the radio on in the kitchen now at all times.'

Leonora could relate to this. 'I miss having someone to text,' she said. 'Before the mobile phones it was fine but once they came in I was ruined. All those funny cat videos the younger teachers still send me, and now I have nobody to send them on to.'

'Is that something with The Twitter?'

'I don't have that. I send them on Viber.'

'Viper?'

'Viber. It's a doodad you can get on your phone. It does messages and calls for free.'

'That sounds good.'

'It really is. It's smashing.'

Jeffrey was done with technology. He'd thrown his computer out two months previously and when his daughter asked, he'd told her he'd sold it.

One of the men who played chess on Sundays had told Jeffrey about all the pornography you could find on the Internet. Jeffrey had read a few dirty magazines in his time, and he'd been to a strip club once, many years ago in Soho. But he wasn't too concerned with it otherwise. The newspapers were always talking about all the bad pornography on the Internet – awful things with children. But this chap promised it wasn't anything like that. Harmless stuff, he told Jeffrey, something to make the nights a little warmer. This chap had been the first widower in the group and he considered himself something of an expert.

A few weeks later, Jeffrey was watching *Dancing on Ice* – they had the loveliest women on that show– and he decided to have a quick look on the computer. The first website he found was a bit confusing, but when he moved the clicker down he saw a video of a naked lady stuffing her face with cake and biscuits and all sorts of junk food and then touching her private parts. There were crumbs everywhere. Jeffrey had shut the whole thing down immediately. Who would be looking for that? He didn't open it again until a month later when his granddaughter begged to be allowed to use the computer. As soon as he'd fired it up, this little box appeared on screen asking him about cookies. He didn't even shut it down that time. He told his granddaughter it was broken, put it in a black bag, and when her mother came to collect her, he took the bus to the end of the line and stuffed it in a public bin near Brent Cross Shopping Centre. He never got any emails anyway.

'Any rubbish? Any empties?'

The lasagne trolley dolly was back, but with a different trolley this time. She leaned over him and took Leonora's plate and glass. She reached for his glass but he wasn't finished. 'I haven't finished with that.'

'Oh sorry. No rush. Take your time.' The air hostess tightened her long blonde ponytail and started sorting through the rubbish, but it was clear she was stalling for time. Her eyes kept darting back towards Jeffrey. She was pretty, not unlike one of the ladies you'd see on *Dancing on Ice*, and he was flattered but he liked his women a little more seasoned. Jeffrey gave her his glass, although it still wasn't empty, and a sympathetic smile that he hoped would let her down gently and encourage her to move the trolley along.

The lady on the computer had been young, mid-twenties

maybe, but it was hard to tell with the faces she was pulling and all that food. How could that ever be a substitute for the real thing? It just made Jeffrey sad. A naked woman on screen was nothing compared to a fully clothed woman, to whom he was attracted, in real life. Leonora was giving him that tingle. There was life in the old dog yet.

'When are you back from your holidays?' he asked, ignoring the foolish feeling that came with posing questions.

'Thursday. Sometime in the afternoon.'

'Well that's interesting because I just had two thoughts.'

'Go on,' said Leonora.

'There's a matinee at the Royal Court next weekend that I'd like to see.'

'Okay. And the second thought?'

'Oh I was just thinking what it would be like to step off the plane and tell my daughter that I met an intriguing woman on board and we've got plans to step out together.'

Leonora returned his mischievous grin. 'Throw in dinner, and you've got yourself a deal.'

'Done,' he said, offering her his hand once more. 'But no small plates.'

'And no early birds,' she said.

'Deal.'

When Leonora's daughter told her to get back on the dating scene, she made it sound as though she were bestowing a gift. As if Leonora needed her children's permission to go for dinner or to meet someone for a drink. For all their technology and TV shows about sex, Leonora often found the younger generation to be rather conservative. When Sarah got engaged, she had come to her mother in floods of tears. Leonora had learned not to be alarmed. The problem, whatever it was, usually wasn't worth half the fuss. This time it was about sex and Sarah was embarrassed to be discussing it with her mother but she didn't know where else to go. She was worried about telling Paul how many people she'd had sex with. 'Her number,' she called it. That generation could never say anything straight; everything was a euphemism. Apparently Paul had only ever slept with one other woman. And so Leonora had gently asked her daughter her number. 'Seven,' said Sarah, shamefaced and on the verge of more tears. Leonora had consoled her daughter, advising that if it was such a concern a white lie could easily be excused. Leonora was the mother and she took her role seriously. She knew when to keep quiet, when to make allowances. Leonora would never tell her daughter that her fiancé's number was the real travesty. Nor would she ever mention that her own number was higher than her daughter's, and that she didn't yet consider it fixed.

She had never been with a black man, or indeed any man who was not white. The idea excited her and she quivered at the thought of dark skin stretched over broad shoulders. He had a smell too, a musk she couldn't describe but found highly appealing. This, experience had taught her, was a very good thing.

They discussed restaurants and swapped numbers as

the plane landed. Jeffrey promised to investigate Viber. When the time came to disembark, Leonora could see a woman barrelling up the aeroplane, hurdling in the opposite direction to every other passenger.

'Dad! Dad!' she shouted, craning her neck around the torsos and luggage of other passengers. 'Just one minute, Dad. I'll get your bag.'

Leonora looked at Jeffrey. He shook his head. 'Alright, Chloe,' he said. 'It's alright.' His daughter had reached Row 27 and began to rummage in the overhead compartment. 'I've got it here,' he said, pulling a small bag from under the seat in front of him.

'Well come on then. We've got a cab to catch.'

'One minute, Chloe. The taxis won't all disappear.' Jeffrey turned away from his exasperated daughter. 'Goodbye, Leonora,' he said, taking her right hand and kissing the back of it. 'I will see you next weekend.'

It was a long time since Leonora had been such an overt subject of jealousy. The daughter gave her a distrustful, startled look and, despite herself, Leonora felt great. 'Goodbye, Jeffrey,' she said, and he ambled down the aisle, his daughter charging ahead.

Leonora waited until most passengers had disembarked. Her own group was probably still grappling with the gangway. As she left the row, she called her thanks to the blonde air hostess at the back of the plane. The woman, who was in the middle of a highly animated phone conversation, balanced the receiver against her shoulder and gave Leonora a remarkably enthusiastic two thumbs up.

It occurred to her then that she hadn't been charged for those red wines. This was as pleasant a flight as Leonora could remember.

TWENTY-TWO

. . . .

Cora felt better than she had in a long time. They'd had an uninterrupted run of Row 27 successes, and she and Nancy were in a stage of rekindled friendship that felt like the platonic equivalent of make-up sex. They kept contacting each other with imagined scenarios for their recent matches: the older couple getting married on a plane; the hippy duo calling their first child Aer (middle name 'Lingus'); or, as Nancy had just texted Cora and she had laughed out loud, the loved-up single parents selling their homes and buying a shared house, not caring where it was so long as it was number 27. And it was Friday, which had a lot to do with her giddiness too.

Aiden wasn't due at the airport for several hours but Cora was already on high alert. She kept thinking back over their exchanges, trying to figure out if he liked her. She thought maybe he did, but every time she considered this she froze. Nothing had changed, but now she'd said it out loud everything was different. What if she couldn't speak normally when she saw him today? His Head in the Clouds badge was pinned to the inside of her jacket collar. Every

283

time she stretched, it pressed against her clavicle and sent a shiver through her. She would see him today. Even Joan's foul mood couldn't bring her down.

'Someone's been at my stool; it's too bloomin' high,' grumbled the older woman, hoisting herself onto the thing for the umpteenth time. 'And did you hear they're letting the part-timers go?'

The self-check-in embargo was coming to an end. The notices had gone up around the airport the previous afternoon. Heathrow's security status had been returned to neutral; self-service kiosks and Internet check-in would be reinstated at the end of May. This meant the end of allocated seat matchmaking and, despite being in denial for several months, Cora was surprised to find she was relatively okay with it. It also meant they would no longer require extra check-in assistants. It'd only ever been a temporary arrangement (even if it had taken Cora longer than most to accept this) but now Joan was calling it a conspiracy.

'Anything to cut costs,' she said. 'Get muggins here to pick up the slack. It'll mean more work for everyone, mark my words. Tight gits.'

'Is everything alright, Joan?' Cora ushered an ignored passenger towards her own desk.

'I just don't fancy doing more than my fair share is all.'

Cora sent the passenger off to Munich and ran a finger under her eyes to catch any fallen mascara. She rarely wore much make-up to work.

Joan kicked the counter unexpectedly. 'Jim's not coming to Sardinia.'

'Oh, Joan! What happened?'

Joan had been mentally packing for her holidays for months. Last week she finally settled on a sarong over culottes – 'more of a breeze' – and she'd organised for her nephew to call in and feed the pigeons. But now Jim was cancelling because his quiz team was up for the biggest jackpot of the year.

'Says he wasn't about to leave The Four Wise Men short.' Joan sniffed, pulling a tissue from her sleeve. 'What about me? I says. What about leaving me short? And do you know what he says? He says to bring my sister. He knows bloomin' well she suffers with her circulation and a two-hour flight would have her ankles the size of water balloons.'

'He should have told them no.'

'I should have told *him* no, the day he got down on his knee with that Christmas cracker ring,' she said, dabbing her eyes. 'As soon as that green mark appeared on my finger, I should have given him the boot.'

'Maybe you can reschedule? Swap your leave with someone else?'

'Serves me right for getting excited about something.'

'Here, I'll go get us a couple of teas. Alright?'

Cora took the sniff as agreement and headed for the staffroom. She stopped a few times along the way, quickly looking around before checking her appearance in various reflective surfaces. Catching herself in the staffroom micro-wave, she shook her head. *Who am I?* But she was smiling so much her cheeks were in danger of engulfing her face.

Cora emerged from the staffroom, a mug in each hand,

to find a small huddle of colleagues and Nancy at its centre. 'Have you heard the news?' Her voice was giddy with gossip as she pulled Cora into the group.

Cora noted the official flyer pinned to the wall behind the air hostess. 'About lifting the self-check-in ban? Yeah, I heard. Those notices went up yesterday.'

'No, not that! Although,' – Nancy dropped her voice – 'I was sorry to see that, Cupid. But no. Something bigger!'

'Come on, Nancy!' said a newbie from Baggage Scanning but the air hostess rounded on him, and he quickly piped down. Charlie winked at Cora. They'd talked on Wednesday – mainly at the same time and to each other's feet – but it was getting better.

'It's Ray,' she exhaled. '*Fight the Flab* has been shut down with immediate effect. The whole show cancelled, just like that.' Nancy snapped her fingers high in the air so the polish glimmered. 'A contestant on the American version had a stomach reduction – got it done at one of those backdoor clinics because he didn't want the show to find out – and he had a heart attack and died right there on the table.'

'Oh god.'

'I know. *And* he'd already paid for it. The backlash in America has been massive, and the producers are pulling the whole thing. Worldwide. Ray's sponsorship deal gone, cancelled, just like that!' Her fingernails caught the light once more.

'Well now, we don't actually know that,' interjected Charlie, but Nancy would not be deterred.

'I know how these things work,' she said. 'I know this TV producer—'

'We know, Nigel.'

'And it's a terribly cruel world. Two minutes out of the spotlight and everyone forgets about you.'

'That sponsorship deal was never definite,' said Charlie. 'And Ray hadn't decided to take it.'

'How is Ray?'

'Ah he's okay,' said Charlie, and Cora noted the direct eye contact as progress. Then a tug of guilt. 'Says he doesn't know how he'll keep the weight off without the extra motivation. He cancelled our lunchtime run today.'

'Well if I think of anything to cheer him up, I'll let you know.'

'Don't forget, Cupid,' said Nancy, giving Cora a meaningful look as she went to leave, 'it's not over til the fat lady sings and I'm on the evening flight to Dublin.'

But Aiden was on the evening flight and Cora had no intention of seating him next to anyone, except perhaps a happily married OAP.

She placed the tea in front of Joan, gave her a quick hug, and set about clearing the backlog. The women worked in relative silence, time moving as quickly as the line. Cora had just checked in a quarrelling couple when she saw Aiden, and another man, approaching her desk. Cora bit down on the insides of her cheeks in a bid to keep them in place.

'Hi,' she said. It was as much as she trusted herself with for now.

'Cora. This is my brother Colm. Colm, this is Cora.'

'Oh hi!' she said, extending a hand across the counter and almost knocking her long-cold tea over the two men. 'Whoops. That was close.'

'I'm going to get the paper, Aiden. He can check in for the two of us, yeah?'

'Sure, yes. Absolutely.' Cora moved the mug away from the ledge. 'I'll get you both seated.'

Colm went in search of a newsagent's and Aiden's entire demeanour changed. Stiff and proper just a moment ago, he let out a loud breath as his body flopped against Cora's counter. 'He was only supposed to stay for a few days but some audit went on much longer than expected. It's been ten long days.'

Cora grinned. 'Families, eh?'

'I owe him. He lets me stay with him every weekend, but ten days. Ten days of him trying to catch me out on something. Little brother syndrome maybe, but everything feels like a fecking competition. Jesus but men can be pathetic.'

'Who knew *you knew* you had so many faults?'

'Oh the list is endless,' said Aiden. 'Could you put us sitting apart?'

'Not a problem.' Cora kept Aiden in Row 27 – she was a sucker for tradition – and put his brother further up the plane.

'Don't you have any?'

'What, siblings?'

'No, I know that: one sister, one brother. But don't you have any faults?'

Cora laughed. 'Where to start. Stubborn, as you already noted. Nosy, as you've also pointed out, directionless, daydreaming—'

'That's not a fault.'

Cora couldn't help it; her cheeks shot up.

'It's not,' he repeated, smiling now too.

'I know.' Cora pulled the stiff collar of her shirt back to reveal the badge. 'I wear it with pride.'

And they stood there several moments too long, wide smiles growing in unison like in a house of mirrors, only dropping eye contact when Colm returned. 'Ready?' he asked, *Financial Times* under his arm.

Aiden, back to the poker-up-his-arse stance, gathered his things. 'Let's go.'

'Nice to meet you, Colm.'

'You too,' said the older brother, a tease in his voice.

The next passenger was on top of them before the men had fully vacated the counter but Cora kept peering over the woman's head to catch the last glimpses as Aiden and his brother disappeared towards Departures. A lifetime of people watching fills you with prejudices; you reduce others to their surface components. How easily Cora had defined Aiden. A few superficial conversations and CV details and she thought she had him pegged. In her own arrogance, she never considered there might be more to his defensiveness than a superiority complex. She was glad she had dug further. It felt good to be wrong.

Cora caught the tail-end of an exchange between Joan and a pinch-nosed flyer annoyed that he couldn't have the seat of his choosing. This was the third passenger Joan had eaten the head off in the past hour. She was in a much better mood now.

'Ray! Over here, Ray!' Joan was waving furiously. 'Did you hear about Big Ray?'

'I did, but it's probably better if we don't—' Cora cut herself off. 'Hi, Ray.'

'I suppose you heard?'

'We did,' said Cora. 'And we were sorry about it. Weren't we, Joan?'

'Was it a stomach stapling? That he died of?'

Ray nodded morosely.

'Sure that's cheating.'

'What does it matter now?' hissed Cora.

'Just trying to get the story straight.'

Ray doubted he could keep going. He said Charlie had been great for the exercise but diet was the main thing and that was where he lacked knowhow and motivation. Joan offered her sympathies and Ray said thanks, but Cora was in the midst of an epiphany. Someone who was an expert on calorie content, who'd been through the weight-loss process, who could do with the company herself . . . Sometimes the universe just fell into place, and today it was playing a blinder.

'Ray, my friend, I have just the person for you.' Cora took a Post-it from her desk and had begun to write down Mary's email address when she noticed two passports sitting on her counter.

'Who's are . . . ?' She opened the burgundy covers to find

a stern-looking Aiden with shorter hair and a wider man of similar features. 'Joan, I'll be right back. Ray . . .' She quickly finished the address. 'Here you go!'

Cora grabbed the O'Connor passports, skidded around her desk, and began to jog towards Departures. They wouldn't get further than that without them, but she didn't want them to have to leave the security queue, come all the way back, and miss their flight. As she hurried across the polished floor she grinned; it felt like she should be on her way to tell some emigrant she loved them and needed them to stay. Cora wasn't quite at that point. But maybe she'd say something to Aiden next week. Not a declaration of undying love, just a heavy suggestion about some restaurant she wanted to try or some film they might possibly agree on. She came to a halt at the security line, nodding to one of the attendants to let her past. She saw the brothers mid-way up the queue and began to shuffle her way through – 'sorry' as she stepped over suitcases; 'not cutting in, just returning something' squeezing through a family; 'official business, pardon me.' She was behind them now, about to tip Aiden on the shoulder when she heard her name.

'Cora,' Aiden was saying.

'Right yes, *Cora*. You two seem very matey.'

'We're not.'

'Don't be so defensive, Aido, I'm only asking. She seems very . . . agreeable.'

Cora shuffled slowly behind them as the line moved up. It didn't sound like Colm was *only asking*. It sounded like he was teasing Aiden. About her.

'And I'm only answering. We're not matey. She's just the check-in attendant.'

'So there's nothing, eh, romantic, between you two?' Cora wanted to kick this smug man in the back of his smug knees. She couldn't see Colm's face but she knew it was plastered with a smirk. 'The uniform's nice anyway.'

Aiden laughed. 'Look, possibly she likes me, I don't know, and I don't want to be rude, do I? But she's just a check-in attendant. Come on, Colm, I'm not that hard up.'

'Cora.'

'Yes, that's her name. Will you stop—'

'No. Cora.' Colm had turned to pull his suitcase and spotted her. He looked rather sheepish now. 'Hey.'

'Cora. I didn't see – hi. Were you—? What are you—?'

'You forgot these,' she said, holding out the passports. Aiden didn't move.

'Thanks,' said Colm, taking them from her.

'Cora—'

But Cora was out of there. She turned so quickly she stumbled over the luggage of a woman behind her. She righted herself on the elastic queue divider, ducked out under it, and continued to walk upright and at a measured pace until she could be sure she was out of sight.

TWENTY-THREE

· ·

LDN -> DUB 7.20 p.m.

Colm slipped into Row 13 and Aiden continued down the aisle without a word. They hadn't spoken since Security.

'Awkward,' was the last thing Colm had said, as Cora ducked under the elastic rope and disappeared out of sight. 'Good thing you didn't fancy her, Aido. Because you would not be getting too far now.'

Aiden shook his brother's hand from his shoulder. 'Don't. Just . . . don't say another word.'

Aiden stopped, as he always did, at Row 27, and slid into the middle seat. He had the whole row to himself. He had asked to sit away from his brother and Cora had allowed him – a quick look around the plane confirmed it – to be the only passenger with a row of his own. He fastened his seatbelt and pulled it tight. Too tight. Good enough for him. He pushed his head into the grove at the back of the seat and shut his eyes tight. He saw her face, not as it invariably was whenever he arrived at the airport, lost in a secretive world, but as it had been in the crowded security line not an hour ago. The rose tint gone from her cheeks, mouth ready to speak but no words forthcoming, and those eyes that saw the possibility in everything (even in him, maybe) like wet glass, reflecting and confirming a version of himself he'd rather not see.

'Cora likes the Irish fella.'

'The Row 27 dude?'

'Yep.'

'Does she realise he hasn't changed his clothes since Bush was president?' George offered Nancy a cracker from one of the snack packs. Now that the interviews were over, and Nancy knew she wouldn't be getting promoted, things had relaxed. 'He probably came out of the womb in that sweater. Are you going to do something about it?'

'No.' Nancy sighed. 'I promised I wouldn't. After last time.'

'So you're staying out of it? Completely?'

'Well I'm not going to *interfere*. I might offer him a coffee.'

George raised an eyebrow. 'Make a little conversation?'

'Nothing special. Just routine. Don't look at me like that, George. I gave her my word.'

Aiden had never seen Cora stand until the day they went people watching out by the taxi rank. Could you believe that? He had basically fallen for a mermaid. Which at least suited the mythological mess he now found himself in, a man undone by his pride. When she came out from behind that counter though. He'd never seen anyone walk like that. All limbs and determination. He'd have followed her anywhere.

Or was he just feeling maudlin and sorry for himself? She was irritating, let's not forget that – every question leading to another, never leaving anything alone. But she had something he had lost. She was curious, she was interested – she was interested in *him* – and he hadn't known to respect it. Always waiting for her counter to be free, finding excuses to let the other passengers skip ahead of him, relishing a quick retort and her indignant replies. That swallow-your-heart-up smile as she revealed the Head in the Clouds pin on the lapel of her uniform jacket. And he'd destroyed it all.

He could blame Colm – as he'd been planning on doing – but the only person he was trying to prove anything to was himself. Hadn't he said as much to Cora in one of the few honest conversations he'd had this year? His brother didn't care who Aiden fancied, who he dated. Why was he so *fixated* on losing? For months Aiden had been flying home, refusing to accept he was miserable. And the best part of it, the only part he looked forward to, was the fleeting encounter, never twice the same, with a woman who could hold her own.

Even with the many questionable things Aiden found himself involved in on a daily basis, this was a novel kind of self-loathing.

Nancy began the in-flight service and considered her game plan. George reckoned she should spell it out to Aiden – he was all heart now he'd found someone of his own. But you don't fall in love through reason, do you? Your heart makes up its mind and then eventually gets around to letting your head know what's going on.

She'd promised not to interfere. But another part of her reasoned that the last three Row 27 matches had been successful – something Nancy put down to the restoration of the rightful world order of her and Cora being mates again – and just because there was only one person sitting in the row this time around, didn't meant they couldn't make it four.

'Coffee, Aiden?'

'Are you going to give it to me for free? Because I do want a coffee, but I want to pay for it. And I want to tip.'

'Okey-dokey.' Nancy filled a plastic mug from the dispenser and took a twenty-pound note.

'No, keep it. I don't want the change. All these months and I've never paid. I probably never even said thank you.'

'You have been flying with us for yonks now, haven't you?' said Nancy, confused by the dramatics but not averse to pocketing a generous tip, something that wasn't technically allowed but protocol could kiss her un-promotable ass. 'How do you find it? Everyone pleasant? Cabin crew? Security officers . . . Check-in attendants?'

'All grand. No, not grand. Great.'

'Good, good. Cause we're all fond of you too . . . Cabin crew. Security officers . . . Check-in attendants.'

'Thanks.'

'In ascending order.'

'What?'

'What?'

'You said – what do you mean, "ascending order"?'

'No I didn't.'

'Yes you did.'

'Don't think so, Aiden.' Nancy shook her head, Merseyside panto frown in position. She pushed the trolley on, folded notes and a few coins forming a slight bump in her pocket. 'Maybe you hear what you want to hear.'

Aiden had never been a quitter. He'd worked hard to get into medicine and he'd worked harder to finish top of his year. Even when it came to spending thousands of pounds on flights to win back a girl who it turned out he didn't actually want and who certainly didn't want him, had he given up? No, he had not. And he wasn't going to give up on Cora – someone he really *did* want, someone he felt panicked at the thought that she may have wanted him too. His heart faltered at the idea of the next forty-eight hours, of Cora going about her business safe in the confirmed knowledge that he was an arsehole. He could feel heat on the back of his neck. The idea of her believing he thought so little of her when, in reality, he thought everything of her.

He was going to make it better. He was going to de-arsehole the situation. He had hurt the very core of her so he'd have to find something at that core that he could make better. He would make it up to her. He had the weekend to figure it out and he would not be getting back on this plane without a plan. Because really, without Cora, what was the point in coming back at all?

TWENTY-FOUR

§heila took a turn on Saturday morning. She got all worked up about the arm, poking at it until she'd opened the wound. Then her temperature started to rise. She was shivering and yawning and the doctors put it down to her reduced food intake and delayed shock. 'It's a lot for a body under pressure,' the specialist told them when she and Maeve arrived ready to set up camp for the weekend. But Cora had her own ideas.

They had taken away Sheila's plants. The carer said they were making her agitated. She kept getting the feeding schedules wrong, even when they were written down, and she refused to let anyone else water them. 'They were starting to smell,' he explained. 'I had to do it. Health and safety . . . She's fine with it though. She seems to understand.'

Sheila, who had a temperature of 102, did not look fine. She barely said a word. Her mother had never fit in in the city; were she a dog, she used to tell the kids, she'd be one of those big slobbery ones who ran the fields all day. The plants had masked the sterility of this artificial home. Bit by bit, her mother was being vanquished. Once they were gone, the rest of her would not be far behind.

Her temperature came down slightly on Sunday and she was smiling recognition at them. Maeve took the morning shift, Cian came in for a couple of hours in the afternoon, and Cora was on duty for the evening. She sat in her mother's armchair and watched the pale, emaciated woman embalmed by pristine sheets as she fell in and out of sleep. Cora struggled to reconcile this invalid with the woman who'd never ironed a sheet in her life, rarely had time for a coffee never mind a lie-in, and had nursed Cora back to health more times than she could count.

'You're getting a break now, Mum,' she said, and the comment hung, undelivered, in the room.

As a child, Cora had done a lot of worrying. She'd worry friends at school didn't like her, that somebody forgot to feed the dog, to lock the back door, that thinking nice things about a woman up the road meant she loved her more than she loved her own mother. She did all this worrying in the dark, when everyone else was asleep.

'You'll have yourself driven demented,' Sheila would say when Cora appeared at her bedroom door desperate to confess everything that was weighing on her mind.

'If I laugh when Cian falls, am I a bad person? What happens if I'm late for school? What would I do if no one was there to collect me? If I walk home alone will something bad happen? Does Maeve love me? Does Cian love me? Do you love me?'

One night, she had worked herself into a state thinking

about death. She couldn't get her head around the 'forever-ness' of it. You were alive for eighty or ninety years but that was only a blip because you were dead for a version of eternity that Cora could not comprehend. It made her head spin.

'Mum,' she'd hissed, standing at the doorway of her bedroom. 'Mum. Please. Wake up.'

From the darkness, Sheila groaned. Cora's father, who slept through all night-time concerns, snored beside her.

'I can't stop thinking and it's making my tummy hurt.'

'What is it this time?'

'Death.'

'Oh sweet Jesus,' murmured Sheila, shaking herself awake. 'You better get in the bed so.'

And they talked through the darkness, Cora sticking her feet between her mother's legs for warmth as she lay out all her concerns around mortality and, since her mother was still listening and patiently responding, she emptied the rest of her conscience too. Sheila never told her to be quiet or go to sleep, she never laughed at the minuteness of the things that made Cora's tummy ache. They talked and they talked until the sun was starting to come up and Cora, finally light of mind, fell soundly asleep.

Cora needed to stand on her own feet, to be a grown-up, yes, yes, but more than that she needed Sheila to tell her everything was okay. She needed her mother to call her sweetie pie and hug her and love her and tell her what to do and who to be and remind her that there was someone who would fight the world on her behalf. There had never been anyone Cora wanted to talk to more than her mother. And she knew they would never have a proper conversation again.

The woman in the bed stirred, the sheets coming away from her shoulders, and Cora stood to gently reposition them.

She was done with the airline. She had decided that on her own. When she thought of her job without being able to designate passenger seating, she no longer relished the idea of going to work. And it was only ever intended as a temporary measure, while she figured out what she wanted to do. So she would hand in her notice and look for jobs. She had applied for two teaching positions this morning and written to the National Gallery on the off-chance they might be hiring tour guides for the summer season.

Her decision had nothing to do with Aiden. She had asked herself this over and over. Friday night's sleep was half dreams of further conversations and text messages and phone calls and every time she woke she checked her phone to clarify what was real, only to remember as she scrolled through her recent calls that Aiden did not have her number. They were, after all, nothing to each other. But she could not get it out of her head.

Just a check-in attendant.

Like a knife turning in her gut. People talked of the heart being ripped out, but Cora felt it all in her stomach. First impressions were to be trusted and hers had been that this man was arrogant, a snob. *Just. Just a check-in attendant.* His words. She was so stupid. And the other bit. She cringed now as she heard it, exactly as it had been. *Come on, Colm, I'm not that hard up.* That was betrayal. She could hardly believe it had come from his mouth – until she saw his face. Guilt and culpability and, worse still, defiance. She pictured him laughing with his brother and she wanted to die.

She was not leaving because of him, because he thought so little of her occupation. She would not tell him she was leaving. She would not speak another word to him. Someone else could deal with his check-ins. Her stomach lurched again. Stupid as it was to miss him, it was like a minor bereavement before the major.

Sheila stirred, as if on cue, waking in frustration with the mummifying sheets. She should not be thinking of Aiden, not when a part of her more valuable than an arm or leg was rapidly disappearing. 'Too hot,' Sheila muttered, pushing the bedding down. She forced herself up and, seeing her daughter, smiled. Cora returned it gladly.

'Sorry to bother you, dear, but would you have a glass of water?'

'Mum,' said Cora, standing to fetch the jug from the bedside table and hand Sheila her spectacles. 'It's me.'

'Of course,' said Sheila, giving a little laugh as she repositioned the glasses and peered up at a relieved Cora. 'Blind as a bat without these things.' She held out her good hand. 'Nice to meet you again.'

The jug seemed to tip itself downwards, shakily filling the tumbler and righting itself again without Cora's help. Her mother maintained a polite smile, an expression intended to reassure but which did the opposite.

'That's grand, dear. Will you tell Andrew I'm waiting?'

Cora continued to stare and her mother continued to smile. Was it her hair, maybe? Would Sheila see her better if she tied it back? Should she stand right in front of her? A lump formed in her throat.

'Mum. It's me. It's Cora.'

'I've been waiting a while now, tell him, and I've plenty to be getting on with.'

Cora pushed her hair behind her ears and stood under the harsh fluorescent tube, but Sheila only raised her eyebrows as if to ask was there anything else. When Cora still did not speak, she directed her gaze towards the door. 'And tell him I need the car.'

Cora slowly picked up her bag. She watched her mother smooth the bedsheets across her lap, and Sheila watched her ex-husband's secretary refusing to do her job. Not knowing what else to do, Cora exited the bedroom. She left a vital limb behind and she walked into the echoing hallway, supposedly to fetch a man Sheila had not wanted to see – or be married to – for thirteen years.

TWENTY-FIVE

....

I **'ll miss you something awful,** but I'm delighted for you. I really am.'

Joan continued to ignore the woman who stood in front of her with a passport outstretched.

'This was meant to get you back on your feet, wasn't that it? And you're walking as well as any of them now. Be thankful you don't have bunions, Cora, that's all I'll say. Anyway, if your heart's not in it why would you spent the rest of your ruddy life doing it? You're young, and there's nowt better than being young.'

Joan's only concern was that she hadn't been there to see Weasel's face when Cora handed in her notice. 'Did he consult his clipboard?' she probed, rubbing her hands with glee. 'Or get out the ChapStick? I'd say that sucked all the moisture out of him alright. I bet he wasn't tapping his little frog feet when you said you were off. I bet he didn't know his arse from his elbow.'

Cora, who had always been a better multi-tasker than her colleague, waved the ignored passenger to her counter and made vague sounds of agreement. She was grateful for

Joan's monologue, for the bickering families, for all the distractions from the letter burning in her breast pocket. Sheila had improved since the weekend. She was back fretting about the scar on her arm, asking over and over who had done it to her and when would it go away. She called Cora by name. She even asked about the airport. But this illness only went in one direction and they could never go back.

'How long until you're gone?'

'I gave my notice on Monday, so five weeks and three days.'

'But who's counting, ha? You're right too. Off to start the next adventure.'

But Cora wasn't counting, not like that. The airport had been good to her. It had given her a much-needed purpose, and friends. But maybe the Aiden fallout had been for the best – confirmation that it was time to go. Charlie and Ray had stopped by on their way out for a run earlier. Ray was back on the wagon, thanks to Mary. 'She's dead helpful, and so funny,' he said, and Cora nodded supportively, trying not to show her surprise. She'd miss the little gang that had cocooned her over the past year.

Her hand brushed across her breast pocket – like a passenger obsessively checking their passport was still where they'd left it. This place was eternally tied to Sheila. Heathrow was a bubble in which everyone knew her mother. Every day someone asked after her, divulging some story or detail Cora hadn't known. She could no longer ask her mother about the past, it wasn't worth the embarrassment when she couldn't remember, so she mined memories at work. What if when this place was gone, the memories went too? She'd been carrying the letter since Sunday night, waiting for the courage to open it.

'So, it seems all is *not* well that ends well?'

Ingrid placed both hands on Cora's counter. She was wearing her usual ill-fitted get-up, a look of urgency across her pristine face.

'How are things, Ingrid?'

'Things were well until I heard the matchmaking was to be terminated.'

'You heard? I only handed in my notice Monday.'

'I mean the embargo being cancelled. But you're leaving? I didn't know that. When?' The Swede tutted. '*Things* are not well at all.'

'Five weeks and three days. But who's counting.'

'I have not been matched.' Ingrid sighed. 'I am unmatchable.'

'You are not unmatchable.'

'The object of the exercise was to match couples. I have been a subject of the exercise for many months and still I am not matched.' Ingrid looked around with her arms outstretched – confirmation that she was here as a single entity. 'The proof is in the pudding.'

'No. Okay, today, I have plenty of time this afternoon.' Cora keyed Ingrid's flight details into the computer. 'Dublin. Plenty of English speakers. You're not leaving for two and a half hours. Plenty of time. I'm clearing the decks. I have two hours left in my shift and it's all for you. We'll find someone good. Someone bloody marvellous. What are you into lately, except the exercise stuff?'

'Sex.'

'Pardon me?'

'Sex. Sex is what I am into lately except the exercise stuff. Lately I've decided I would like to have some sex.'

'Alright. I can work with that. So we need someone you want to have sex with. Handsome?' Ingrid nodded. 'And not too old . . .' The Swede inclined her head ever so slightly. 'And . . .'

'A solid man.'

'Okay, and by that you mean . . . ?'

But that was it. That was her only request.

'Solid, right. On it.' Cora's hand again travelling to her pocket, she pushed the letter down further, relieved to have a reason to ignore it for a couple more hours. 'Here you go – 27A. Have a pleasant flight.'

Cora went through the Dublin passenger list automatically eliminating females, husbands, anyone younger than twenty-eight and older than forty-five. She was down to eighteen candidates. Seven were blackballed for profile photos or status updates that pointed to relationships. Two were gay. Cora would miss this. She was good at this. She searched for information on the remaining nine and settled on a shortlist of three. She'd wait until the men presented themselves at check-in. She was going back to intuition.

'I'll look after the Dublin flight, Joan.'

'Righto.'

And so they began to arrive. More Irish people than English, several groups of friends destined for the Guinness Storehouse, a small troop of excited scouts, and a young couple barely on speaking terms. Option One – a mechanic from Kent – was a friendly chap and handsome, but he was significantly shorter than Ingrid. Personal preference perhaps, but: blackballed. Not long after him came Option Two.

'Francis O'Meara,' said Cora, waiting until she had opened his passport. His profile picture showed a handsome but inexpressive man. In person, he was equally striking and friendlier.

'Frankie, actually. Only my mother calls me Francis. And airport officials,' he added, a slight smile behind the stubble.

'Welcome to Aer Lingus, Frankie.' Cora had done an extensive search on this man but all social media information seemed to stop a few months back. His LinkedIn told her he was working as an engineer in Dublin – or at least he had been until January. Perhaps he was in London for a job interview. 'Work or pleasure?'

'Flying visit, just.'

'Anything interesting?' she pressed.

'Ah.' He threw his eyes up. 'Family and whatever.' But there was a softness to how he said it.

'Wife?'

'Mother.'

'Smashing.' He was the right age, he was indisputably handsome and his eyes, a dark blue, were flecked with kindness. In the queue behind him Cora spotted Option

Three – arguably better dressed and easier to track online. But there was something about Frankie. She liked how he stood, wide and firm. Like he had nothing to hide. She thought he might qualify as 'solid'.

'27B,' she said, placing the boarding card in his wide hands.

It turned out to be the right choice. Option Three was not good; he was one of the complainers. He lectured Cora slowly and loudly on how if he couldn't check in online, he should be able to specify his seat at the airport. She said she'd do what she could, and then put him in the very back row between two of the scouts.

With the Dublin check-ins finished, Cora turned off her counter light and slid down from her stool. Her shift had finished twenty minutes ago and there was no more work she could think to do. The staffroom was empty. She changed her shoes, removed her things from the locker, and sat at one of the three white tables, turning the slightly crumpled envelope in her hands. She pulled gently at the seal, thinking how her mother had always liked the taste of envelope adhesive. She used to lick closed their letters to Santa and march the three of them down to the post box. How many more Christmases would they have? How many more turkeys and hams? How long until she could not swallow? Cora inhaled deeply and just as she began to tear the envelope open, her phone rang. Maeve.

'Is it Sheila?'

'Yes.'

'What's wrong?'

'It's good news actually, for a change. She's as good as I've seen her, in fact.'

'Really?'

'In a long time, yes. She had a new doctor in with her, a specialist, and he says he can get rid of the scars on her arm. He said a skin graft would likely be too much for her and there was a chance of infection, but he's going to make up a cream that should vastly reduce the marks. You should see her, Cora. She's made up.'

'I thought the Rowan Centre wasn't going to pay for any cosmetic treatment?'

'They're not. This chap is a volunteer. He rang the centre this week offering his services. How's that for good timing? I thought he seemed a little young but I looked him up and he's won awards. He's one of the best burn doctors in the UK. How lucky are we he didn't call a few months ago, or volunteer at another centre? Very lucky. Cora? You still there?'

'What's his name?'

'I already looked him up and he's legit, more than legit.'

'His name, Maeve.'

'Alright. Hand on.' She heard her sister put down the phone and her mind began to race. Then the receiver being taken up again. 'Doctor Aiden O'Connor. He's Irish.'

Her stomach dropped.

'Sheila really took to him. Kept playing with her hair. Somewhere in her mind I think she was flirting.'

He had been to see her mother. He had gone uninvited to the research facility – and everyone had fawned over him.

She tried to piece it together but it didn't make sense. What was in it for him? To barge into her life after humiliating her and start throwing his weight around. Was he showing off? Was he messing with her?

'Cora? Hello?'

'Tell him we don't want the help.'

'What? Why in heavens not? Sheila is delighted. And it's free. Anyway, it's not up to us. They had the consultation this morning and he's going to begin the treatment – non-evasive – next week.'

'What clinic is he with?'

'Hang on . . . It's called . . . Blackhall Suites. Harley Street.'

Cora, already on her feet, flung the phone and half-opened envelope into her bag, and stormed out of the staffroom.

TWENTY-SIX

·······························

'I'm here to see Aiden O'Connor. It's urgent.'

'Have you an appointment?'

'No, but he'll want to see me. Cora Hendricks.'

'If you don't have an appointment he won't be able to see you today. I can book you in for next week? A consultation, is it?'

The woman's eyes hovered a moment too long on Cora's forehead. She brushed her hair over her face. 'Can you just tell him I'm here? Cora Hendricks.'

'As I said, he's booked solid all evening.'

'Doctor O'Connor is treating my mother – a woman with Alzheimer's incapable of sound judgement – and if you do not let me see him, I will stand outside this place and tell everyone who comes within a kilometre radius that Blackhall Suites advocates abuse of the elderly.'

The receptionist paused. She got up from her desk. Cora shook her head at the watching security officer. *I'm going nowhere.* A minute later the receptionist returned, with Aiden following.

'This is a surprise – a good one. I'm glad to see you, Cora.'

'Can we talk in your office?'

'Of course. It's grand, Mandy. She's a friend.' Had Cora been a little less enraged, she might have laughed.

She followed down the corridor, not wanting to walk with him, not wanting to start talking only to be interrupted by unexpected turns or distracted by faltering directions. Aiden's office was minimalist, like she'd once pictured his apartment. There were no certificates on the wall or photographs on the desk. It could have been anyone's.

'I never got around to decorating.' Aiden pulled the door behind him as he trailed her into the room. 'You don't need to be Freud to figure that one out.'

Cora exploded. 'What do you think you're doing going to see my mother? Do you think me so incompetent I can't take care of her? Or is this another chance to show the world how great you are? You're a doctor, you're a doctor – and I'm *just* a check-in attendant.'

'Cora, I—'

'Why would a man with such disdain for me want to spend time with my mother – my sick and vulnerable mother? What sort of mind game is that? Have you not humiliated me enough? Do you even realise how humiliated I was? Laughing at me with your brother. I thought – But no.' Cora winced, still incapable of recalling the comments without a physical reaction. 'I felt so stupid.'

This time Aiden waited until he was sure she was done. 'I'm sorry, Cora.'

'Is that it?'

'I never wanted you to feel stupid. I'm the idiot. My

314

brother always gets to me. I shouldn't let him but he does. And I wanted to make it up to you so I thought I could help with your mother. I wanted to do something for you. Jesus, I like you. A lot. More than anything in this city.'

Cora looked around the room, a sneer in her voice. 'Not a lot of competition there.'

'I wanted to help, if I could. I know how much Sheila means to you and god knows it's better than anything I'm doing here.'

'I don't want you near my mother.'

Aiden looked at her, a plea in his eyes that Cora refused to meet.

'I'm sorry—'

'Leave her alone and I'll forgive you.'

'I'm sorry but I can't renege on my promise. I'm her doctor now and I've a duty of care. Sheila is happy about having her scars treated and the Rowan Centre has already agreed.'

'You're an egotistical snob.'

'I know.'

'You think you're better than everyone, and you're not.'

'I know that too.'

'How dare you scoff at my job, when you don't even like what you do? At least I'm proud of my work!'

'You're right. You should be.'

Cora floundered. 'Good.' She focused on him now finally, unfamiliar in his formal attire. He looked well, so clearly attractive, and it infuriated her further. 'So will you leave her alone?'

'I'm a pompous egotist but I'm also her doctor. I can't.'

'You're unbelievable! Jesus.' Tears of frustration built behind her eyes as she struggled not to blink. 'Have you not done enough?' She had let herself like him; she had let herself *tell people* she liked him. 'Can you not just leave me alone? Hell!' She tried to steady her voice. 'I don't want you to speak to me and I don't want you to come near me. I won't be at the airport much longer anyway; I've handed in my notice. Which has nothing to do with you.'

'I won't be there any more either.'

'What? Actually, I don't care. But good, that's good news.'

'I'm not flying back to Dublin any more. I'm volunteering in London for people like your mother instead. The whole thing was ridiculous. I was miserable. The only good thing about flying home was seeing you.'

She managed only a whisper: 'What are you trying to do?'

'I'm trying to say sorry. I'm trying to tell you that I like you. A lot. I like you a lot, Cora. I think you're one of the best people I've ever met.'

'You hardly know me.'

'I don't know your birthday or if you're a dog person, no, but I know that I want to stand and sit beside you as much as possible. I want to be around you because you're kind and funny and magnetic. I like your face – the big cheeks that engulf all your other features when you smile – I like the way you think, the way you walk, I even like the way you insult me. And I never like that. I was an arrogant arsehole and I'm sorry. I'm trying to get you to forgive me.'

Cora willed herself not to blink, not to let the dam break. For a moment, she almost believed him. Her eyes started to sting. 'I don't trust you. I don't . . .' Cora placed one hand on the table. She spoke slowly, the only way to stop her voice from cracking. 'I came here to talk about my mother. If you want to make it up to me, you'll leave her be.'

'I think when you calm down you'll—'

And there it was. 'Don't tell me to calm down! Don't—' He moved towards her and she moved away. 'Don't talk to me.' In the corridor now – shinier than the airport, oozing money and arrogance – she walked fast. Out on the street. Where was she going? Home. She needed to go home. She walked on. But she couldn't get the conversation, the sequence of events right. She grappled for her phone. And then she stopped. She couldn't call her. Even if it hadn't been about her. She could not call her. There it was: the stomach-churning truth. She could never call her mum again. Cora closed her eyes, suddenly aware of the tears prickling her cheeks. She sat at an empty bus stop, hand still in her bag. She redirected it away from the phone and took out the envelope. She wiped at her face, took two deep breaths and ripped it open.

My dear sweetie pie,
It's hard to imagine all that will happen as I sit here writing this, feeling so sturdy, so evergreen. But my branches are weakening and my leaves are shedding. The doctors have confirmed it. One by one they are dropping off. And I need to tell you all that seems impossible to forget before they have all gone.

I want to tell you that I love you. That's all
this letter is: 'I love you, I love you' written over
and over in different ways. Your mum loves you.
Whatever else gets lost, that bit is unforgettable.
It's engraved in my bark, it's at the tips of my
roots. I'm so proud of you, Cora. Do you know that?
You're stitched into me.

I'm sorry for the awful things I'll have said
to you by now and all the important details I've
forgotten. How is that possible? When now I can
conjure up a thousand images for every stage
of your life. But my branches are weakening. I
know. And I'm sorry for everything I will miss,
for every time you need me and I'm not there. I'm
sorry for abandoning you, Cora.

Please forgive me.

And please listen to me. Because I want to tell you
a few things I fear you may have forgotten.

1. You are worth so much more than you give
   yourself credit for. That's a fact. Listen to your
   mother.
2. Yours is a big heart. It's always been like that.
   And a heart that big is bound to get caught
   in the crossfire, but that's okay. If it breaks, it
   mends. It is there to be used.

3. You have always had great tenacity. As you should, as I taught you. But remember that pride comes before a fall. None of us can do it all on our own.

4. Some people are worth the risk. This is very important. I've seen you shrink from the world and it's no good. Do you hear me? We all get scared; the test is to carry on regardless. Give people a chance, my sweet girl. Put your trust in them.

And remember, for ever and always and long after that: your mum loves you.

X

TWENTY-SEVEN (A)

LHR -> DUB 2.30 p.m.

Ingrid had been watching him from the moment he boarded the plane. As he passed the first row, she could distinguish broad shoulders and a general hairiness. Then she lost him behind another passenger, which was a feat because he was definitely above average height. By the emergency exit, she'd registered the manly stubble and watched him help an elderly couple put their luggage in the storage compartment. He had no bag of his own. With every row, the stakes grew and she did not glance away for fear the magnet would break and he'd be sucked into an earlier row.

When he stopped, nodding and sliding in beside her, careful not to spill into her personal space, Ingrid was fairly certain that what she felt was her heart flutter. Cora had done well.

'How's it going?'

Ingrid thought for a moment. 'Average to good.'

He laughed. 'You're not Irish, anyway.'

'No,' she said, cautiously defensive. 'I'm Swedish.'

'It's just no one in Ireland ever answers that question.

How's it going?'

'Why not?'

'Ah, they use it like "hello". And if someone does answer it, they just say "grand". Everyone is grand. I often thought what it would be like to stop someone and say, "Well actually, I'm glad you asked. Come here till I tell you everything that's been getting me down for the past few months."' The hairy man chuckled. 'An honest answer, like.'

'And what would your honest answer be?'

'Probably grand.'

His name was Frankie and he was farming 'temporarily', but didn't go into further detail. He'd come to London that morning to drop off his mother – she was going on a holiday and didn't like to fly alone – and he'd be back to collect her in a few days. That was it. He was a man of few words. Which was attractive because he was attractive. Ingrid was aware of the double standards allowed to beautiful people, but she was not immune. Mostly she talked.

When Nancy appeared with the coffees, Ingrid was relieved. She'd gotten into a bit of a monologue about the optimum time slot when presenting a conference paper.

'Free? Are you sure? We paid three euro on the way over.'

'It's only free in Row 27,' Ingrid told him.

'Never heard of that,' he said, taking the UHT milk from Nancy. 'But sure, make hay while the sun shines.' He removed the lid, his hands dwarfing the paper cup.

'You wouldn't be making much hay in this weather,' Ingrid gushed – nervous, excited, the flutter now in her loins. 'More like silage!'

She was referring, of course, to the unusually high humidity, which had been the focus of all weather reports that day. But Frankie didn't laugh, just took a sip of his coffee. She'd always found it hard to gauge humour.

'I grew up on a farm.' She tried again.

He swallowed his coffee. 'They've farms in Sweden, so?'

Ingrid frowned. Hadn't he heard of their famously long growth seasons?

'Ah I'm only coddin' with you.'

'Codding?'

'Messing,' he said. 'Joking, like.'

'Codding. I see.'

'Sure of course they have farms in Sweden.'

Of course they had farms in Sweden. Jesus, Mary and Joseph, Frankie. Was that meant to be a joke? Hadn't there been a contingent of Swedes at the ploughing championships? And on the last night they took them out on the lash, to show some hospitability, and the session ended with all the Irish lads drunk as skunks, singing 'go home to your sexy wives' over and over at the bemused Scandinavians. Frankie didn't mention that though; he wasn't sure the story worked in sobriety. He was a bit rusty at this. Between the farm, the pub, the creamery and an occasional mass, Frankie hadn't spoken to a woman – other than the one who gave birth to him – in the four months since he moved back home to help with the farm.

'What is your mother doing in England?'

'Visiting a sister in Bromley. She only does it every five years but even then can't bear to fly on her own. I hadn't flown in months. Hadn't been in Dublin in months.'

'Do you live far from Dublin?'

'Not too far. 'Bout hour and a half. I was working above in Dublin but had to head home after Christmas.'

'Why?'

They were very direct, the Europeans. Asked a lot of questions.

'They needed a hand on the farm. My dad passed away and Ma couldn't handle the place on her own.'

'I'm sorry for your loss,' she said and Frankie couldn't help smiling at her studious solemnity.

'These things happen. He was almost eighty.'

'And he was still working!'

Frankie laughed. 'See now, farming in Sweden can't be like Ireland. Nobody retires where I'm from. They're all obsessed with the land. Afraid some foreigner will toss them off it again if they turn their back for a minute.'

'But don't the children take over?'

'Yeah, well.'

They fell into silence.

'We probably should have,' he said finally. 'But nobody wanted to.'

'So why are you doing it now?'

'Ah.' And this time he left it at that.

Ingrid enjoyed a challenge, and now she'd gotten him talking she had a new one: understanding what he was saying. But she liked the seasick rhythm. Up and down and crashing back up again. And excessive hair was a sign of virility. Which she enjoyed too.

'I've never been to an Irish farm. Even though my work is concerned with agricultural policy and Ireland is the largest beef exporter in Europe and in the top three for dairy.'

'Is it?'

'Yes. Is that not common knowledge?'

Frankie shook his head.

'Interesting. Well yes, it is, and yet they never do farm visits. I'd like to see one. Peculiar how all decision-making for rural areas is done in urban settings.'

'You're more interested than me.'

'You're not interested? It's your livelihood.'

'Temporarily. I was into it when I was younger, driving the tractors, helping with the harvest and all that. But I was an engineer until my dad . . . like I said. And I'll be going back to it. Once we convince Ma to sell.'

'Difficult?'

'Says the only way she's leaving is in a box.'

Frankie was bored of talking about the farm. They didn't talk much at home but when they did, it was the only topic.

When he was in Dublin, he'd barely thought about the place. Another life.

He knew the conversation was lopsided but he'd never been good at direct questions. He asked Ingrid (nice name) about farming in Sweden – good and general, nothing awkward – which led to the one she grew up on and, without really asking, her parents. It turned out conversations were like riding a bike; once you get going it all comes back.

She was smart and funny, though possibly not on purpose. He'd pulled a girl from Sweden when he was in college. Ingrid was even better-looking. And he wasn't laughing *at* her. Not at all. Her sincerity made him happy.

'Do you get back often? To Sweden, like.'

'Once in a pale moon.'

'A blue moon?'

'Yes. A blue moon.' He could see her thinking and he grinned.

'I don't know why it's blue either.'

'Maybe somewhere they have blue moons?'

'But not very often.'

And she smiled too.

Ingrid talked at length about Ireland's position as a dairy farming nation and its high rate of greenhouse gas emissions from the agricultural sector but she worried she was delivering it wrong.

'I'm talking too much.'

'No, you're grand. It's interesting.'

Ingrid considered this. 'It's difficult to know what other people find interesting.'

'You've got a sort of practical passion. It's nice.'

'I haven't even told you about running – that's my big passion.'

'I'm listening.'

'Do you run?'

Frankie shook his head. 'You'd see them out on the streets in Dublin. But what is everyone running *from*, that's what I'd like to know.'

Ingrid grinned. 'At the beginning, you are running away. From being sick or lonely or how you look. But once you get into it, you're running towards something: happiness or health or a longer life.'

'See, now. Even that. Very interesting.'

She glanced at him. He was smiling but he wasn't teasing. She tucked her chin into her neck and let the warmth wash over her.

'Could I visit your farm?'

'My, er . . .'

'For a farm visit. If it was convenient.'

'It's just it's not really my farm. It's my mother's.'

'Would she object?'

Frankie knew exactly how his mother would react to a foreigner on her land: with great fecking suspicion. Not that she feared her son being stolen away, but rather that this beautiful woman with a successful career elsewhere would have her eye on Maureen O'Meara's few dozen acres.

Good thing she was in London so.

'What she doesn't know won't kill her.'

'I'm in Ireland for two days,' said Ingrid. 'I have meetings until 4 p.m. tomorrow and then an hour and a half of travel, allowing twenty minutes for rental pick-up . . . I could be there for 6 p.m.'

'I'll throw on some dinner so.'

'You cook?'

'We have modern men in Ireland, you know.'

She went pink. 'I never said—'

'I know. I'm only messing.'

'Coddin'?' She looked straight at him. He found the urge.

'Yeah. I'm only coddin'.'

And then he gave in. He leaned over, lingering a moment lest she objected, and placed his lips on hers so quickly it sounded like a rubber sucker being pulled from an udder.

'Jaysus. Sorry.'

Ingrid leaned forward, hiding her face as she rummaged in her briefcase.

'On a plane and all. Sorry, Ingrid.'

But when she resurfaced she handed him a pen and paper. 'I'm going to need your address.'

And as he wrote the familiar directions – 'right at the post office, two lefts, and a sharp right at the bend'– she leaned in and whispered, with that endearing, formal sincerity: 'Thank you, Frankie. That was lovely.'

TWENTY-SEVEN (B)

. . . .

It was more than a week since she'd stormed into Aiden's office and she hadn't heard from him. Which was what she'd asked him to do. Friday had come and gone, but he had not. Which he'd told her would be the case. All of a sudden he was infuriatingly true to his word.

Aiden had been back to the Rowan Centre to see her mother. (Another promise he insisted on keeping.) Maeve had been there but Cora had made up an excuse. He'd applied the ointment once, showing the staff, Maeve, and Sheila how to do it in the future. It was straightforward, Maeve said. So that was it. There was no need for him to go and see her again. Unless something went wrong. And, of course, Cora didn't want something to go wrong.

'Penny for them,' asked Joan, arriving for her shift two hours after Cora had started hers. Terminal Two was dead.

'Nothing. Just thinking.'

Cora had an interview next week at the Tate – a co-ordinator for kids' summer camps – and she was thinking about that, but mainly she was thinking for the millionth time that maybe she'd been too stubborn. She kept thinking about what Aiden had said. And her mother. The more time passed, the more she wanted to trust him. Couldn't she have just taken him at his word? She didn't want to shrink from the world.

Beside her, Joan was whistling. Loudly. The cartoon representation of a postman carrying good news. 'Anything to tell me, Joan?'

'Well now that you mention it, yes. Sardinia is a-go!'

'Really? That's great. Who'd you get to take Jim's place?'

'No one. He's coming. Two of the Four Wise Men got busted for selling knock-off washing machines.' Even if Joan had managed to keep the glee from her voice, the manner in which she rubbed her hands together gave it away. 'They tried to delay the start of the sentence but no joy. And no stand-ins know as much about history and the classics. Jim's beside himself naturally – been out wallowing with the pigeons. Poor sod.'

Cora smiled.

'I do love him really. Though god knows why. Any road, a bit of colour on that belly and he'll forget all about it.'

It was possible, wasn't it, that Aiden meant what he said? About being sorry, about liking her. *A lot*. He'd said he liked her a lot. But Cora had always trusted her instincts. He barely knew her. How could he think she was the best thing in this city? He clearly hadn't been to the National Gallery. She convinced herself it was a line. And yet she knew him as little as he knew her, and she had liked him. *A lot*. And she hadn't liked anyone in a long time. How can you be sure what is instinct and what is fear? With each passing day, this horrible sensation grew – a sensation she was starting to recognise as regret.

She saw Ray across the floor and waved. He blushed. They'd met only five hours ago; Cora was heading into the bathroom to clean her teeth and Ray was leaving after a shower. He now spent as much time at Cora's apartment as she did, only for most of it he was cloistered away in Mary's room. And then there was Ingrid. She'd stopped by Cora's counter on the way back from her Dublin conference with Frankie, who it turned out was a farmer, in tow. He was collecting his mother and Ingrid, looking like the proverbial cream-getting cat, already had her next flight booked to the Emerald Isle.

All this lifted Cora's spirits. The happiness of others did nothing to detract from her own. It wasn't like there was a finite amount in the world, and when a lot was taken by other people there was none for her. You make your own happiness. And the only thing that stood in Cora's way was herself. It wasn't that she couldn't forgive, it had just been easier not to.

Cora watched Ray disappear behind the escalator, probably off to start his shift. In a semi-trance, she stared at the last spot she had seen him, fragmented feelings whirling through her mind. The daze wasn't broken until someone else appeared from the shadows, heading into the terminal.

Is it possible to will something into being? Cora had never considered it before now, before she recognised Aiden O'Connor coming towards her.

'I know you told me not to talk to you.'

'I – yes.'

'But I thought I'd make one last attempt before I did that. I finished the treatment with your mother.'

'I heard.'

'I think it'll work well.'

Cora said nothing.

'I came out two days ago but you weren't working. Your colleague said you'd be in today.' He glanced towards Joan, who was openly eavesdropping.

'I meant to tell you some chap was looking for you, Cora. Must've got distracted by the holiday. I'm off to Sardinia next week.'

'Very good,' said Aiden. 'It's meant to be nice. Very clean water.'

'I've work to be getting on with so—'

'What are you talking about, Cora, this place is dead!'

Cora threw Joan a look but the older woman continued to position herself like she was the third point in this conversation.

'I'm sorry.'

'You said.'

'I really am. I'm sorry. Tell me what I can do to make you forgive me.'

'It's fine. I forgive you.' Joan's chair creaked. Cora did not want to discuss it, not in front of other people. 'Is there anything else?'

'I wanted to say . . .' Aiden lowered his voice and Joan leaned further forward again.

'Look. You've said enough. Let's just leave it, okay? I forgave you and you agreed not to talk to me, so let's just stick with that.' Cora was going red now. Passengers were starting to arrive and while they didn't seem to see Joan, who practically had the popcorn out, there was a family making a beeline for her.

'Cora, can we—?'

But the various generations were upon her, arguing in Spanish and English about who had the passports and how many children there were, and Aiden was pushed to one side. She'd hurt his feelings – not quite like he'd hurt hers and she shouldn't care but she did.

'It's seven, Papa! We're not taking Maria.'

'Then why is Maria here?'

'That's not Maria, Grandpa! That's Gabrielle.'

Cora took the available documentation and counted the passengers. The final three passports were located – the last one extracted from the mouth of a toddler – and she did her best to accommodate their contradictory seating requests.

When they finally left she noticed that Aiden had too. She stood up on the footrest of her stool and surveyed the terminal but she couldn't see him.

'Where did he go, Joan? Did you see where he went?'

'Who, pet?'

'Aiden – the man, the man who was looking for me.' But the older woman shook her head, busy herself now – several minutes too late – with customers.

'Will you – I'll be back.' Cora hopped down from the stool. 'I won't be long.' She started to walk quicker, ignoring

Joan's response, turning her head and whole body as she went, trying to spot Aiden in the crowds that had suddenly appeared. She hesitated outside the men's toilets, wondering if it was worth waiting, but she couldn't risk losing the time. She looked in Costa and WHSmith, her walk now a jog. She stopped at the underground entrance, looking around her once more, careful not to miss anything in her panic, before she jogged down the conveyor belt. Her heart was pounding like it was a sprint. She'd lost him. He'd come back and she'd made him think she wasn't interested and she'd sent him away. He had given her a chance and she'd been too stubborn, too proud, to take it.

She stumbled on the escalator, straightened herself and kept going. She didn't want to be scared. She wanted to be able to tell him that she liked him too, a lot, that she liked his smile and his hair, she liked him in a suit and in that stupid rugby jersey, she liked his know-it-all-ness and she did actually like that he knew a lot, but she also liked that he was kind and considerate and, yes, that he'd made her mother happy and that he made her happy – irritated and incensed but happy too. She even liked his stubbornness and how, in ways, including her reluctance to admit it, they weren't all that dissimilar.

She got to the platform to find it empty and the gentle breeze of a recently departed train. She looked up at the real-time display – the Tube was arriving in five-minute intervals. She'd just missed one. She stood on the platform edge, the end of the line, and dropped her hands to her side. Fuck. She did a 360 and stared again down the dark tunnel as if, what? The Tube might reverse back into the station? Fuckidy, fuckidy, fuck. She'd lost him. It hit her then, like a wave breaking inside her; like she'd ruined her entire life. A wildly exaggerated assessment, and she knew even then it would lessen, but in that moment there was nothing she wanted to do.

Cora turned and slowly made her way back towards the terminal, back up the escalator, the conveyor belt, back past the shops and cafes, the arrivals gate, the crowd of expectant faces and chauffeurs with iPads and handmade signs.

Already it was less. It was fine. She told herself she'd be fine. She'd learn from it. It was a lesson – in her own pride, her fear, her reluctance. And then the wave again. A crashing tsunami of what-ifs. The drowning sense of dread. What if she had just told him? What if she had allowed him to like her, to have her, to sit beside her all the time and listen to all she wanted to tell him? Side-by-side, a little team. What-if.

Walking across the terminal floor, she saw the airport differently. It was not a long-term surrogate, this place, and she knew that was why she was leaving. A place so transient could not be her grounding; a place so sterile could not be a womb. At the Aer Lingus counter, Joan was dealing with a passenger but there was no queue. Cora retook her seat, nodded her thanks to the older woman, and tried to force a smile. Coming around the corner were two familiar faces: teenage siblings from the multi-generation Spanish family that had just checked in. Cora looked about her desk for a forgotten passport or bag or teddy bear but there was nothing.

'Cora Hendricks' said the older girl, the one with the best English.

'Yes, how can I—'

'I not finished.' The teenager shushed Cora and cleared her throat. 'Cora Hendricks, as you can see, I am not talked to you.'

Cora frowned. She didn't dare interrupt again but something was lost in translation.

'Because you told me not to do that. It may not seem like it but I have always listened to you. The first time we met you told me about, ah . . .' The Spaniard leaned over to her younger brother, standing awkwardly beside her, and took a piece of paper from him. 'Ah *si*! You told me about a dream you had the night before where you were a pilot on a massive purple plane. You read me your horoscope that morning and asked if I thought your dream meant you were dealing with a great deal of responsibility.'

This story was familiar . . . This dream . . . Yes! She had told Aiden about it, and he had responded glibly that it probably just meant she worked at an airport and had seen a pilot the previous day.

'And . . .' The younger brother piped up, grabbing the page back as he read – 'You insisted on reading my 'oro-scop-ay.'

'Horoscope,' his sister hissed.

'Horoscope. Even though I told you repeatedly that I did not believe in them. You did not listen to me, but that is not my point. My point is that I listened to you. I even remember what the . . . 'oroscope said.'

'It said,' the sister resuming oration as Cora looked around but could see no familiar faces, 'that I would be tested. But if I took the challenge on headfirst, it would stop looking like a bad thing and become something wonderful. You're a challenge, Cora Hendricks. And I remember everything.'

'*El final*,' whispered the boy and his sister reluctantly let him take the paper from her. 'If you do not want me to talk to you, that's okay. But I want to hear more from you. I watch you at the counter and wish I could be part of your world, which always seems so much more interesting than the one the rest of us are living in. I want to hear everything you dream, everything you think. Even if it's you pulling me up on my nonsense. I want to hear all of it. Because I'd rather get insults from you than kisses from anyone else.'

The siblings stopped and looked at Cora expectantly, proud of their oratory.

'Am I – is he – do you want a reply?'

The boy looked at his sister and she looked back at Cora. 'You will give him insults?'

'I – if that's what he wants.'

They didn't budge.

'Yes. I will give him insults.'

The girl whistled, her gaze at the wall to the end of the Aer Lingus row, and the siblings stood where they were until Aiden appeared. They swapped the page-long speech for two twenty-pound notes, and hurried off giggling.

'Can I talk?'

Cora looked at Joan, who had half an eye on her customer and the other one and a half on Aiden. Further up the row, the rest of the attendants were also staring at the man who stood several feet from Cora's counter. She looked at him too, sheepish and vulnerable, like she'd never seen him. He brushed curls from his face and shifted awkwardly. Cora got down from her stool, forgetting about the watchful eyes, refusing to feel fear as she walked out from behind the desk and slowly moved towards him.

'Do you still want to stand beside me?' she said, stopping directly in front of him.

'Always.'

'And will there be more cheesy rom-com gestures?'

'If you promise there'll be more arguments.'

'I'm not the one who starts the arguments.'

'Mmm.'

'Don't mmm me. You're always doing that. Mmm is not a word.'

He smiled, dimple pronounced, and she melted a little. 'That's my girl.'

Cora was in uniform and she was on duty. But what were they going to do, fire her? She took another step towards him, stood on her tippy-toes though it was not necessary – she just liked the sensation, the precariousness of it – and then she kissed him, resolute but careful, on the mouth. She quivered on her toes but she did not come back to earth until their lips had parted.

'Can we get out of here?' he whispered.

'I still have three hours on my shift.'

'Right. Of course,' he said, eyes open now. 'I'll wait.'

'For three hours?'

'Sure. I'll sit over there and pretend to read a paper or my phone but mainly I'll watch you.'

Cora laughed. 'No thanks.'

'Tough luck, sweet cheeks. This is a public space.'

Cora looked at him, long since given up on trying to remove the grin from her face, but he didn't yield.

'Alright,' she said with a shrug. 'If you insist.'

'I do. Three hours,' he said, pulling his phone from his pocket. 'Better let the clinic know my meeting is going to run late. Mr Gordon-Oxley's neck will have to live with gravity for another day.' And he started to move towards the benches.

'I'll just go back to it so.'

'And wave over at me every now and again,' he said. 'Big, crazy waves. We're both out of here shortly.'

'So why not act like total dolts?'

'Exactly.'

Aiden went and took a seat in the waiting area, and Cora returned to her desk.

'Everything alright?' asked Joan, gasping for gossip as the rest of the attendants craned their necks behind her.

'Yep, all good, thanks,' said Cora, her cheeks starting to hurt.

The next passenger approached, passport in hand, and Cora glanced over to see Aiden watching. She smiled as he half raised a hand, held it in the air for a moment, and frantically started waving from side to side as if in the midst of an epileptic fit. Cora dropped her gaze and laughed. How much easier it was to chance looking stupid when there were two of you taking the risk. If it breaks, it mends. She looked up again.

'Now,' she said, beaming at the woman with the out-stretched passport. 'Where are we off to today?'

I am grateful to the existence of public libraries – particularly Hornsey Library in London – for giving me places to write and to people-watch. To Sharon Carlyle, who agreed to answer a complete stranger's questions about airline particulars. Any accuracies are thanks to Sharon, all inaccuracies are down to the limitations of reality. To my agent Liz Parker at InkWell Management Literary Agency for her never-ending enthusiasm and to Juliet Mahony at Lutyens & Rubinstein. To my editor Sara O'Keeffe at Corvus (Atlantic Books) for kind and very constructive direction. To my mam and dad, the greatest match I know. To Mary for initial feedback, Carol for persevering reads, and Colm for everything.

And, finally, to all the friends and family whose lives I pilfered for material but, most of all, to Teresa Shortall. The one woman whose story I wouldn't dare to steal. At least, not yet.